Praise for Lucy Parker

"This story made me tremendously happy. I liked this book so much, I read it twice."
—*Smart Bitches, Trashy Books* on *Act Like It*

"This was a book that made me feel safe. It made me feel safe in the author's hands, safe in the characters' hands, safe in the story's hands."
—*Dear Author* on *Act Like It*

"Well written, with very human characters and an entertaining plot, this debut novel is highly recommended for romance lovers."
—*Library Journal* on *Act Like It*

"Every bit as vibrant, funny, sexy and poignant as the first book—quite possibly even more so, on all counts."
—*All About Romance* on *Pretty Face*

"This is a slow-burning romance since Luc and Lily want to be professional. The author writes really great and cute sexual tension.... This author definitely has a way with words."
—*Smexy Books* on *Pretty Face*

"When you find yourself laughing out loud, wiping away tears, and rereading passages you just read, you know that you've found a real gem among a sea of contemporary romances. *Pretty Face* by Lucy Parker is a witty and engaging look at the London theater world."
—*Harlequin Junkie*

**Also available from Lucy Parker
and Carina Press**

Act Like It
Pretty Face

making up
up

LUCY PARKER

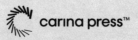
carina press™

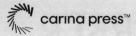

carina press™

ISBN-13: 978-1-335-00705-6

Making Up

Copyright © 2018 by Laura Elliott

Recycling programs for this product may not exist in your area.

www.CarinaPress.com

Printed in U.S.A.

For my nieces, Riley and Charli, with love.

May you always find happiness
and unexpected moments of magic.

And don't read past this page until you're older.

In memory of Pat, George and Ray,
my grandparents. Still missed. Always loved.

Chapter One

When one of the most talented aerial performers in the West End suddenly slammed into the side of a fire-breathing dragon, crushing his metallic wing and snapping her own forearm like a matchstick, quite a few people cheered.

Trix Lane was about six feet away from her cast-mate when the collision occurred, hanging upside down from a hoop, and for a moment she had the dizzying sensation that *she* was the one falling.

The audience continued to applaud as Paige's hands jerked free of her aerial straps and she tumbled the rest of the short distance to the stage.

Trix watched, helpless, as the straps sailed upwards almost in slow motion, leaving a ghostly, repeated pattern in the strobe lighting, like a time-lapse photograph. The black crystals on Paige's costume caught the swirling beams of light in an obscenely pretty way.

And as she lay dazed on the floor, the chorus continued to dance around her, high-kicking and jazz-handing their way through a wink-wink-nudge-nudge number about the therapeutic benefits of love and sex.

Trix really hoped that the extremely badly timed ripple of laughter was directed at the trio of oblivious Masked Fools, who continued their cheeky banter with the crowd.

The Festival of Masks was loud and chaotic from the opening sequin-wiggle to the last romantic clinch. It was the show with an identity crisis, according to one long-ago critic, unsure whether it was a carnival, a rock concert, a very dark fairy tale, or just a slightly smutty night out. The orchestra was now building to a crescendo, and laser beams of colour dissected the darkness around the theatre, dipping and weaving. In the early days, Trix had sat in the stalls during rehearsal a few times, and the view from there was like being caught in a kaleidoscope of fractal art.

With as many as thirty performers onstage and a dozen in the air during the finale, navigating around swooping mythological creatures and eye-tricking illusions, it probably wasn't surprising that most of the audience were either looking elsewhere when the accident happened or thought it was part of the act.

And it all happened so bloody quickly.

Trix swung through the last moves of her own routine out of sheer habit, pulling the momentum from Jono Watanabe's firm grasp as he swung her outward in a strong arc. Her appalled gaze met his in the instant before he released her. She drew her legs in for a double rotation. When she caught the bar of her hoop again with the small of her back and rolled up to sit, she hit every transition right on the beat with the ease of constant practice.

Below, the perfectly choreographed pattern of the dancers faltered just a little as the cast realised, one at a time, what had happened. Trix looked over at Jono, who had his left arm and leg hooked around the bar of his glittering trapeze. He was always so grace-ful that the position would look effortless from the ground. Up here, in the heat and strange sense of iso-lation, Trix could see the bunched muscles quivering down his side. He stared back at her, sweat beading on his shaved head, apparently at an equal loss as to what to do now.

The golden rule of theatre, always, was to keep going. Ad-lib through a forgotten line, chin up after a dodgy note, dance past a stumble.

Obviously, nobody onstage was sure if it was ap-propriate to keep booty-shaking around the unmoving body of their castmate.

In the air, the dragon hung off-centre, one wing slanted at a lopsided angle.

The atmosphere resonated with a feeling of unreal-ity as things came to a close, highlighted by the cliché of the band playing cheerfully on.

Marco Ross, their current stage manager, was so hardnosed that if it had happened mid-performance, Trix wouldn't have been surprised if he'd just lassoed poor Paige's ankle, dragged her into the wings, and thrown her understudy into the spotlight before the news could reach the orchestra pit.

Fortunately, it happened with only a few seconds left to run, although for the first time in three years, an even-toned voice came over the speaker system to ex-plain that there would be no curtain call for tonight's performance.

Trix, Jono, and several of the other aerial perform-ers had to wait above while the partitions descended around the circular stage. Under the stark glare of the houselights, voices blended into a headache-inducing racket.

When her feet were back on solid ground, the relief of hearing Paige's voice through the clamour made Trix's hands shake as she unhooked her wires. She'd been playing Pierrette for so long now that it was as routine as scrambling an egg or brushing her teeth. A grim-looking rigger checked her equipment as he took it from her.

The crew was so stringent about safety practices that the chances of a collision midair ought to be infinitesimal to nonexistent.

As usual, the universe spotted complacency and delivered a swift kick up the arse.

Or, in this case, a crashing blow into a giant robotic dragon. Paige had managed to take the main impact on her arm instead of her skull, thank God, but several things were no longer pointing in the right direction. Since her castmate was having a bad enough night without Trix doing a full-body shudder and then stress-vomiting everywhere, she swallowed hard on rising acid in her throat and crouched down at Paige's side. Her fingers hovered above the other woman's knee, afraid to touch her and risk hurting her more.

The house medic was trying to examine her while they waited for the ambulance. Apparently he had a death wish.

"Am I in pain?" Paige repeated. Her jaw was clenched tight, and she had to force enough space between her gritted teeth to speak. Sweat dripped from beneath her crystal headdress and pooled in the hollows of her shoulders. "How about I take the bone sticking out of my arm and skewer your tiny little balls

with it, and we'll compare notes? How about that? How are *your* pain levels after the testicle kebab, you piss-biscuit? Zero to ten?"

When she wasn't dealing with compound fractures, Paige "Pissbiscuit" Lawson was the sort of person who put a fiver in a swear jar if she said "bugger" in public.

She was going to be mortified when these moments of her life were posted online under the guise of fly-on-the-wall realism.

At Trix's side, Jono also looked at the *West End Story* film crew, everybody's constant shadow for the past month. They were hovering with their cameras and drooling into their ring lights at the thought of the views on this episode.

Without a word, Trix and Jono moved together and stood where they could block as much of Paige from view as possible. When a camera shifted position, so did they, ignoring the irritated noises behind them.

For a reason he chose not to share, Marco had signed off on this so-called web documentary about the backstage reality behind West End "glamour." The online series had been pitched to the cast and crew as an impartial account of sweat and sacrifice. So far, surprising exactly nobody, the result was sex, scandal, and spats, cunningly edited to look a lot more interesting than it was.

Trix suspected that Marco fancied himself as the next silver fox to go viral on social media, which would explain why he regularly walked into the shot with his pecs out, even though he hadn't personally performed onstage for about two decades and had no need to be semi-nude at training. He could just as easily stare in withering silence and bark out his blatant insults with his shirt on. His job description seemed to centre around raising his voice every time he had something demoralising to say, making last-minute and usually inconvenient changes to training schedules, and failing to see the humour in any joke in the history of funnies, even the ones scripted into their own show.

Nobody could be that obnoxious every second of his existence. Even fate would lose patience and start dropping pianos in the vicinity of his head. Perhaps Marco was a surprising ray of sunshine outside the theatre.

He came to stand over Paige and the medic, his lips compressed, his admittedly attractive silver hair sticking up in agitated spikes. There were probably invisible birds circling his head right now, tweeting *lawsuit, lawsuit, almost killed one of your principals, lawsuit*.

This would still be the moment to set aside the implications for the show and offer some human empathy to the member of the team suffering horrific pain.

"I don't care whether you're playing the lead role or that kid who juggles with fire balls," Marco said flatly. "When you're on the stage, your mind is *engaged*. What the hell happened out there? Do you know what a bloody hassle this is going to be?"

And maybe Marco never brought the sunshine. Maybe Marco was just a perennial wanker.

"I'm probably going to spend the next month fielding calls from parents about their traumatised wee kiddies," Marco muttered, and Trix inhaled sharply.

Nobody knew the extent of Paige's injuries. Nobody knew whether her career had just ended permanently. Nobody should really be bringing "wee kiddies" to see a show with a strong burlesque element and highly sexual plotlines; they might have magic tricks, but they weren't a pantomime. There were several brutally frank things she wanted to say to Marco at that moment.

Generally she found it easy to get along with people, even working in an industry full of big personalities and even bigger egos. Marco was one of only three people who had ever annoyed her on such a fundamental level that it made her skin itch.

The paramedics arrived after a few minutes, and Trix got out of their way. "We'll meet you at the hospital, Paige."

Paige was heading swiftly into a state of morphine-induced marshmallow, by the look of it. "I think Jono's going to puke," she said indistinctly, and Trix spun around.

Jono's face was still shiny with sweat, and he did look very definitely green under the strong lights. "No, I'm not," he retorted with complete indignation, and then threw up all over himself, the floor, and Trix.

This was one of the times when it would be nice to be taller than five foot, and not presenting the top of her head as a target.

Naturally the doco crew caught the entire thing on camera.

Tonight had blown all other performances out of the water for the title of Worst Ever, an honour previously held by the popping button incident, which had exposed her left nipple to a packed house. Although quite a lot of people had missed the action that time, too, since her breasts were essentially microorganisms: too small to be seen by the human eye. On the plus side, she'd never been hit in the face by her own tits while doing a straddle mount on the hoop.

Everyone had at least stopped gawping at Paige's departing stretcher now. And Marco looked disgusted and left them to it, so that was something.

Poor Jono was so mortified that Trix should probably stop giggling, but at this point things were so horrifying it had flipped her inappropriate-laughter switch. Exam rooms, bad news, projectile vomiting: all cues for her face and vocal cords to act independently of her brain.

Her costume would have to be put through a carwash before the drycleaners would touch it, and it was possible she'd end up as bald as Jono if she didn't see some shampoo soon and things had time to congeal. Since neither of them could look much worse, however, she delayed a bolt for the showers long enough to give him a quick hug. The feathers of his costume were soft and silky against her fingers.

"Some people will do anything for internet fame," she teased, and he groaned low in his chest.

"Stop. I can't look at them. I can't look at anyone." He dropped his head the considerable distance to her shoulder. "I'm going to need you to stand in front of me for a while. Until my hands stop shaking. Then I can dig a pit and subside into it."

"I come up to approximately your knee. My services as a human shield are useful only to toddlers." Trix gave his back a consoling little pat. "And I know I have a decent butt, but I would really prefer it if my friends didn't stand behind me while I'm in the shower."

Jono straightened to his full height. His eyes were still shadowed. "Holy shit. When she fell…"

"I know." Trix's knees felt like she'd spent intermission doing tequila shots.

That instant of time, with the thick straps seeming to float and Paige's eyes wide and panicked, was fixed in her memory like a still from a horror film.

"I guess we're in for a major cast shake-up." Despite the dodgy stomach, Jono was a more rational thinker than Trix, whose brain was currently stuck on hand-wringing and nervous bouncing. He gulped. "Bones outside of body. I don't think she'll be back on Wednesday."

Trix forced herself to stop jiggling about like a manic wind-up toy. "She might not be back at all." It was a sobering realisation. They put everything they had into a career that could end in a split second, but it was always one of those "it won't happen to me" prospects, easily pushed aside in the sweat and adrenaline under the lights. "Cassie will have to take over as Doralina."

Which was unfortunate. Paige's understudy was a pill. If Cassie bollocksed up a cue, she had a habit of looking from the nearest performer to the audience and pulling an exaggerated face, inviting the assumption that the other person was at fault. If she ran someone over with her car, she'd blame them for denting her bumper.

"Maybe. Maybe not." Jono scrubbed his hand over his mouth. "Cassie's trying to wriggle out of her contract."

Trix was attempting to pull the sticky scraps of her costume away from her skin without giving Jono an eyeful. It took a moment for the implication to sink in. Her head snapped up so quickly that she felt a tendon pull taut in her neck. "What?"

"Apparently Cassie's trying to leave. They'll probably have to reaudition the role, in that case, and the second understudy will get a massive promotion in the meantime." Belatedly, Jono's own brain caught up. "Shite. Is that still—"

"Me." For an instant, Trix thought her own stomach was going to follow Jono's projectile example. "It's me. I'm second understudy for Doralina."

The Night Wraith, the most technically difficult and physically demanding role in the entire production. She *had* agreed to learn the cues and the basics of the routines this year, solely because it meant a few extra quid a week. It was another never-going-to-happen scenario that had funded her weekly Sunday roast at her local pub. She was supposed to be the Prince Harry of the situation, well down the line of succession.

She had to force her speech out of a chest that felt as if steel hands were gripping her lungs and electrocuting her heart. "Is that definite? About Cassie?"

"No." Jono was completely oblivious to her building panic. He knocked his fist gently against her shoulder. "But I heard it from Allie, so..."

Her friend in the wardrobe department was the oracle of company gossip, and could usually predict hook-ups, engagements, and promotions at least a week before the news went official. If Allie said it was so, there was a bloody good chance that Cassie was on her way out.

In Trix's current frame of mind, Jono's genuinely delighted, supportive grin looked like the Grinch's malevolent leer. He sketched an ironic bow. "Check you out! Leading lady. Hell, yeah!"

She couldn't move her own lips into anything resembling a smile. In the past, she'd have been split right down the middle between horrified concern for

Paige and guilty excitement. Now…terror. Nothing but terror.

"It's not definite." Her mind reverted to instant, protective denial. "Cassie might not leave if she knows she's got a shot at weeks of mainstage performances—" *Weeks. Oh, hell…* "—and if Paige is going to be out for months, minimum, Marco will want to recast the role externally."

Marco couldn't stand Trix. He had an especially patronising tone reserved for the occasions when he was forced to address her. Usually as "Pinky," which was an accurate description of her hair colour but not of the finger she was tempted to raise in response. There was no way he'd want her headlining. That glorious saviour of a man.

"There won't be time to recast by Wednesday, so if Cassie's out, you'll definitely get a run in the limelight. How bloody fantastic." Jono was so thrilled for her. He was such a good, unobservant friend. A renewed frown crinkled his brow. "Although I still don't understand what happened. Paige is always on point with her timing—"

He suddenly focused on the hovering camera crew, properly registering their presence, and his usual patience and politeness fractured. "Seriously, do you have to do that now?"

"Yep," said the one who had a cold. The blithe response came out as "Yeb."

There were three cameramen for the invasive webseries, whom Trix distinguished only as Sneezy, Coffee Stealer, and Pen Clicker.

"Don't worry, mate," Pen Clicker said, finding a

loose thread on his shirt to fiddle with. "We'll edit out anything that's not relevant."

So far, the doco crew's definition of relevancy differed wildly to that of everyone who was reluctantly starring in it.

Unlike certain other productions, which had to use public nosiness to fill seats by turning costar relationships into a marketable commodity, *The Festival of Masks* consistently performed to full houses. They didn't need PR tricks, and they definitely didn't need a team of glorified vloggers constantly shoving a camera in their faces and asking questions like: "Wouldn't you rather spend Saturday night with your mates at a club, or having a night in front of the telly?"

Short answer: hell yes, sometimes she would, but she'd already lucked out in scoring a role in a production that only ran performances Wednesday to Saturday, with a scattering of shows for charity or the super-wealthy on other days throughout the month. Nights out weren't off the table, if a person didn't go overboard on the cocktails when she had training or a show the next day.

Trix had been relieved to see that she hardly appeared in the *West End Story* pilot, and assumed she'd been written off as the weird pink-haired chick, only good for a couple of establishing shots. Then the second episode had kicked off with a montage of her at training, repeatedly catching her foot on the hoop during a split pike, a move she could usually do with one hand literally tied behind her back.

Her role in the series seemed to be defined as anonymous twit who was overdue to get her roots dyed, and long may it continue.

"Meet you out back in half an hour and we'll go to the hospital?" Jono looked at her more closely. His hand lowered to rest on her arm. "Are you all right? You look a bit—" Sneezy ventured near them with an external microphone, and Jono jerked his head impatiently. "Jesus! Would you piss off?"

"Come on." Firmly, Trix caught hold of Jono's elbow and tugged him away. "Much-needed showers."

"If you show up at the hospital," Jono said over his shoulder, "you ambulance-chasing, film-school dropouts, I will bloody well call the police."

They ducked around a couple of chorus dancers, who were among the many people choosing to cool down where they could watch the drama unfold.

"You realise that after that footage is creatively edited, you're going to come off as a cross between Darth Vader and Don John."

"Good," Jono retorted, holding open the door to the backstage corridor for her. "Better than coming across like Dogberry's even more gormless son. After she watched the first episode, my mother called to ask if it wasn't difficult to perform on the trapeze without a spine."

People from the cast were crowded throughout the green room, grabbing snacks, talking on their phones, or lying semi-comatose on the couches. Allie and other members of the wardrobe team were collecting stray items of clothing that had been carelessly discarded between acts.

The room was busy, but there was a clear path to the two men standing by the water cooler. Marco stood with a rigid spine, looking stony-faced. He'd probably been reading his social media feed. Not a good day for him, either. There would be far more accusations of shoddy safety protocol than compliments about his hair.

He was talking to a veritable mountain of a man with closely curling dark hair, warm brown skin, and the muscle definition of a clean-eating superhero.

On the shortlist of the three most insufferable people Trix had ever met, there was Marco, there was her vile ex-boyfriend Dan—and there was Irritant Number One. The original wanker. The pop-up dickhead who made a surprise appearance every ten pages or so in the picture book of her life.

Fate had a habit of tossing him in her direction at regular intervals. Either when things were going well and she apparently needed a reality check, or when everything was already a crap heap and she made the mistake of uttering the fatal question: *could this get any worse?* For someone who wasn't an entertainer, he never missed his cue.

A couple of metres away from him, Trix stood still.

His gaze travelled with mild curiosity over the assembled performers and swung to clash with hers.

Trix saw in her peripheral vision that Allie, who had known them both for years and witnessed many of their more voluble encounters, was wincing.

For a moment, she was completely at a loss for words. Then she shook her head. Well. Sure. What more fitting way to end this absolute ballsack of a day?

All she needed now was to find Dan lurking in the shower cubicles and she'd have a complete set. *For today only, you can have all three bastards at once, for the low, low price of your sanity and self-esteem!*

Sarcastic observation, universe, not a challenge or a request. For the love of God.

He was still looking at her, his expression enigmatic.

She grimaced. "You're like a less particular version of Beetlejuice," she said flatly. "I don't even need to say your name. One passing thought and you materialise out of nowhere."

A gleam flickered to life in the almost black irises. "On your mind, was I, Tinker Bell?"

Leo Magasiva. Top London makeup artist. Wizard of special effects. Possessor of beautiful voice and aggressively hipster beard.

Pop-up dickhead.

Beatrix Lane.

The extremely short bane of Leo's existence.

She had been laughing up at someone, a tall Japanese guy with a shaved head and folded angel wings strapped to his bare back. Nothing new there. Trix was a relentless flirt.

Although it had been a very long time since he'd personally experienced that facet of her personality. Flirting required a level of goodwill normally reserved for people you didn't want to drop-kick off a cliff.

She turned, her eyes still dancing. Her smile vanished the moment she saw him. As usual, whenever these fun little encounters occurred, she looked as if she wanted to mount his head on a pike somewhere. She offered him her idea of a hello.

Out of habit, Leo studied her makeup with an impartial interest that obviously raised her hackles even more than his return greeting. Her evil expression would be more effective if someone hadn't upended the contents of a sick bag over her pastel-pink head.

She played the broken porcelain doll, Pierrette—the weakest of the principal roles, in his opinion. The character was an irreverent troublemaker with a lot of the best lines, but she was too annoying to be likeable.

He was saying nothing about typecasting.

The makeup brief for Pierrette was full-body, high-lighted by the fact that Trix wasn't wearing much more than sequins and stockings, but it was relatively simple. He assumed that Trix had been given a tutorial and did at least some of it herself. Given her current bedraggled appearance, it was difficult to tell what sort of job she made of it. But she had a laser eye for spotting weaknesses and pointing them out mercilessly, so she ought to be quite accurate with small tools and intricate detail.

For a show like this, with such a large ensemble cast, most performers would have to do their own makeup. The contracted makeup artists would usually only have time to focus on the most extensive transformations. Which in this case would be the troupe of acrobats who played the Shadows, the Mirror Man, and Doralina the Night Wraith, who had apparently just suffered a serious arm injury.

He was shortlisted for the current vacancy in the theatre's makeup department, and had been invited to watch tonight's show from the lighting box to refresh his memory of the characters. He'd seen the production at least four times over the past couple of years, so he'd ducked out before the final number to check the facilities backstage. Word had quickly filtered through that there had been an accident, initially with no details as to who was involved. *He'd* been extremely aware of his heartbeat for a minute or two, so God knew what it had been like for the cast and established crew.

Although, obviously not all that traumatic for the production's stage manager, who seemed to be missing the genes for tact and sensitivity. In one breath, Marco Ross had murmured something about his concern and then sniped that the injured woman had nobody but herself to blame for her broken bones. It did sound like human error, but it still wasn't a good look for the SM to be openly trashing his cast.

"If you come in tomorrow morning, I'll have the contract for you," Marco said, leaping over the part where he actually made a formal job offer. Leo was still debating whether he would accept it. He badly needed the cash infusion, but there were several bloody strong deterrents, one of whom was poking out her full lower lip and radiating disdain.

He tightened his jaw. The very sight of her raised an uncomfortable jumble of emotions, jabbing an insistent finger at sleeping bitterness and regret.

Marco ignored Trix and her angelic companion, who had apparently been involved in the same vomiting spectacle. His voice contained nothing but impatience. "I'll need you on board for Wednesday's performance. After Paige's fuck-up, we're going to have to make major changes in the cast, and I don't need anyone else mucking me about."

Somewhere, even the Sith Emperor was looking at this guy's management style and thinking "Bit harsh."

Trix's expression didn't change—it was conveniently already set to a high level of "fuck you"; she just expanded the target—but he saw her body stiffen.

Even though she regularly hoodwinked people into thinking she was a sassy little spark of kindness, Trix had never been afraid to stand up for herself, or for anyone she thought was getting a raw deal. Her case for the defence was uniformly short, brutal, and laden with profanities. It was a quality he would admire more if he weren't usually on the receiving end.

He fully expected a blunt response to Marco's lack of empathy, but she balled up her hands and kept her mouth shut.

Cautious, pragmatic, and completely out of character.

Marco caught Leo's slight frown, but misinterpreted the reason for it. He offered a half-arsed and mostly unnecessary introduction. "Leo Magasiva, new recruit in makeup and special effects." He inclined his head towards Trix and Angel Boy. "Pierrette and Oscurito."

"Oscurito" rolled his eyes, and Trix had the expression of someone who needed to sneeze, which Leo mentally translated as "I have an actual name, you mannerless bastard."

"Who both need a shower," Marco added distastefully, and, well—yeah.

"Leo and Pierrette have met." Allie spoke up for the first time, tucking her brown hair behind her ear. She had been gathering scraps of sequinned fabric very slowly, keeping an avid eye on them. She obviously expected them to start circling one another and snarling like crotchety Rottweilers. Years ago, fate had stuck him at the same school as Allie and Trix. Allie had conned him into a lasting friendship via a series of irritating knock-knock jokes in chem lab. She'd outgrown the jokes, but they'd stayed mates through the years.

Trix had messed with him in a far less endearing way, kicking his feet out from under him before she'd skipped off to some flash boarding school. Their budding…whatever had crashed and burned a long time ago.

Allie was openly grinning, enjoying herself a little too much. "They've met several times, in fact."

Something of an understatement. Trix bounced in and out of his life like one of those fucking carnival games. Their usual style was to cross paths, cross swords, and then cross their fingers that it was a long time before they saw each other again. Spending time under the same roof never did much for their respective blood pressure.

Unfortunate, then, that his only immediate job prospect was on her long-time show.

"At least twenty times in the past few years alone," Trix said gloomily, and he countered, "At least twenty-one."

Their eyes met.

"You have a habit of blocking out all memory of the McCallisters' christening three years ago." Mournfully, he murmured, "The cautionary tale of the delayed ceremony and the absolutely trolleyed godmother. Poor little Xander. So young. So innocent. So entirely unprepared to be ditched in a nativity crib and lost for almost a quarter of an—"

"At least twenty-one times," Trix snapped, a warm flush appearing through the smeared white paint on her cheeks. "And that isn't the only occasion I've tried to erase from my brain."

Marco's phone rang, and he glanced at the screen and scowled. "Meet me in my office in ten minutes."

He shot the order in Leo's general direction before he walked out of the green room to take the call.

With the boss out of earshot, Trix crossed her arms, and the sequins across her chest shimmered under the light. "The last time I saw you, I believe you had a clear goal for the future and it didn't include showing up here to do my lipstick. What exactly prompted this career move?"

It was really very unnatural for that many acidic comments to be contained within such a small person.

"If I recall correctly," Trix went on, clearly articulating each word, just to make sure the biting antipathy didn't go over his thick head, "your plan was to devote yourself entirely to the legitimate world of film, where people would worship your talents to your satisfaction. I didn't expect to see you slumming it back behind the curtain."

Interesting. If he clenched his jaw hard enough, he could successfully stop his left eye twitching.

Allie coughed into her fist. "I'm guessing you haven't been browsing the gossip sites much this month."

"No." Trix sounded reluctantly interested. "I have not. Why? What did you do? Or should I say who? And I hope the poor, misguided woman wasn't married."

The reason Leo had been unceremoniously fired from a high-profile film set, and was currently having his name trashed in tabloids from London to Newcastle, had nothing to do with a woman.

The person whose head he'd exploded into a swollen mass of open sores had been male. He'd also been furious, and not shy about shooting his mouth off to the producer and the press.

End result: one hell of a career setback.

You cause one A-list actor to blow up like Violet Beauregarde and people think you're incompetent.

Quite a few of those pointing fingers should turn in the direction of the celebrity, who'd known he had a serious cosmetic allergy and failed to mention it either verbally or on any of the three forms he'd signed for that exact reason.

Bloody actors.

The professional bullshitter he'd known the longest raised her eyebrows expectantly. Her hazel eyes were flickering with an unholy gleam. The sort of expression that a squirrel might adopt on spotting a particularly intriguing nut.

Standing in a room full of people who were going to let him touch their faces, Leo didn't really feel like telling the amusing anecdote of how he'd accidentally maimed the last sucker. Assuming that Trix could—and almost definitely would—look it up for herself, he shifted tactics. "I'm surprised you don't know. You seem to keep fairly close tabs on my career, Tinker Bell."

"I prefer to have an idea of your whereabouts," she agreed readily enough. "It's like watching out for potholes when driving. And don't call me that. It's patronising and it makes you sound like a prick."

This was more like the Trix who bristled over perceived injustice and caused a wise man to shield his sensitive areas. Metaphorically speaking.

"I don't know." In a staggeringly ill-judged move, Angel Boy stuck his head over the parapet and said, "It's kind of cute. Suits you." Then the ballsy bastard actually nudged her.

There was a brief pause.

With a burst of manly comradeship, Leo cut in before Trix could raise her delicate foot and boot the dude into next week. "Speaking of names…"

He needn't have bothered with the save, because apparently threats of bodily harm were reserved for him. Patronising comments from anyone else just resulted in a thin smile and an ungracious introduction. "This is Jono Watanabe."

"I'd offer a handshake, but I needed to be under a shower about ten minutes ago, and I don't think anybody but Trix would be prepared to touch me right now." Jono nodded from Leo to Trix. "So, you're all friends already?"

Trix made a noise that would be a dead-on impression of someone dropping a spoon down a garbage disposal, and Allie patted Jono's arm. "I know it's hard to believe," she said to nobody in particular, "but this one actually makes his living following cues and interpreting body language."

Jono looked slightly blank. Apparently Trix's current taste in men ran to a pretty face and not a lot behind it. Not much had changed there, then.

Trix adjusted the top of her costume, which appeared to be staying up by a literal thread. "We should get moving," she said abruptly. "Even if we can't see Paige tonight, I want her to know we were there."

There was something in her eyes that Leo didn't like.

When he saw people upset, he usually had one instinct, to the dismay of those who didn't enjoy being spontaneously hugged by a large bearded bloke. However, physical contact with Trix would be the equivalent of cuddling a roll of barbed wire. It was fortunate for all concerned that the green room door swung open and hit the wall, making everyone jump and drawing Trix out of her worried preoccupation.

"Ew." A girl in a dressing gown strolled past them, holding a Venetian-style mask. "Don't walk through the wings, peeps. There's blood, and sick, and God knows what else on the floor."

Trix tugged at her top again, a move that exposed more than she'd probably meant to; then she quickly folded her arms across the skimpy fabric and looked at him accusingly, as if he'd been the one to hook a finger into it for a quick peek.

Somewhere behind him, someone murmured, "Hey. That's the guy from the paper, right? The hot beardy one? Who practically killed—"

What a time to be alive.

"I need to get this costume off before it permanently melds to my skin." Trix slipped her fingers through the crook of Angel Boy's arm. She gave him a sympathetic little squeeze, before she looked up at Leo and her elfin face turned sour enough to curdle the milk in every latte in the room. "I think the last dregs of my optimism hit the floor with Paige tonight, so I'm assuming you're accepting this job."

Leo shifted his attention from her hand, which was smudged with greasepaint, patchy with freckles, and curled around a muscular forearm. "Was there a 'congratulations' lurking in there?"

"Your ego has never needed outside validation. It's one of the many ways you astound me." Trix's response was delivered with such sweetness and fervour that it almost masqueraded as a compliment.

Allie scratched her nose, conveniently covering her

mouth in the process. Even the bald, winged boyfriend seemed to pick up the undercurrents this time. Once again, he cut in with an exuberantly friendly remark. Bit of a human puppy. "Trix and I have been with *Masks* since opening night. Best company in the West End. You'll never work with nicer people."

Cut to Trix's narrowed stare for a ludicrous contrast shot. Leo's lips twitched. "Impressive track record," he said mildly. "A lot of performers are too restless to commit to a multi-year run. Too…fickle. Speaking generally."

Trix's spine straightened so quickly that she gained a few much-needed millimetres of height. "And sadly, some of the Y chromosomes floating around are such superficial knobs that they're lucky to be offered any work at all." She casually removed a crusty speck of mascara from her lashes.

She was really wasted in musical theatre. Anyone who could bury that much loathing beneath layers of vocal honey was just itching to be cast in a violent whodunit.

Snide dig aside, she wasn't wrong. He took issue with the "superficial knob" element, but with his current PR problem, he *was* lucky that Marco Ross was such a documented bastard. People in the industry weren't queuing up to work for him at short notice, which was probably why he was prepared to overlook Leo's well-publicised shortcomings.

He grimaced. This was a paid gig that came with the chance of subsidised rent in company accommodation. And the show had enough non-performance days that he'd be able to stick to his plans to enter the UK SFX makeup artistry championship this month. In the interests of his future career, he needed to win that title. In the interests of paying the bills in astronomically expensive London, he needed a job. Right now.

"So. You on board, Mags?" Allie asked him when Trix had sashayed off, plastered to the side of her unnaturally good-looking castmate.

He glanced at her, running restless fingers through his hair.

A shot at steering his career back on track, for the small price of having his ego shredded on a daily basis by the pink peril.

His reply was heartfelt. "Shit."

Allie pursed her lips in a silent whistle. "Fasten your seatbelts, folks. It's going to be turbulent."

Chapter Two

When Trix woke up on Sunday morning, she could hear birds singing.

Less idyllically, there were loud voices outside in the street, and someone was crashing about and swearing in the lounge. Probably one of her flatmates attempting to cook something more arduous than a bowl of cereal again. The stovetop still hadn't recovered from Pancake Batch #18.

She rolled over, yawning. She'd thrown off her fuzzy blanket in the night and it was bunched down at the end of the bed, trying to strangle her feet. Even when she'd got home from the hospital at two a.m., it had been warm outside. Now, at just before nine, it was sweltering. A strip of sunlight between the blinds was warming her lilac-painted walls, creeping along the wooden floorboards and raising a line of sweat across her bare back.

This was the hottest London summer for years. All over the city, everywhere she went, people were complaining about the heat wave. When it passed, they would all suffer selective amnesia and start to make disparaging comments about the rain, agreeing that they were a bunch of chumps for shivering damply in

England when there were places that actually saw the sun. Good times.

Her phone vibrated on the bedside table and she reached for it, tilting the screen to read the message. It was from Natalie, the assistant stage manager.

Emergency meeting at ten. Marco's office. Try not to be late. He's been here since 7 and breaking all existing d-bag records.

She tried to suppress the immediate flip of panic in her stomach. This didn't definitely mean that Cassie was out. It could be standard, dull protocol. The principals were always called in for a debrief if there was even a temporary change of cast. Everyone had their own style when it came to the choreography, and if you were out of sync with the timing, it looked messy and usually resulted in awkward hitches and repositioning.

It did *not* usually result in someone doing a header straight into the nearest prop.

Trix couldn't get over Paige, of all people, letting her concentration slip like that. It wasn't even really a *rookie* mistake. When there were multiple artists and props in the air at once, timing was crucial. It was Aerial Newbie 101 at LIDA, the London Institute of Dramatic Arts. Concentration and spatial awareness. And Paige was a veteran, the most experienced artist in the show.

Her wife, Carly, had been a notable no-show at the hospital. Trix wondered if she was the underlying cause of Paige's state of mind, which had resulted in a split-second action that would have a lasting impact on the rest of her career. She was facing months of rehab on her arm, and she specialised in a discipline that relied heavily on upper body strength.

Seriously. The bloody fucked-up things people did when they were in love.

Or thought they were in love.

Her gaze rested briefly on her wardrobe. The door was partly ajar because she hadn't bothered to fold her last load of clean washing and had just stuffed everything in and hoped for the best. There was a time when that display of laziness would have been strongly criticised, the poison diluted by a tone of fond exasperation and a smile she'd thought was sincere.

One of her old sketchpads had slipped from a shelf and fallen open on the rug. Thanks to the legacy of Dan's disparaging comments, she hadn't picked up a pencil in ages. The same way she'd put numerous other things on hold that were a fundamental part of her personality but hadn't measured up to his conception of the perfect girlfriend.

She was going to draw something this week. Anything. She'd get back into the swing of things playing Hangman if she had to. She could think of a cathartic caricature to put in the noose.

Crash.

"*Fuck.*"

The sound of something else smashing in the lounge, followed by a familiar voice, catapulted Trix out of past regrets and into more pressing problems. She was out of bed and firmly tying the knot of her robe in about three seconds flat. One quick look in the mirror to make sure there were no nipples or remnants of sleep on display, then she left her room and hurried down the narrow hallway to the lounge.

The Old Wellington owned this terrace house and had divided it into three four-bedroom flats. Without the reduction in rent that the company offered current employees, there was no way she'd be able to afford this part of the city. The only downside: communal kitchen, living area, and bathroom. Two of her flatmates were large, muscular men who liked to burn things in the oven, optimistically hope that someone else would clean the loo, and take suspiciously long showers. The fourth bedroom in their flat had been vacated last week, and Trix had been crossing her fingers that the next person on the waiting list was a very quiet, tidy woman. Preferably a feeder who liked to bake chocolate chip biscuits.

Instead—*this*. Talk about going from the sublime to the ridiculous.

She took a moment to question her place in the universe, the existence of karma and Higher Beings, and the span of his beard. Each individual hair was particularly springy and upbeat today. *To Kill A Mocking Beard*. New title for her memoirs. "I should probably be more surprised."

Leo rose from a crouch, holding a broken photo frame. His piercing dark eyes looked at her from under thick brows. He cleared his throat. "You should also probably wear something under your robe if you're going to stand in front of a window in summer."

She moved into the shadow of the bookcase before folding her arms and crossing one leg in front of the other. "As usual, what a gentleman."

He set the frame down carefully on the coffee table, examining it with a frown. "Amongst my many gentlemanly attributes," he said, "I have these things called eyes. And if you're going to put *your* attributes right in front of them…"

She was trying to think of a really scathing retort, preferably something so cutting that he'd immediately pick up his things and leave while sobbing piteously, when something *moved* on the coffee table. Something that also had things called eyes and was looking straight at her from underneath a piece of newspaper.

"What the hell is that?"

Leo followed the direction of her gaze and made a noise in his throat. Gently, he extracted a pygmy hedgehog from its hiding place and deposited it back on top of the newspaper. The adorable little squidge looked tiny against his massive hand.

We do not squee over anything to do with this man, ovaries. Rein in the hormones immediately.

"That is Reginald. Who is non-allergenic, makes much less noise and probably less mess than you do, and will usually be living in his vivarium, not on the coffee table."

"Reginald."

His beard—she assumed there was a chin under there somewhere—lifted ever so slightly. "Reggie."

Trix looked at him unblinkingly. "Reggie. Reggie the Hedgie."

"He's my sister's. I didn't name him."

The tips of his ears were flushing. Trix felt a brief flicker of genuine amusement. "Uh-huh."

"He's more dangerous than he looks," Leo threatened. "Smirking women usually ignite his killer instinct. I'll try to keep him contained, but I make no promises."

"Death by snuffles. Got it. I'll watch my back." She looked around at the sheer amount of *stuff* everywhere.

"Just to be clear, so I don't throw up my hands and give up on life prematurely—" she took a step back and almost fell over one of his suitcases "—does the fact that I can no longer see the carpet suggest you're moving in?"

He looked at her with the admiration that had been entirely missing from his perusal of her nonexistent tits. "Scotland Yard lost its brightest star when you went into show business. It's going to be just like living with Jacques Clouseau."

"You're moving in. Here."

He dropped the obnoxious flippancy and picked up two large suitcases. With one hand. "For the time being." He didn't sound thrilled. "I've signed an eight-week contract with the show, on two conditions. One of which was this room."

Judging by the face, he hadn't checked the other names on the tenancy agreement.

"Did the other condition involve me joining the queue at the Jobcentre?" Trix asked sarcastically, and he straightened to look at her.

"Startling revelation, I know, Tinker Bell, but I don't base all my major life decisions around you." He gestured with his bags. "Which room?"

"End of the hall, last door on the right." Directly opposite hers. Dear God.

Manners kicked in, and she picked up a box and followed him. He tossed both suitcases on the bare mattress in his room and turned.

"I see you still play rugby," she said absently, handing over the box of mud-encrusted trainers and gear. Leo had been the hero of the rugby team at their school in Buckinghamshire, although he'd blown out his knee the year she'd won a scholarship to boarding school in London, and—

And he'd suddenly gone completely rigid. The expression in his velvety eyes was a complicated mix of…what? Regret? Discomfort?

The pained body language was a bit unnecessary. She'd placed the pile of old shoes and dirty laundry politely into his arms; she hadn't slammed it into his testicles.

When he eventually bothered to answer her single attempt at small talk, his voice was cool. "I still kick a ball around now and then."

"Yes," she said sweetly. "I suspect I'm shortly going to have that impulse myself."

With a narrowed look, he returned to the lounge to collect more of his crap. "And our other two flatmates are—"

"Acrobats, gym addicts, carb thieves, and usually out of the flat by six."

"So am I." Leo lifted another box, rested it on his shoulder, and spoke with the exact level of optimism she felt herself. "It'll be like we're hardly living together at all."

Since she was about to stub her toe on it, Trix picked up a clear plastic case full of brushes, which turned out to be much heavier than it looked. "Considering the general trend of the past twenty-four hours, I wouldn't count on it. I think one of us did something to piss off the universe, and my amazing powers of deduction suggest most likely you."

Or not.

Trix came extremely close to spitting a mouthful of water all over the papers on Marco's desk. He'd already seen her covered in someone else's vomit, so she'd probably hit peak gross-out levels last night, but his opinion of her could apparently still plummet even more.

She looked from his scowling face—really excelling at the motivate-your-staff aspect of management there—to Natalie, and the head trainer, Steph.

She'd known the most likely outcome of this meeting, but she didn't enjoy being right.

"Cassie's already left," she repeated. She reached forward to set the glass of water down on the desk.

"To join a company in Australia," Natalie confirmed. The assistant stage manager was an attractive woman in her forties with very green eyes and very purple hair. Since Steph had just put blue tips in hers, the three of them looked like a *Jem and the Holograms* tribute band. "Apparently she met an Aussie while she was doing a bus tour last Christmas and they're sick of doing long-distance."

"Did she break her contract? Are you just accepting her resignation?" And yes, Trix was looking for any possible out right now, even at the expense of romance.

"It was up for renewal anyway, and she's chosen not to continue with us," Natalie said neutrally, and Marco muttered something inaudible. He was probably summoning his flying monkeys.

Trix's hands seemed to float up to press against her cheeks of their own accord. A little spontaneous imitation of *The Scream* emoji. "You want me to take over as Doralina."

She knew the Night Wraith choreography in theory; every so often, she sketched it out in an understudy rehearsal, skipping over the really difficult moves, and barely holding some positions for even a second.

"There's no dialogue to learn, at least," Natalie offered, trying to be helpful.

Doralina was a unique principal role in that she never spoke. She just swooped through the other characters' nightmares in a series of death-defying feats of endurance and flexibility.

And occasionally sang.

"There is the second-act solo, though," Natalie added, reading her appalled mind. "One of the voice coaches will be here shortly and we'll see where we are with that."

Trix slid one hand up to her forehead, then ran it over her tousled hair. She wasn't tone-deaf. She was classically trained and had a good voice.

She also hadn't had a performance solo in over three years.

In fact, the last time she'd sung alone onstage had been at her audition for *Masks*, when she'd put her name down for all the principal roles. Aimed high. Nothing ventured, nothing gained. At that point in her career, she'd lacked experience but apparently not confidence. According to the director, that ballsy disregard of her own limitations had secured her the role of the irreverent Pierrette.

She'd pirouetted across the boards on opening night with stars in her eyes and rock-solid transitions, seeing herself somersaulting right up the career ladder and heading for bigger and brighter things.

What the fuck had happened to that Trix?

Her heart was trying to punch out of her chest. Her hands were shaking. And a symphony of voices were commentating in her head, all basic variations of *hell no*. Marco's. Dan's. Leo's. Her own.

"I can't." The words materialised out loud, and she

imagined them hanging in the air, as if she'd written them in fire with a sparkler.

Steph came to sit on the edge of the desk in front of her, blocking her view of the other two. She leaned forward, resting her hands on her thighs. She was all compact muscle and strength, and exuded competence. "You can," she said emphatically. "Pierrette is far too easy for you now, and you haven't been pushing yourself enough for ages."

"I'm used to the hoop." Trix closed her fingers around the thumb of her opposite hand, digging her nails in. "Doralina is almost entirely straps and silks." She'd always enjoyed both straps and silks, but she hadn't been doing much of either. Each discipline tested different muscle groups and skill sets, and the hoop was where she felt most comfortable and confident in her ability.

If she ever wanted to reclaim the pieces of that past Trix, there was only one option. She would have to push herself. One new challenge and one step at a time.

This was more of a fucking huge leap. Across a burning pit of lava.

"We'll take out the most advanced transitions until you've found your feet—or your wings," Steph said, "but you can absolutely handle it. I've seen you do a lot of Paige's moves when you're just messing about at training. If you can do it for fun, you can do it for the audience. You definitely have the upper body strength for her routines."

Trix wondered if Steph was politely suggesting that for such a short person she had the shoulders of a rugby prop.

"You've got a very similar build to Paige, and your

size is an advantage for this role." Steph grinned in a flash of white teeth. "You're like a little whippet when you build up momentum up there, and you can't tell me you don't enjoy having more room to move than you get on Pierrette's hoop."

A flashback of Paige soaring above the stage, beautiful, graceful, powerful, every muscle locked tight in a culmination of years of experience, before suddenly jerking, fumbling her grip and slamming into the side of the metal dragon. Then tumbling down like a rag doll.

Steph read her mind. "What happened to Paige is not going to happen to you. That was an entirely avoidable accident."

"We'll audition candidates before we permanently recast the role, but we'll need you in the meantime." Marco looked as doubtful as she felt about her unexpected little rise up the ranks. "Dana will fill in as Pierrette."

"And I think we should just formally promote Trix and Dana to the roles right now." Natalie sounded uncharacteristically belligerent. That probably had more to do with wanting to thwart Marco than an overwhelming belief in Trix's career prospects.

"No," she said hastily. "Hold the auditions." *As soon as possible.*

Steph put her hands on her hips. "Don't rule out the possibility of expanding your horizons before you've even given yourself a chance."

Trix lowered from a suspended headstand into a back lever, her weight held by her straightened arms, her body facedown parallel to the ground.

"Control," Steph said, her eyes intent on Trix's form.

She felt a quiver run down her arms, a muscle shift, and she released the hold, dropping her legs to the ground. She wasn't even going to attempt the side planche, which would twist her body to the side so that one arm crossed behind her back. With technique this poor, she'd rip the labrum out of her shoulder socket.

Steph bent to run experienced hands over Trix's shoulders and arms, massaging the muscles there. "We'll stick to the standard meathook there for now."

In other words, as they'd had to do for most of the choreography in this routine so far, they'd sub in all the moves that *looked* impressive but were actually comparatively easy. Flash over substance.

The voice session had been borderline acceptable. Trix had managed a decent rendition of Doralina's power medley, and was under instructions to rehearse it even in the shower, which she was sure would thrill men and hedgehog alike.

"This is partly self-sabotage," Steph said. There was no judgment in her tone, but Trix inwardly flinched. "You can and have done all these transitions a dozen times. I'm not sure what happened to knock your confidence this past year or so, but a little self-belief wouldn't go astray right now."

Trix said nothing, and Steph patted her on the shoulder. "We'll work on it." She checked her watch. "After you take a break. Water, food, stretching. Meditate it out. We'll meet back here in thirty."

Trix waited until Steph's bouncing ponytail disappeared through the outer door before she got to her feet, gave herself a shake both literally and metaphorically, and reached for the straps again. She was not going to be beaten by a couple of strips of nylon and her own inadequacy.

A few minutes later, she landed solidly on her butt for the third time in a row.

"Shit." She flopped backwards on the mat and dropped her arms over her sweaty face.

The padded ground in the gym muffled footsteps, so she jumped when a deep voice said, "Eight out of ten. The landing could use some work, but the language was colourful."

"Why do you hate me, fate?" Trix asked without opening her eyes.

"I don't want to jump to conclusions here, but I'm starting to get the impression you're never that glad to see me." Leo nudged her foot with the tip of his boot, and she reluctantly cracked her lashes open. "Heard about the promotion. Congratulations."

"I am not in the mood for your sarcasm right now."

He raised that annoying judgy eyebrow. "You don't seem to be jumping for joy. In fact, there wasn't a lot of vertical lift going on, period. What's the technical name for that dismount?"

"Piss off," she said without rancour. She was too dispirited and too knackered to emote.

He had a thick file of papers tucked under his arm, and when he shifted his stance, the thin fabric of his T-shirt pulled taut across his wide chest. It was a novelty to see a guy actually wearing a shirt in this building. Pecs aplenty. It would be a good slogan for the theatre's website.

"Point me in the direction of the choreographers' office and I will."

She did, listlessly, and he cocked his stupid, handsome, hairy head.

"Cheer up. Not everyone thinks you were in cahoots with the dragon to secure your rise to fame."

That did summon an expression from her, and his face changed as well.

"I'm joking, Trix. Jesus."

As a slightly politer version of the hand gesture she wanted to make, she dropped forward to rest her head on her legs and made a flicking movement with her fingers.

"Are you stretching or trying to tickle me?"

"I'm getting in character. Channelling Doralina and her incredibly useful ability to make men disappear."

"Something you have in common lately, from what I've heard." His voice was light, but there was a note in it that made her look up.

"Excuse me?" she said dangerously.

His firm lips tilted at one corner. "People keep assuming I'm avidly interested in your love life. Three-date rule, is it? Before you apparently kick them so hard into the friend-zone that Manchester United's talent scout comes knocking on the door."

If he made the mistake of turning his back on her before her temper simmered down, he was going to experience her penalty kick for himself.

She got to her feet and snatched up her towel. "None of your business."

"No." He surprised her by *almost* sounding apologetic. "It's not. I told them to sod off, and I shouldn't have repeated that garbage, even in a crap attempt at winding you up." Then, just as she thought he was almost tolerable for a few seconds, he shot himself in the foot by adding, "If you want to date half of London, you should be able—"

Trix had a fanciful vision of herself swelling with outrage until she floated into the air like a helium balloon. "Well. Gee. Thanks for your blessing, Mother Superior."

He had cut himself off anyway, and winced slightly. "That was meant to be something along the lines of personal preferences being nobody's business but our own. Somehow it came out in Sanctimonious Arsehole."

"It *is* your most fluent language."

"I'll take myself off to the office now."

"You do that."

By nine o'clock that night, sitting across from her best friend over the remains of a pub dinner, Trix was more of a shrivelled balloon than a helium balloon.

"Sorry I was so late," she apologised again. The fairy lights on the brick wall behind them cast stars across the surface of her beer. It was oddly relaxing.

Her current state of lethargy was also helped by the alcohol content, and the fact that her arms and legs felt like stretched playdough.

Lily rested her chin on her palm. Her platinum blond hair was falling out of a messy knot and she wasn't wearing any makeup. And as usual, she looked like she'd just stepped out of an ad for really expensive perfume. "You already apologised twice. It's fine. But you look *knackered*. I'm thinking you should be in bed, not waiting for— Who's the band?"

"Matt Flynn. And I am knackered. But I don't feel like going home to stew in my own anxiety."

"Are you not doing so good right now?" Her brown eyes concerned, Lily pushed her sundae dish away. Her engagement ring caught the sparkle of the fairy lights. It was elegant, and beautiful, and a little bit quirky, like its owner. Her fiancé, the top West End director Luc Savage, knew her very well.

In fact, she was radiating a distinct air of just-shagged-my-man-and-it-was-*phenomenal*.

Trix coughed. "You weren't late yourself this evening, by any chance?"

A tinge of pink filled Lily's cheeks. "I might have been *slightly* late also. Don't change the subject. What's going on? Is it just the new role? Because you can absolutely do it."

"Or I will absolutely fail."

"You're not going to fail." Lily made a philosophical flowering gesture with her hands. "And what *is* failure, really?"

"Everyone getting up, leaving, and demanding their money back, leading to the show folding, the theatre closing, and years from now, us looking back at this conversation as decrepit, probably tipsy old bats and realising that this was the moment when my life officially sunk into a cesspool?"

"All right," Lily said after a moment. "That wouldn't be ideal. Apart from the tipsy old bats part, which sounds like a fucking hoot. Luc'll be approaching crypt-keeper status by then, and I confidently expect him to be a miserable old git, but hopefully a sprightly one."

Luc was a good fifteen years older than Lily, but her experience with intergenerational dating had turned out a hell of a lot better than Trix's. Of course, Luc wasn't a total dickhead, which helped.

"Seriously, you're not going to fail. It's about time you had something new to do work-wise. You were always the one who wanted lots of different experiences. Try it all, until you find something that feels right? Live in the moment, make your own happiness, dream big?"

Younger-Trix had been an extraordinarily *peppy* person, apparently. Until she'd encountered an actual test of that optimism and folded like a collapsible deckchair.

Lily hesitated. "It would be totally natural if you wanted a fresh start now that you're well past the breakup with—" Her voice trailed off.

The D-word that they *still* danced around, thanks to Trix almost destroying their friendship by falling for a complete twatnozzle and then acting like one herself.

Dan. Douchebag. Disaster. Deepest regret. Choose a term and insert here. They all applied.

Picking up her fork, Trix looked down at her plate as she traced a pattern in the leftover gravy with the tines. "Yeah. It's been almost a year now." And it felt like a lifetime. Someone else's lifetime. She *should* be well past the breakup by now. Dan was out of her life, and in hindsight he'd never been in her heart, just wormed into her brain and hormones. So it should be out of sight, out of mind, everything back to normal.

During their final post-breakup showdown, she'd been so infuriated that she'd stormed around to his flat and given him a verbal shredding—a release that had felt better than any of the admittedly good orgasms she'd had with him. After which, she'd thought she would just spring back to being the person she'd been before, as if he'd been a temporary blip. Slithering his way into her life, imploding her entire sense of self-respect, and then forcibly ejected and forgotten.

Telling him exactly what she thought of him had been cathartic, and closed the chapter of him being *physically* present in her life, but the high of that moment had faded quickly.

She could cut out the shrapnel, but the scar didn't just disappear.

Lily was watching her with uncomfortable perception. "Are you still talking to the therapist at the theatre?"

"Yes." She was contractually obliged to. *The Festival of Masks* employed an interdisciplinary team of trainers, physiotherapists, and a clinical psychologist as part of their safety practice. It was all intended to minimise injury and cast turnover.

It would probably be more effective if she could get up the courage to do more at her monthly sessions than crack self-deprecating jokes and evade all questions. Handling the work, sure, no problem. Nope, no worries in her personal life. She was seeing a handful of nice men now and then. Top-quality blokes. Wasn't getting her heart broken. No hang-ups whatsoever. Nothing to see here.

"You don't still have feelings for him, do you?"

The fact that Lily could genuinely worry about that was a sign Trix really *did* need to make some changes.

She snorted. "*Fuck no.* I'd rather chew off my own hand than ever see him again. It's not about Dan, as a person, anymore. It's about me, and the fact I could ever have thought I was in love with someone like that in the first place."

She'd let him strip so much away before she'd realised what he was doing.

Weak. It made her feel weak, even thinking about it.

And she'd never, *ever* thought that about herself before him. She'd never seen herself that way.

"I still don't know why you forgave me," she said suddenly, setting her glass down.

Dan had despised Lily. He'd done his best to drive a wedge between them, and she'd almost let him do it. To the person who'd been fiercely loyal to her since the first day they'd met at boarding school.

She had been awful to Lily, and she'd never forget that, even if they were still sitting together over a beer seventy years from now.

"Hey." Lily hooked her pinky finger through Trix's. "Who slept in my bed with me when I had nightmares at school? Who drove me all the way to Glasgow for an audition? Who made me see the funny side of being stuck in a contract playing the biggest bitch on prime-time TV? Whenever I need help, you're there. It was one really shitty page in what I hope is a very long book for both of us. And it is *not* your fault. It's all on him." Lily was emphatic as she spoke the words she'd tried to drill into Trix a hundred times before. It was easier to listen to them than it was to believe them.

Lily's grip tightened on hers. "We're forever, you and me. You and Luc are my soulmates. You're my family."

Trix blew out a quick breath. Her eyes were stinging.

"We're good, Trix," Lily said firmly. "We'll always be good." She gave their joined hands a little shake. "And we'll keep on keeping on until *you're* good, too."

"Oh, shit," Trix said after a throat-clogged pause. "I'm going to cry in The Irish Rover. Change the subject fast. Final wedding plans. Update me."

Lily gave Trix's fingers a last squeeze before she picked up her own drink. "No idea," she said through a mouthful of lager. "You'd have to ask Célie."

Lily and Luc had intended to have a simple ceremony and dinner, until his mother, the French singer Célie Verne, had asked if she could take over the organisation. Within the space of a month, they'd picked up a full wedding party and over two hundred guests, who would all be heading to an estate in Cornwall next month.

Trix had broached the subject of time off from the show for bridesmaid duty, which Marco had approved after he'd found out it was Luc Savage's wedding, because he was a sycophantic arse, and she was holding him to that capitulation regardless of what role she was playing.

"She calls every day to get final approval on stuff, but she's pretty much handling the whole thing," Lily said, "and I'm so grateful, that if we ever have a lifestyle that would suit a dog I may have to name it after her."

"Should I be at all concerned that I don't have a dress yet?" Trix asked, reaching out to snag one of the soft-centre chocolates that had come with Lily's sundae. Self-care with caramel. She was all right with that.

"Célie's on it. She asked what your taste is. I said feathers, virulent shades of orange, and a shit-ton of tulle."

"Excellent."

Through the hubble-bubble of voices in the pub,

Trix heard a guitar warming up. "Matt Flynn's set is about to start."

Lily craned her neck, trying to see. A whole group of businessmen who'd been gaping at her from the bar, tongues hanging around their knees, almost fell off their stools trying to get a better gander down her top. She remained oblivious to the perving going on nearby. "Do they have a warm-up act?"

"It's a pub gig, Lily. Not a rock concert at the O2." Trix shook her head in mock sadness. "All this hob-nobbing with the rich and famous. You're just becoming so very… Mayfair."

A stale pretzel hit her on the back of the head, and she grinned. Her fingers tapped on the table with the rhythm of the violin.

Amusement vanished when a barmaid moved away from a booth near the entrance and she saw who was sitting there.

"Unbelievable."

"Problem?" Lily leaned forward. "Oh, Leo's here." She cast a mischievous glance sideways. "What a happy coincidence to celebrate the two of you moving in together."

She started to raise her hand, and Trix took it down with a speed that would impress many a rugby scrum half. "Don't even think about it."

"Yeah, and by the way, oldest and dearest friend," Lily said, twisting in her seat, "what's *that* about? You've known Leo since you were kids? And in the entire time I was working with him, you didn't find it necessary to mention that fact?"

Lily was currently playing Elizabeth I in the Tudor play *1553* at Luc's theatre. Leo had headed their makeup team for the opening month as a favour to Luc, who unfortunately had the bad taste to be friends with him, and Lily had made some rather unsubtle suggestions at the time. Trix had practised selective deafness.

"I thought you were total strangers. And he was clearly interested—"

"Interested in having as little to do with me as possible."

"—and he seemed so nice and quiet and gentlemanly that I figured it would be a textbook case of opposites attracting," Lily finished, grinning at her and ignoring her sour interruption.

"Ha-ha. 'Nice.' 'Quiet.'"

"I spent three solid hours with him when he was doing the design for my Elizabeth makeup, and all he said was 'yes,' 'no,' and 'stop moving your eyebrows.' He was the original big, brooding, and silent type."

"Oh, he shuts up when he's *working*. He can only focus on one thing at once, so it's the only time he keeps his pithy little comments to himself."

"You know," Lily said thoughtfully, "it's interesting. Luc's known Leo for a few years now, and I know a lot of people who've worked with him, and everybody else seems to have a really high opinion of him."

"Nobody more so than Leo himself, I'm sure."

"Kind-hearted, they say. Intelligent, they say. Funny. Good manners, even."

Trix wasn't sure what her face was doing, but it made Lily hastily press her lips together.

"I find it odd that in ten years of deep, meaningful, often drunken conversation, you never once mentioned this epic tale of insults and hostility." She took another comprehensive look in Leo's direction. "With one of the sexiest men on the planet."

"I don't waste my time talking about irrelevant things," Trix said loftily and completely untruthfully.

"He was at your school in Bucks? You've obviously kept in touch." And Lily was obviously going to cling to this distasteful subject like a mouse clutching a piece of Stilton. Her perfect, classical nose was all but twitching.

"Not by choice," Trix muttered. "He's a bloody Jack-in-the-Box. Pops up all over London. We were having a pretty good run these past few months before the universe decided to kick me in the teeth, but usually, everywhere I look, there's Leo. Weddings. Christenings. Train stations. The biscuit aisle in the supermarket. The bus to the King's Road. Your production party." While she was trying not to look back at the far booth, Trix saw that he'd found himself a friend, a girl with endless legs and curves, flawless-looking brown skin and masses of black ringlets. She leaned towards him across the table, her brows pinching together. "My local pub."

"Well, he's living nearby, so it *is* technically his local now, too," Lily pointed out reasonably.

"Nearby? Judging by how long I had to wait before I could have a quick shower tonight, he's going to be living in my bathroom."

"You wouldn't have to share a shower with anyone if you'd just rented my flat after I moved in with Luc."

She and Lily lived in different stratospheres, not just different boroughs, when it came to finances. "It was a really nice offer, Lily, but I couldn't afford to live in a three-bed flat in Chelsea in a million years."

"The rent was less than you were paying in your last place."

"The rent you invented out of thin air was peanuts," Trix said bluntly, "and I appreciate your loyalty and crap idea of property investment more than I can say, but I'm fine in the company house. Even if there does seem to be a universal law that if you get two or more twentysomething guys in the same flat, everything starts to smell of man sweat, even though I know for a fact that all three of them take thirty-minute showers."

Lily stared at Leo's booth again. "Is that Leo's girl-friend?" The question was suspiciously casual.

Trix didn't bother to turn her head this time. "Probably. Gorgeous and grumpy. Just Saint Leander's type."

Lily's expression suggested that she was struggling to contain about fifty questions at once. She closed her lips into an incredibly aggravating smile.

"Don't even." Trix was goaded, against her better judgment. "This is not a 'we-bicker-because-we-want-to-bang' situation. It's a 'he's-a-tosspot-and-I've-learned-my-lesson' situation."

"I don't believe I mentioned sex," Lily said sweetly. "What an interesting direction your mind took."

A dark wave swamped Trix without warning. All the conversation about Dan had roused enough bad memories. She didn't feel like revisiting teenage humiliation. "Leave it, Lily."

Every trace of amusement fell away from Lily. Her eyes flickered. "Did he hurt you, T?"

Lily had witnessed enough of the shit with Dan that she was probably imagining all sorts. Trix forced a smile. "He bruised my fragile teenage heart, that's all. I thought he— Well, I thought wrong."

Suddenly, in her mind, she saw Leo's smile. The genuine, real deal, not the sarcastic version he usually threw her way now. Laughter in his eyes, a warm glance that lingered on her face. A deep, teasing voice. Even at fifteen, he'd had a man's voice.

The sexiest guy on the planet.

Pity he'd turned out to be such a prick.

"You know he's invited to the wedding?"

She'd suspected but absorbed the confirmation with a groan. "I hope Célie has tequila jotted down on her clipboard, and lots of it."

With a wry look, Lily tilted her head towards the door, where Jono had just come in with a couple of friends. "There's Jono. We like *him*, right? Can I call him over or will you lunge forward and wrestle me to the table again?"

Jono had already spotted them and was coming over, his really fit friends following behind. It was a trio of twinkling eyes, closely shaved chins, and greetings devoid of all traces of sarcasm. How refreshing.

"Hey, Trix. Lily. Room for a few more?"

With a narrowed stare at Lily the Smug, Trix returned Jono's friendly smile. "Always."

Deliberately, she moved her chair so her back was squarely to the door.

At this rate, Leo was going to end up surprised if he opened a door and Trix *wasn't* on the other side of it. Gym door: Trix, repeatedly messing up an aerial move. Bathroom door: Trix, wrapped in a towel and audibly tapping her foot, all freckles and attitude. Pub door: Trix yet again, now practically sitting on Angel Boy's lap.

What a treat for the eyes while he was trying to

enjoy a beer, listen to some live music, and wonder what vicious, fanged demon had possessed his baby sister while she'd been out of the UK.

"Are you even listening to me?" Cat asked, in what only a saint wouldn't describe as a spine-grating whine. She drummed her painted nails on the table.

He'd ordered her a piña colada from the pub's limited cocktail menu. It had been her drink of choice since she'd first raided a bottle of white rum from their grandmother's booze cabinet, age fifteen, but apparently only the "socially inept" drank those in New York.

"New York good, London pile of shit, you're only here under duress, and you have no interest in taking up the summer internship with *The Festival of Masks* wardrobe department that I had to negotiate as part of my contract and call in a massive favour with Allie to secure." He set down his beer and looked at her questioningly. "Does that about cover it?"

Cat leaned back in the booth and folded her arms. "You don't have to be a dick about it."

Pots and kettles and glasshouses and stones came to mind, but with a lot of restraint he only said, "Not trying to be a dick, Cat. Just trying to understand."

How could a twelve-month fashion design course turn the fairly normal twenty-year-old he'd driven to the airport into this pain-in-the-arse doppelgänger?

"It's not like I *asked* you to get me a job in the theatre," Cat pointed out.

She had literally been asking exactly that for the past three years, but whatever. Don't argue with the doppelgänger.

"Anyway, I didn't say I *wouldn't* do it," Cat went on

with massive condescension. She wrinkled her nose
and propped her chin on her fist. "I suppose it's better than nothing."

The thousands of fashion students who would pull
out their teeth one by one for a shot at interning backstage in the West End would be glad to hear it.

Matt Flynn, one of his favourite local bands, were
hitting their stride with a song about troublemaking
women, and he could fucking well *relate*.

He flicked a glance towards the back of the pub
again. The place was filling up, but he could see a
flash of pink hair in the low light, and could swear he
heard a giggle above the guitar chords.

"Who do you keep looking at?" Cat twisted to look
over her shoulder, and the crowds conveniently parted
to clear her view. "The blonde with the tits or the one
cosplaying Nymphadora Tonks?" She picked up the
piña colada and took an absent-minded sip, obviously
forgetting it was loser juice. "Neither look like your
type."

"According to you, my only type is desperate, delusional, and preferably deaf." When she was just being
an annoying sister rather than an entitled brat, Cat
would probably find that she got on like a house on
fire with the Tonks lookalike.

They were both gold-standard ego-shredders.

"Uncannily accurate description of all your exes,"
Cat retorted, with a cruelly short-lived flash of a smile
and her usual sense of humour. Then the demon descended again, with a crabby demand: "What does
the job pay?"

What the job would *cost* was beginning to seem like
the more relevant question. Short answer: a few more

threads of his rapidly fraying professional reputation if his sister brought this attitude into the Old Wellington.

Covertly, beneath the table, he pulled his phone from his pocket. He needed to work on his sketches for the SFX championship before he went to bed tonight—one creation good enough to get him through the qualifying round, and a showstopper for the final—and he had to finish making a list of materials.

Cat scowled when he told her the hourly wage for the internship, which admittedly wasn't great—apart from a handful of the biggest names, even the full-time performers didn't earn serious money in theatre—but it was more than a lot of people made, whose work was more arduous than hers would be, and the experience was beyond price. And he'd put their modest inheritance from their grandparents into a trust for Cat that gave her a small amount of additional income each month, so unless she expected to *buy* from all the designers she looked up to, she should be able to afford her rent.

"Are you serious?" she demanded. "I could make way more than that working at a corner café in Manhattan."

He seriously doubted it.

"I don't remember anyone actually dragging you back from the States by the hair," he commented mildly. "If you wanted to stay that badly, you could have."

As she had each time he'd ventured into dangerous territory this week, she bristled, stuck her lower lip out, and changed the subject. "Do you still need me to model for you for this competition?" She didn't sound enthusiastic about that, either.

Too bloody bad. She'd agreed to act as his model

weeks ago. Or his blank canvas, as he tended to think
of the clients he worked on. He kept that term to himself. People found it oddly insulting.

Back when he'd first started training in makeup and
special effects artistry, he'd practised on his mates, his
girlfriends, people from the club where he'd worked
part-time as a bouncer—essentially, anyone he could
bribe with a free lunch into sitting still for a few hours
while he slathered them with paint and latex. These
days, he had several people on his contacts list he
could call up and actually pay, but when he'd raised
the subject during a terse long-distance conversation,
he'd imagined Cat would be grateful for the extra cash.
And neither of them had to be at the theatre until mid-
afternoon that day, so she would still be free to come
to the morning qualifying round with him.

"Yes," he said firmly. It would be a hassle to book
someone else now at such short notice, but more im-
portantly, if Cat's obnoxiousness indicated some sort
of personal crisis, she could deal with it where he could
keep an eye on her. Not by maxing out her credit cards
in Covent Garden. "Preliminary round is Wednesday
morning at the Grosvenor Arena. Eight a.m. Sharp."

Things didn't officially kick off until half-eight,
but Cat had inherited their Nan's sense of timekeep-
ing, and he couldn't afford to have anything go wrong
with his entry. The stakes were off the scale. Winning
the title always came with industry kudos, but with
a top studio executive taking over as head judge this
year, the prize included a one-on-one meeting with her,
and the chance of a two-year contract on her latest net-
work series. The show was heavy on special effects,

shooting nine months of the year in the States, and a fast-track to patching the holes in his frayed career.

"Nothing turns out the way you think it will," Cat muttered into her glass, with a bitterness that made him lift his head sharply.

She looked determinedly away, clearly not willing to engage.

On the other side of the room, Trix got up to dance to an Irish rock song and laughingly let Angel Boy twirl her by her outstretched arms.

"Yeah. Well." He picked up his own drink again. "That's life, isn't it?"

Sláinte.

Chapter Three

On Monday afternoon, after playing musical chairs with the casting, they had a full rehearsal for the first time since tech week. The aerialists and acrobats had to train most days to stay in condition, but they didn't usually drag in the entire cast and a skeleton orchestra to keep them company.

So very *many* people to watch Trix doing such a very mediocre job.

By the time Marco had shouted his way through the first act, she was quite happy to maintain eye contact with him while she sang Doralina's power lyrics about punishing the follies and vanities of man.

He stalked around the stage, getting in everybody's way, conferred with one of the voice therapists and then snapped, "A robot could deliver that performance. Feel the *vengeance* behind the words. Doralina holds the power of destruction within her grasp, and only that thin thread of morality keeps her from eviscerating her enemies."

Trix ought to have nailed this role immediately, because she and Doralina were clearly sisters of the soul.

"You're flat," Marco continued to berate her.

Undeniably true, but she suspected he wasn't talking about the contents of her sports bra.

Nearby, Jono slowly lowered himself back to a vertical hold on the trapeze, biceps bulging in a show of effortless strength. "I think she sounded great," he said loyally, without a single falter in his concentration.

"And she's doing significantly better with the first-act rope routine," Steph added.

Everyone continued to ignore Marco's grumbling, which was standard practice, and Trix appreciated the support, she really did, but she was starting to feel like the kid stumbling along at the back of the egg-and-spoon race to the accompaniment of pity cheers.

She missed the final transition in the easiest of the straps routines, and just hung there for a moment, legs dangling, toes incongruously pointed, the spotlight throwing starry pinpoints into her vision. Dust was dancing in the air around the stage. She could see the orchestra still playing, but in that instant, there was nothing but a roar of white noise and ghosts of the past in her ears.

"I think it's admirable that you keep trying. Some people would realise they were wasting their time and just give up. Are you ready yet, darling? I don't want to be late again. Unfortunately, people aren't quite as laidback in financial circles as they are in the... dance world."

Air quotes around "dance world," every time, so that she was pretty sure most of Dan's friends in the "financial circles" thought the Old Wellington was a brothel.

Echoes of passive-aggressive laughter.

Taint of her own gullibility.

Trix drew in a long breath, for a second seemed to be unable to release it, and dropped out of the hold so that her feet hit the floor squarely.

"Ten-minute break," Natalie called from her seat in the front row, and as far as Trix was concerned, the lighting crew should shine an angelic golden beam down on her purple head.

Her hands were shaking again, and her stomach was queasy, and there was sweat under her ears that had nothing to do with the physical exertion of the routines. This was more than normal stage nerves. She needed to get out, alone, and fast. Before her heart physically propelled itself out of her chest.

A group of burlesque dancers were lounging around in the wings, wearing giraffe onesies and eating crisps while they waited for their cues, and Trix squeezed past them enviously. She thought she returned their greetings as she shoved her feet into her shoes, but her ears were still buzzing and her vision was going blurry, and she ignored the faint sound of Jono calling her name.

Backstage, all the noise seemed to coalesce and the chaos faded into a peripheral fuzz, so that the only person Trix could focus on, as if she were standing at the end of a tunnel, was the beautiful girl with amazing curly hair who was saying loudly, "If she's supposed to be the star of the show, she's a bit shit, isn't she?"

She was working so hard to control her breathing that it didn't seem the slightest bit strange that Leo's girlfriend from the pub last night was here in the theatre now. Publicly slagging her off.

Trix turned abruptly and continued her power walk to the back hallways. She didn't stop moving until she'd pushed through the outside door to the rear alley, which was hot, dirty, and smelly, but thankfully empty.

Letting out another breath that ended too quickly in a small squeak, Trix dropped to a crouch on the uneven cobblestones and pressed her forehead into the palms of her hands.

She was going to have a heart attack. She was going to have a heart attack and die right here beside a dustbin that stank like mouldy old socks.

I'm fine. I'm okay. I can do this. I can do this. IcandothisIcandothisIcanIcanI—

...can't.

Leo stopped by the wardrobe office on his way back from a meeting with the lighting director. The lighting scheme for the show used a lot of blue filters, which didn't transmit enough red and tended to turn pink-based makeup into grey corpse flesh.

The lighting crew didn't want to change the status quo.

He didn't want burlesque dancers who looked like they'd just lurched out of a coffin.

"Hey, Allie," he said, poking his head through the door. The office was an L-shaped room and contained so many clothing and fabric samples that it could have looked like a celebrity's overstuffed closet, but both senior costume designers were Type A perfectionists and had their space organised with military precision. Someone had obviously had an anal-retentive orgasm getting carried away with a label-maker. There was even a triple-tier of drawers labelled "Pasties—Small, Medium, Large."

He removed his gaze from that after an extended

pause, and refocused his mind. "How's your afternoon been?" Blatant subtext: *how has Cat's afternoon been, and have you justifiably murdered my little sister and hidden her body in one of these trunks?*

Allie's return smile was a shade too wide. *Shit.* "Oh, my afternoon's been great, how about yours? And on a completely unrelated note, there's a set of ceramic dishes I want. They're hand-painted and expensive. I'll text you the link."

Leo winced. "That bad?"

She made a nostalgic humming noise. "Remember the good old days when I'd come around to your Nan's for tea, and Cat would want to impress me, and she'd be all sweet and cute and we'd set the table together? Let's just say that if I pick up a butter knife today, she really shouldn't stand within reach."

He shook his head. "I'm sorry about this. I don't know what the hell happened in New York, but she can't bring it into work. I'll have another word with her."

"And sadly, that was the last time anyone saw him alive."

He grinned. "Hand-painted and expensive, was it?"

"*Very* expensive." Allie looked at him ominously. "And this is only Monday. My poor shattered nerves. My wispily thin skin. Expect to add another eyeliner tutorial to the compensation package by Friday."

"It's been ten years, Allie. If you still can't draw one black line on your eyelid without turning yourself into a cartoon burglar, it might be time to move on in life."

"I will not be defeated!" she declared, flipping him off with derogatory affection. "I *will* master the perfect feline flick by thirty."

Leo checked the time as he ducked back through the doorway. He'd skipped his afternoon break, so there was enough time to get to the art supply shop on the next block before his debrief with Marco. Should probably pick up a coffee, too. The caffeine buzz might give him enough patience to hold his temper.

Wending through the backstage hallways, he smilingly shrugged off the attempts of a teasing-eyed burlesque dancer to gauge his relationship status, and caught an armful of props from an overburdened intern before they crashed to the floor. He also caught sight of Cat, propped up in the entrance to the green room. She was repeatedly running a length of sequinned fabric between her fingers, but unless she was attempting to generate enough heat between her skin and the polyester to remove the wrinkles without an iron, she wasn't working. She was looking up between her lashes, and swaying back and forth slightly, and trying to flirt with Trix's Angel Boy. Jono. Leo really should remember his name. Since Trix seemed to be cuddling the guy every time he saw them, Angel—*Jono* would probably be hanging out at the flat.

Wouldn't want to be rude.

He considered interrupting but kept going. With someone else listening, it wasn't the ideal moment to suggest, politely and reasonably, that Cat either tell him what was wrong, and whether he needed to kill someone in the States, or drop the attitude and do some work.

There was time enough later to be called an interfering, unsympathetic arsehole.

The fastest route to the art shop was via the back alley behind the theatre. He swung the outside door open and almost fell over Trix, who for some reason was meditating by the rubbish bins.

Several staggeringly brilliant observations about that came to mind, but they all dried up when he got a proper look at her. She was cross-legged, white-knuckled, and making weird little hitching noises in the back of her throat, like a squeaky tricycle was being wheeled past.

Christ.

She wasn't meditating. She was having a full-blown anxiety attack.

Getting down on his haunches beside her, he cupped a hand around the back of her head. Her tangled pink hair was silk-soft under his calloused skin. It fleetingly crossed his mind that this was the first time in years he could remember touching her. Jesus, she was little. His hand looked and felt huge and unwieldy against the delicate bones of her skull.

"Trix?" He wasn't sure if she was even aware that he was here. He ducked his head and put his mouth by her ear. "Trix."

Her eyes jerked up to meet his. Enormous green-and-bronze pools of bottomless panic.

An invisible thread between his gut and his chest pulled taut. He kept his voice very level and firm. "You're all right. Just breathe in. Slowly. Hold. And breathe out. You're okay, Trix. You're fine."

One of her fists came up and grabbed a handful of his shirt, squeezing the fabric tightly. He detached her grip and linked his fingers through hers, holding her hand against the steady beat of his heart, keeping his own breaths deep and even. With his free hand, he reached into his pocket and pulled out his phone.

He unlocked it and thumbed through his apps until he found the one he was looking for.

"Here." He held the screen up so she could see it and then set the phone gently on her lap. "Keep your eyes on the circle. Breathe in for the first half, breathe out for the second."

She shot him a mulish look—stubborn even in the middle of a panic attack. But she watched the screen. And she didn't let go of his fingers while she breathed with it.

He wasn't sure how long they sat there. It was stinking hot in the alley, and it bloody reeked—evidently, this was the place where rancid cheese and rotten eggs came to die, but his other hand somehow came back to rest on her head, and after a while a strange sense of peace came down around them like a cool breeze.

It was the brief truce between battles in the middle of the war. As soon as she had full vocal capacity back, she'd no doubt make use of it. But it had been a shit of a month, apparently for her as well, and right at this moment he was surprisingly content to just sit here and listen to her slow, steady breathing. He stroked her hair.

Always, always, that little flicker of…

With a jerk, he moved his shoulders, as if he could physically tear that sensation from his skin; it was like the tickle of silk gliding across his nerve endings, simultaneously addictive and fucking unbearable.

Eventually, she shifted beside him, and he opened his grip so she could take her hand back.

"You all right?" he asked, careful to put no inflection into the query.

He expected to be told to go and make violent love to himself, to put it nicely, but after a full ten seconds

of ignoring him, she said without looking up, "Guess
not. Yet."

"This happen often?"

"Never." Her hand was slightly unsteady as she
pushed a lock of hair back behind her ear, revealing
the sharp, bony angles of her jaw and cheek. Her face
was completely bare today, and she had even more
freckles than he remembered. They were pinpoint dots
scattered across her skin, clustering in places like con-
stellations, which seemed fitting since she had a tattoo
of small black stars down the side of her neck.

He was fairly sure that if he got a ballpoint pen and
played join-the-dots with the freckles on her cheekbone, he'd end up with an outline of the Millennium
Falcon.

He was also fairly sure what she'd do to him if he
tried.

Resting one arm across his lap, he said, admittedly
reluctantly, "Do you want to talk about it?"

He figured and hoped that would be a resounding
no. The peaceful atmosphere had faded fast, to be re-
placed by a thick sense of urgency that was driving
him to get up and out of range of seeing, smelling, or
touching her until he'd got his equilibrium back.

In this instance, derision was a beautiful sound.
"To you? No." Her conscience must have been prod-
ding her, because she followed up with a subdued,
"Thank you."

For some reason, the underlying note of "*the fuck?*"
in her voice and her obvious bewilderment at the whole
situation needled under his skin. "You don't have to
sound quite so staggered. Whatever you think, I'm not

a complete dick. I wouldn't leave *anyone* alone in an alley gasping for breath."

She removed her fixed stare from her pink trainers and glared at him. "I didn't imagine you were helping me out of personal concern for my well-being," she said, taking his words the wrong way as usual, and *yes, please continue to be a snarky, wilfully obtuse, pain in the neck.*

That was their comfort zone, and he was good with it.

Standing, he automatically extended a hand to help her, but she was already scrambling up. Neither of them was making eye contact.

"Don't tell anyone." It was a sudden rush of words. Quietly, she added, "Please."

"I wouldn't. Ever."

She cast him a quick glance. She was still holding his phone, and she thumbed out of the anxiety app and was handing it back to him when her attention was arrested by his background pic. Her dark eyebrows went up. "You like *Galaxy Agent.*"

He owned the books, watched the show, was part of an online forum, and planned to go to the fan festival on the South Bank soon for the launch of the new volume. "Yeah."

She studied him. "Obsidian Knight or Red Queen?"

Without a word, he tugged up the sleeve of his shirt. At the centre of the tattoos on his right biceps was the Obsidian Knight.

Trix lifted her hand as if she were going to touch his arm. With the most minuscule of lip-curves, a gesture that was only distantly related to a smile, she twisted around and gathered up her hair so he could see the tiny Obsidian Knight tattoo on the back of her neck.

If he didn't think about who it was attached to, that was one of the sexiest things he'd ever seen.

"You realise that's going to be goddamn annoying to cover up every night." Not really. He could turn a five-foot-nothing woman into an eight-foot yeti if he had to; covering a tattoo was child's play.

Trix let go of her hair and turned back. "I've seen you completely change someone's appearance with a brow pencil and a roll of double-sided tape. Your massively inflated opinion of yourself has *some* justification. Professionally speaking only. I think you'll cope." At those last words, a cloud passed across her face.

He had moved farther into the alley—if he hurried, there was still time to get to the store and back without causing Marco to burst too many blood vessels—but he stopped. "You'll cope as well. And if it's the new role that's causing you this much grief—well. Maybe your opinion of yourself isn't inflated *enough*." His mouth quirked. "Professionally speaking only."

She blinked, as if she didn't recognise him, or a single syllable that was coming out of his mouth.

Something else they had in common.

Trix trudged home from the Tube at six o'clock that evening with legs the approximate consistency of gelatine. When she was dating Dan, he'd usually had a car collect her from work, which had made her feel like she was in a film for a while. Until she'd realised that his thoughtful gesture was because he wanted to be sure she was going straight home and not bouncing off to shag somebody else, and that most of those films were probably meant to be cautionary tales about predatory men and the dazzled fools they picked up at parties.

She was quite happy to take the Tube again now, jelly knees and all.

God. She'd had a panic attack.

At work.

In front of Leo.

Who had actually been really...*kind* about it. She'd still struggled with the rest of the rehearsal, but at least she'd made it back to the stage, and she owed a lot of that to him.

How massively unsettling and out of character.

But it wasn't like she was going to trot along at his side for the rest of her life so he could hold her hand whenever things got too much for her. For one thing, they were not friends, and what the hell.

She needed to be able to handle this herself. Help *herself.*

She was going to get through this.

She was not going to lose the person she'd been for a quarter of a century before she'd even met Dan to the lingering influence of that manipulative weasel.

She had downloaded Leo's app, though. Whatever methods worked. And the methods she wanted to employ right now were couch, wine, and the worst reality show she could find.

Unfortunately, when she opened the flat door, was hit by a wave of stuffy heat, and followed the scent of Eau de Men to the lounge, the couch was already occupied.

Three male heads attached to three space-hogging male bodies swivelled. Leo's eyes were sharp and interrogative; her other flatmates, Scott and Ryan, just looked as they usually did. A combination of friendliness and guilt. Like golden retrievers that were happy to have the rest of the fam home, but couldn't hide the fact that they'd been raiding the pantry.

"Let me guess," she said, dropping her bags on the floor and stretching out her left hamstring with a groan. "There's no booze and no chocolate biscuits."

"I'll go to the shops tomorrow," Scott said, with unfailing optimism. He bounded off the couch and stretched, too. He was shirtless and the movement caused an undulating effect from pecs to abs, like setting off a row of dominoes.

She was unmoved. He'd nicked all her comfort food again. There weren't enough happy trails and V-shaped pelvic muscles in the world to compensate.

"We were just reaching a consensus," Ryan said, also getting up. "We're going to head to the park and kick a ball around for a bit, then get some fish and chips and enjoy the weather while it's here. You coming with?"

Trix hesitated, her eyes tracking back to Leo. He was blank-faced now, and said nothing.

"There's a tiny breeze out there," Scott coaxed. "Unlike the airless cube here. Come on, T-rex. We haven't had a friendly match in ages. And you look half dead, so you can have a nap in the fresh air after dinner, while our temperamental *artiste* sets up his easel and draws pictures of lipsticks *al dente*."

"The temperamental *artiste* is sketching competition entries in an attempt to save his flagging career, you bell-end," Leo said. "And unless you're making fucking spaghetti, it's *en plein air*, not *al dente*."

"Same thing."

"Not even the same language, mate."

Trix interrupted the man spat. "As fun as this sounds—" She frankly thought she and Leo had been forced into close enough company for one day, and imagined he wholeheartedly agreed.

To her surprise, after a noticeable pause he stood, pushed his hands into his pockets, and shrugged. With the enthusiasm of someone anticipating a root canal, he said, "You probably shouldn't sit here by yourself; you'll just overthink everything."

Yes, she would.

And in the interests of positive steps forward, she *had* told herself she would start drawing again this week, if there was an opportunity. She could bring her own sketchbook…

Bit childish, isn't it… She slammed down a mental door on that encroaching echo of Dan's voice.

Scott took her silence as agreement. "Good, we're all going, then. Usual tackling rules?" he asked with a teasing glint. "Anything goes?"

Leo came to a dead halt in the middle of gathering his sketchbooks, and studied Trix from the top of her head to her scuffed trainers. "Yeah, I don't think so. We'll skip the tackling."

Trix exchanged glances with the other two and shook her head sadly. Just when she was beginning to credit him with some natural smarts, even a few good self-preservation instincts.

Ryan laughed out loud. "Well, we'll see, mate. Give it five minutes and then you can let her know if you can't handle it."

An hour later, Trix took Leo down yet again with

a front scissor kick. Having to do countless front split balances on the aerial straps was doing her *some* favours in life. She was very limber in the thighs today.

He hit the ground, rolled, and came back up to his feet in one motion. People who rejoiced in that much height and physical presence shouldn't be that graceful. It was just greedy, snatching all the genetic blessings on offer.

However, as someone who regularly bounced off crash mats, she could appreciate the artistry of a good fall.

He looked at her levelly, and she pressed her lips together to repress a smile. There was a definite hint of amusement lurking in his eyes. She arranged her face into an expression of intense sympathy. "Didn't you used to be, you know, *good* at this?" He'd been tipped to go pro at one point. "Too many greasepaint fumes over the years?"

Too late, she remembered his reaction last time she'd mentioned his rugby-playing past. It was an instant replay; he went strange and stiff again.

"More like dodgy knee." The amusement had vanished. "It's never quite forgotten the experience of being flattened under Damon Holland. What he lacked in brain space, he made up in body weight."

She'd known he'd been injured during a game, but she hadn't realised he'd been taken down by his own team member. "Damon Holland?" There was a blast from the past. Which unfortunately ruffled the surface of her own bad memories where Leo was concerned. "What, did he lose his balance in the scrum?"

"No," Leo said evenly. "He waited until the ref was distracted, slammed his boot into my Achilles tendon, and then 'accidentally' tripped over my leg and landed on my knee."

"What?" After Trix had left for London, Allie had kept her updated on the news from Bucks, but evidently she'd left a few things out. "Jesus. Why?" She adjusted her hold on the ball, hugging it to her chest. "Did you nick his girlfriend or something?"

Leo and Damon had always had an intense rivalry on the team, but she didn't remember them being at the point of physical brawling.

If she'd thought his reaction was odd before, it was nothing compared to his response now. He made a rough sound in his throat, a cross between a laugh and a snort, and shot her a completely incomprehensible look.

However, all he said was, "Come on. Dinner will be here shortly and I need to redeem myself."

"Understatement of the decade."

He moved so quickly she didn't see him coming. His hand came down and the ball shot up out of her grasp. "If you're referring to anything but the game, Tinker Bell—" She made a lunge for the ball and he held it on the tips of his fingers, high above her head. The soft cotton of his T-shirt rode up his raised arm, faintly smudged with grass stains. "She who fires the first arrow is responsible for the war. *Galaxy Agent*, volume two."

Trix feinted around him, poked a fingertip into a sensitive spot on his ribs that made him jerk reflexively and drop his arm, and snatched back the ball. "He who rewrites history is a self-serving, insulting dick. My memoirs, chapter one."

She took off with the ball and heard him swear behind her. A Labrador bounded up to them and non-verbally joined her team by latching on to the hem of Leo's shirt and trying to slow him down. A burble of laughter left her, and Leo couldn't hold back a chuckle.

He tried to tackle her in a very ineffectual, don't-hurt-her-she's-just-a-girl way, and she employed a scissor kick again. Leo reacquainted his arse with the grass, and the Lab peeled his lips back in a gummy, drooly dog-chuckle.

What a good boy. Clearly streets ahead of human males in the intelligence stakes.

The dog's smiling owner jogged over to reattach his lead, and Trix tucked the rugby ball under her arm and stood over Leo. "I just don't think you thought this through."

He rolled over and stretched his big body out on the grass. "I'm waving my imaginary white flag. My ego and other parts of me are now battered beyond repair by the ruthless professional athlete." He folded one arm beneath his head and placed his other hand mockingly over his heart. "I will never again underestimate a woman's athletic ability and capacity for violence, or worry that she's so short someone will step on her and crush her like a bug. Any reluctance to play contact sports with women in the future will be entirely out of fear for my *own* safety."

Then he swung his leg and knocked hers out from under her, managing to break her descent with his forearm so that she ended up on the ground with no impact at all. "However," he said, looming over her, all beardy and sweaty and genuinely grinning, "my masculine ego is still fragile enough that I'm not going to be the only one knocked on my arse."

Trix laughed again. Unprecedented behaviour in his presence. This whole day was weird. "Always harping on me being short." She dug her fingers into the grass, plucking at daisies. With the sun still burning down on her front, even after seven in the evening, the earth was nice and cool against her back. Leo was usefully blocking the light from shining directly in her eyes. Her own personal eclipse. "Have you considered that maybe you're just unusually large?"

"Body-slammed again?" Scott goaded Leo, reappearing with Ryan and an armful of greasy, deep-fried deliciousness from the chippy across the road. "Should we revisit that conversation about a veto on tackling to protect our defenceless, delicate flower here?"

"Is that Trix or Leo?" Ryan joked, carelessly tossing his parcels of chips onto the grass and then following them down. "This is definitely not a trainer-approved dinner, so don't be uploading any fancy shots of your battered cod on social media, Trix. We keep our diet on the down-low."

Trix plucked a freshly fried chip from the paper, blew on it, and bit in. "Excuse me, condescending mansplainers. My photo feed is shots of quirky doors and windows, and other people's dogs. Yours, before I stopped following you to preserve my eyeballs, was bathroom selfies and post-coital portraits. Which of us is the over-sharer here?"

Ryan patted his stomach, then shoved an entire battered fish fillet into his mouth. "Sharing this body is my civic duty," he said, while chewing. His dark skin was beaded with sweat. "Fuck, it's hot."

Scott was turning a crispy pink under his mop of red-gold hair. "But is it the weather, or are we feeling the heat on our two local celebrities here? That is the question."

Still sprawled on the grass, Leo opened one eye. Trix frowned at Scott over her chip. "What does that mean?"

Scott thumbed something into his phone and turned it to face her. "Look who's a popular girl on social media, then."

Ryan handed *his* phone to Leo. "And look who's not a popular boy in the tabloids."

Trix took Scott's phone and stared at the screen. "Hashtag Jinx?" she repeated. "*Jinx*?"

"The latest episode of *West End Lies* went up today, and apparently the doco crew have decided they need a romance plot for extra smut points. You and Jono made the epic mistake of trying to incorporate the *Dirty Dancing* lift into his trapeze routine when you were arsing about at training a couple of weeks ago. Tag, you're it. Clearly shagging."

"And the tweeny-boppers are all aboard the Good Ship Jinx," Ryan said, grinning heartlessly. "Can't wait for the episode when the footage of Jono regurgitating his dinner all over you goes live."

Scott gripped Ryan's arm. "The *romance*, Ry."

Ryan clutched his chest. "My heart. The feels."

Trix scrolled through comment after gushing comment in disbelief. The sentiment ranged from "They look so cute together" to "OMG, so bendy—bet they get freaky in the sack." Someone had made a GIF of their laughing fail at training. They'd been *GIFed*. And "Jinx" was a bit of a stretch as a nickname for their so-called relationship.

Although, an accurate representation of life lately.

"Bloody hell," she said, studying the stills from the

hatchet-job the camera crew had done on the editing. "Could they make it look like we're any more averse to wearing clothes? Take a shot every time Jono takes his shirt off."

"All the better for you to squeeze his pecs, my dear." Scott wiggled his eyebrows at her.

"I was not *squeezing his pecs.*" Except in this photo. In which she appeared to be doing uncomfortable things to his nipples. Awkward. "I don't go around casually groping my poor friends. Or strangers, for that matter. If I was standing like that, we were about to do a lift."

"Not in the soft little hearts of the nation's impressionable youth, you weren't." Ryan was giggling like a particularly annoying little girl. "They'd rather have the fairy tale. And really," he added sanctimoniously, "don't we *all* want that, in this clusterfuck of a world?"

"And apparently the fairy tale," Scott said, "is you. Theatre's adorable little Thumbelina. About to bang the hot acrobat like a snare drum."

"Yeah, you're both gits." Trix gave Scott his phone back. "Damn it. I was so okay with my micro-second appearances so far."

It was hard to get too worked up about it; it was so ridiculous compared to the more pressing issues on her mind. She was just glad Jono wasn't in a committed relationship, as far as she was aware, and she definitely wasn't, so there was no one to take it too seriously.

"Bloody *people.*" She and Leo made the exact same remark at almost the same time, his tone less joking than hers. Synchronised misanthropy. What next.

"Aww." Scott looked back and forth between them. "Look at you two, with your cute little matching sketchbooks and your burning hatred of mankind."

Trix's nosiness surpassed her better judgment. She assumed Leo wasn't circling quite the same type of rumour mill. If he was involved with the tactless supermodel from the pub, he wouldn't need any imaginary girlfriends on the side. "You haven't blown up any *more* clients, have you?"

She had done a bit of web-browsing on Saturday night, filling in time while she waited for news about Paige. Obviously, it was a very serious and potentially life-threatening issue when somebody had a bad reaction to cosmetics. She had a couple of skin allergies herself, so she could sympathise with the actor who'd expanded like an overinflated football. It was also a definite black mark on Leo's otherwise goldplated reputation.

So for all of those reasons, she did feel guilty about finding the whole thing absolutely fucking hilarious.

She'd made a pretty poor attempt at hiding her amusement, and Leo's sidelong glance was sour. "Not yet, but two days and counting until the next performance. Give me a chance." He tossed Ryan's phone back to him. "Just more of the same rubbish in the tabloids. It's life, isn't it? People take a grain of truth and sow an entire field of bullshit."

"What a beautiful quote." Trix ate another chip. "You should have motivational T-shirts printed."

"You and Trix could form a support group," Ryan said. "VOIB. Victims of Internet Bullshit."

"Except Trix's situation isn't really bullshit." Leo reached for one of the bottles of beer Ryan had bought and removed the cap without a bottle opener. Apparently lids just took one look at his rampant masculinity and gave up.

Trix flipped open her sketchbook and reached for a pencil. She considered that little comment, but after ten seconds of musing, it still didn't make sense. "What?"

"You and Angel—Jono." Leo's throat moved as he took a swallow from the bottle. It wasn't a good brand anyway, and the beer was probably warm and claggy by now. One could only hope. "Not really something out of nothing, is it? You're obviously...close."

Anyone with an IQ higher than point-five would see the warning lights flashing around them right now. Even Scott and Ryan, who Mother Nature had probably made so handsome because it was the only way they would survive natural selection, pulled identical "yikes" faces.

"'Close'?" Trix repeated pleasantly, and Ryan yanked out a piece of greasy newspaper that was wrapped around the outside of the chip parcels as old-timey decoration and pretended to become engrossed in reading it.

"Every time I turn a corner, you two are hanging all over each other." Leo grimaced, as if the beer had been as rankly reminiscent of bathwater as she suspected. Then, odiously, he tilted the bottle towards her in a salute. "Not that there's anything wrong with that. As Ryan said, everybody loves a lover."

"How about we leave Ryan out of this," came the voice from behind the newspaper.

"First of all," she said, and Scott muttered something that sounded like "*abort mission, abort mission.*" Trix wasn't sure which of them he was talking to, but ignored him. "Jono is not and never has been my *lover.* And secondly, what happened to people being able to do whatever they want with their own bodies and everybody else keeping their prying noses out?"

Leo looked faintly exasperated. "You *can* do what

you like. I couldn't care less if you're a total celibate or shagging every person on the show—"

Scott coughed out something that may have been *"Double lie."*

"—I'm just pointing out that you can't really get annoyed if people assume you're more than friends with someone when you clearly *are* more than friends."

It was unfortunate that this was a particularly sensitive topic for her. She'd had an earful in the past about how women couldn't possibly be platonic friends with men without at least one party wanting to move the relationship onto a mattress. Dan had been totally paranoid about her friendships with other men in general, and with Jono in particular.

She'd found herself making excuses then, and sometimes actually cancelling plans.

Now, it just pissed her off.

"Correct me if I'm wrong," she said, propping an elbow on her sketchbook so she could stare him down properly. "But you're an extremely touchy-feely person." It was one thing they had in common, being naturally physically affectionate. Obviously not with each other. "How many times have you casually hugged Allie over the years? You two hang out together. You go to dinner. You go to concerts. If I had to describe your relationship, I would go out on a limb and call you 'friends.' So if we turn your reasoning back to you—how many times have *you* seen each other naked, or wanted to?"

"That would be zero. As usual, you're completely misinterpreting my point. It's got nothing to do with friendships between men and women. That goes without saying; you can be mates with men, you can be mates with women, and sex has nothing to do with it.

I was referring to you as an individual, and one specific man. Who you obviously have chemistry with."

They glared at each other.

"And it was such a nice peaceful evening," Ryan said mournfully, still behind the paper.

Trix did not have chemistry with Jono. Doralina hopefully had *some* chemistry with Oscurito, because there was stage-snogging between the characters, and dance moves that could reasonably be described as grinding.

Jono, the nonfictional man, was a *friend* who would keep his lips and hips to himself as soon as the curtain went down. And who occasionally vomited on her head.

He was like an incredibly sweet little brother, always seeing the best in everybody. There were zero sparks between them; and Leo didn't just sound delusional, he actually sounded a bit jealous.

That was both ironic and confusing, since he'd once been shatteringly clear about his opinion of her. Dating-wise. There had been nothing to *misinterpret*. Her memory had stored the exact shape and sound of every syllable that had dropped out of his spotty teenage mouth. Unlike compliments, which were lovely but ultimately forgettable, insults took root in her psyche for eternity.

Her heart beating a little too heavily, Trix felt it like a physical blow when her eyes met Leo's again.

Her *head* knew what had kicked off the resentment between them—and whose bloody fault it was, no matter how many irrelevant *Galaxy Agent* proverbs he busted out, ta very much—but apparently her treacherous body had much lower standards below her neck.

After all this time, after every snide look and sarky

comment, every jab and jibe, every man she'd met since, there was still this inexplicable…hum in the atmosphere.

She was a grown woman and it would be childish and *weak* to get up and bolt from his disturbing presence, so she took the adult route. And turned her back to draw nasty pictures of him.

Her first venture back into illustration took the form of a comic strip, *Galaxy Agent* style. She even coloured it. Her caricature of Leo was pretty accurate, if she said so herself. Because she hadn't forgotten how good he'd been to her for a very short time today, she drew him as a superhero. A superhero who'd got his massive, swelled head stuck in the Pit of Prejudice, like Winnie the Pooh after he'd eaten too much honey and wedged himself in a door. Another caped figure sat nearby, twirling her pink hair and swinging her legs with a total lack of concern.

When they got back to the flat in the quickly darkening dusk, she slipped it under his bedroom door.

If he chose to also see a parallel with blowing up the diva actor's head on the film shoot—

Well, she was an artist of many facets.

Chapter Four

Before she was even dressed on Wednesday morning, Trix's stomach felt like she was halfway down a plummeting drop on a rollercoaster.

Tonight was her first public performance as Doralina. Then three more in a row before she got a few days' reprieve. She'd even dreamed about it last night. Most people seemed to suffer insomnia when they were stressed; Trix turned into Narcolepsy Nancy, dropping into a defensive coma at every opportunity. Unfortunately, she slept deeply but not peacefully. Her latest nightmare was a repeating loop of Paige's accident, but with Trix in the strike zone. She'd heard the crack of her arm breaking, and could swear she'd even felt a shadow of the pain.

She'd gone to see Paige in hospital yesterday, after a full day of intensive rehearsal. The other woman had been subdued and withdrawn, which Trix realised was because Paige was in pain, out of a job, potentially having marital difficulties, and probably not in a mood to smile at the woman who'd pinched her role while she was under the knife.

The voice of stress, however, suggested that Paige's

silence was because she knew Trix was going to be absolutely rubbish and was too nice to tell her.

Pulling the wardrobe open, she dug through the mess, looking for her most mood-boosting clothing. She was meeting Jono at her favourite café at half-past seven. To have a platonic breakfast together and somehow manage not to shag one another senseless while they ate their bacon and eggs.

She scowled at her closed door, as if she could laser-eye right through it and zap Leo wherever he was lurking. Although he'd probably left already. If someone were still asleep, she'd hear it. All three men snored. It was how she imagined it would sound on Mount Olympus if Zeus got really pissy and started throwing lightning bolts into huge, echoing canyons.

When she padded out of her room, hoping there was still hot water in the shower and that Leo might have left his door ajar so she could have a quick peek at Reggie from the hall, there was a piece of paper taped to her own door.

Carefully, she detached the tape from the wood without ripping the page. A small smile indented the corners of her mouth as she looked at it, and widened as she took in the details.

His drawing style had matured hugely over the past decade. He'd done a full-colour job as well, a professional wash of paint over the bold black lines. The saga of Superhero Leo and Superhero Trix continued. In his instalment, the Trix figure had just knocked illustrated Leo off his feet. Instead of Monday's rugby ball, she balanced a minutely detailed globe on one hand. She was launching into a grand jeté to leap across a ditch towards another patch of land that was signposted as Welcome to Conclusions—Population: 1.

He'd drawn her jumping to conclusions.

And with the world at her fingertips.

She still felt oddly... *fizzy* half an hour later, when she met Jono outside the café.

He was holding two takeaway cups of coffee and looked at her quizzically as he handed her one. "You look like you're in a good mood. I thought you'd be a nervous wreck this morning."

"Thanks," Trix said, raising the cup. "And I am a nervous wreck. I'm just hiding it well with my mad acting skills." She really did not want to discuss how short the time was until curtain. She was on orders to relax and not psych herself out this morning, and she was trying. "Is breakfast off, then, if we're having portable caffeine?"

Jono cleared his throat, and Trix eyed him in sudden suspicion. He was looking a bit...shifty. "What's going on?" She hesitated. "This doesn't have anything to do with our newfound internet fame, does it? Do you want to keep your distance for a while?"

Jono's face cleared. He smiled at her. "God, no. We should have expected that. Those things always want a love story, don't they?" He added teasingly, "And as we are by far the most attractive people in the cast..."

"At least it's only a web-series. I don't think we're going to have *London Celebrity* camped out on our doorsteps any time soon. Although I might stay off social media for a couple of weeks."

"Probably a good idea," Jono said, but he sounded distracted. He glanced at his watch.

"If you have to be somewhere, we can just meet up

later at the theatre," Trix suggested, slightly puzzled as to why he hadn't just texted to say he was busy.

"Actually, I did have an idea for something we could do this morning to take your mind off tonight." He looked shifty again.

"It's not illegal, is it?"

"What? No! Of course it's not." Jono looked genuinely shocked.

"Oh, well. I suppose we could do it anyway. What is it?"

"A…friend of mine is doing a sort of modelling job this morning, and I thought it might be cool to go and watch."

"Uh, Jono…" If Jono had a very *not* platonic "friend" who could make him blush like that, and she'd asked him to come to a private modelling gig, she might not be that appreciative if he brought someone else along. "If you're seeing someone and she invited you to—"

His cheeks flushed even more. "We're not seeing each other. And she didn't invite me, exactly. She just mentioned it, and it's a public event, so I thought it could be…fun."

He was actually stammering. Trix hadn't seen him so obviously gone over someone in ages.

"Still," she said, trying to put it tactfully, "this sounds like something you might want to do by your—"

"I don't want it to look like I'm *following* her or something. If you come, too, it'll just look like a couple of people from work showing up for moral support."

Trix did have quite a few hours to fill in before she had to be at the theatre, and she did want to keep busy.

"Okay," she said. "One wingwoman at your service. Lead the way."

As Jono ordered them a taxi, she wondered who he had a thing for at work. There was a girl in the chorus who flirted with him, but he was usually just discouragingly polite to her. When the car arrived and he opened the door for her, she asked him who they were going to morally support from a non-stalkerish distance.

He said something to the driver through the window and got into the car beside her. "Cat. The new intern in wardrobe."

Click. Trix snapped in her seatbelt and looked up sharply. The new intern in wardrobe.

A.k.a. Miss Permanent Good Hair Day and her vocal opinions about Trix's sub-standard performance.

A.k.a. Leo's tall, leggy pub date.

She wondered if her mad acting skills were up to the task of faking a sudden migraine or nosebleed.

It took an embarrassingly long couple of minutes for her brain to connect the rest of the dots.

Shit.

"Jono…what exactly *is* this 'modelling' job?"

Jono cleared his throat. "The qualifying round of the UK SFX competition." He continued to stare fixedly out the side window. The blush was spreading down his neck. "Should be cool, right? Not often you get the opportunity to see that many top special effects artists at work."

Shit.

She was spending her morning off as the uninvited cheer squad for Team Leo.

"I'm sure Cat will be stoked to see us there," Jono said with desperate optimism.

Trix said nothing.

"And Leo, I bet he'll appreciate the support."

Silence.

"Please don't murder me in the back of a taxi. The clean-up bill will be eye-watering."

The Grosvenor Arena was a relatively new build and the facilities were better than last year's venue in Cardiff. Contestants milled around their workstations, spectators wove in and out while they were still allowed behind the barriers, and the judges were clustered around the central platform where bands would play live music throughout the heat. A voice over the loudspeaker was summoning people to the registration desk and doing a periodic countdown. Leo recognised most of the registered artists, and spotted a few familiar faces amongst the models.

He did *not*, however, spot his sister.

A muscle ticked in his jaw as the PA system cheerfully boomed out a twenty-minute warning until the official start-time. He checked his phone again, but Cat hadn't replied to any of his texts.

In the past, if she had been MIA after promising to meet him somewhere, he'd have called out bloody MI5 looking for her. At this particular point in their lives, he was assuming she was out for a casual breakfast with someone she'd met clubbing. Or she could be jetting off to Paris to press her nose against couturier windows, for all he knew. Either way, he highly doubted she required assistance.

She was apparently not in the mood to *offer* it, either.

He'd had a quiet word with her yesterday about her

attitude around the theatre, and asked her again to tell him what was wrong, and she hadn't spoken to him since. He'd still thought she'd show up today and just sit in sulky silence.

He thumbed uselessly through the rest of his contacts, but gave it up when he reached the Ds. Chances of getting someone else here and registered in the next nineteen minutes? Pretty much nil.

He swore as he returned his phone to his pocket. One shot at this TV contract, and it was flying out the door before he'd even lifted a brush.

"Problem?" enquired a syrupy voice. The concern threaded around the word was about as convincing as election-year promises from a politician.

Turning, he managed a smile. It would probably have scared small children, but at least his mouth moved. "No. No problem. How are you, Zoe?"

Zoe Mitchell was a special effects artist who hailed from his home county. She was a beautiful woman and they should have a lot in common, and he usually lasted about three minutes in her company before he found himself fantasising about the fiery pits of hell opening beneath her feet and dragging her home.

She viewed herself as his strongest professional rival, even though they worked in different spheres and rarely competed for the same jobs. She'd always made a strong attempt to grab the title but didn't quite rank as the most irritating woman he'd ever met.

He wondered if Trix had woken up and found her drawing yet.

"Oh, I'm doing extremely well, thanks," Zoe said, baring a lot of teeth at him in return. "Just wrapped up a project in Amsterdam."

"Great place to work."

"Yes, isn't it?" She pulled another moue of false sympathy. "Heard about your little trouble on set recently. Bit of a rookie mistake, no? Overlooking an allergy that severe?"

He'd once gone on a date with this woman. He'd met her at a convention, they'd both had a lot to drink, and it had seemed like a reasonable idea to go to dinner and a club after.

It was a decision he'd regretted before the waiter had even brought the menus.

She'd since married a Welsh sound editor Leo had worked with a couple of times. The man looked smaller and more hunched every time Leo saw him. He'd probably resemble a shrivelled, joyless walnut by their fifth anniversary.

Ever since that time, Zoe had chosen to see every high-profile job Leo got as rank corruption and nepotism.

And he'd chosen to see her as a shit-stirring troublemaker.

"I didn't realise you were entering this year," he said, changing the subject. He did his best to sound as if it were a happy surprise.

"No, I don't bother much with the competition circuit anymore." She did a one-shouldered shrug. "My schedule is too full. But the prospect of winning a face-to-face with Sylvia George was too tempting to pass up. I talk to her people whenever I'm in town, but the woman is just *so* busy that she's always in the place I'm not."

Leo suspected that happened to Zoe quite frequently, with all sorts of people, not just the top studio execs.

Bet she has bad luck with phone calls, too. A mysteriously high rate of disconnections after she announces herself.

She said something else, in the saccharine tone that usually accompanied a vicious insult, but he'd stopped listening, his attention caught by a familiar flash of pastel pink.

Brilliant. Exactly what the morning needed.

If Trix was going to appear absolutely bloody everywhere he went, he might as well scoop her up, wrap her legs around his back, and carry her about with him. Save them both some time, and...

...

...

...hell.

Interesting mental image.

It was probably a good thing that Angel Boy materialised in front of him then, Trix tagging along behind with obvious reluctance, before his mind could take him any further down that path. It was fraught with perils. It was the equivalent of the chainsaw-bait moron going down to the basement in a horror film. Rational people everywhere screaming *"Don't go there. You masochistic fuckwit."*

Zoe abruptly turned and walked off mid-insult. She'd spotted the judges and was arrowing in to harass them instead, but Leo preferred to think she just faded quietly away when ignored, like many of life's horrors.

He focused on the other two. "Hello," he said, and lifted an eyebrow at Trix. "If you're here to cheer me on, I'm afraid I'm going to have to insist on pom-poms."

Yeah, cheers for that, brain. He had not intended

to say that. He'd *intended* to resist the compulsion to needle her for a while, focus on the issue at hand of the invisible sister and nonexistent model, and leave things at a short "Hello."

She prickled all over and went glowing-eyed like an angry lioness.

He really shouldn't take any sexual interest in someone looking at him as if they were debating the most painful way to lop his balls off.

Jono murmured something in response that was probably friendly and polite, because he seemed like a very decent guy despite his propensity to put his hands all over Trix, but she had apparently been rendered speechless with annoyance.

Leo worked with entertainers and their correspondingly fragile egos all the time; he'd learned to develop a thick skin and a deaf ear, and was usually well compensated for not rising to the bait, no matter how provocative.

Trix was the only one who shot all his shields to pieces, apparently just by existing in his presence.

And it pained him to say it, silently and without witnesses and probably never again, but even though she undeniably looked for the worst in him every time, it was *possible* that he occasionally acted like a bit of a dickhead around her.

"Sorry," he apologised abruptly. "Scratch that comment from the record if you can."

Trix blinked her wide hazel eyes at him, the murderous light in her irises fading ever so slightly. "Did you just apologise to me?" she said after a moment's stupefaction.

He smiled faintly. "Caught me with my defences

down. I'm about to drop out of the competition, and behind the polite murmurs of 'too bad, so sad,' several people in this room will be rubbing their hands together and cackling."

Trix frowned. "You're dropping out? Why?"

"Because the 'make up' aspect of the championship is not supposed to mean telling the judges you have a model to work on when you don't."

Jono, who had been peering around the room so intently that it was distracting, looked back quickly. "No model? What happened to Cat? Is she sick?"

"Of me? Yes. In the generally accepted definition of the word? I doubt it. She's just not here."

"Well, didn't you text her?"

Leo managed to maintain his expression of "This sucks, but it's not *impossible* that I'll recover my career from the trash heap without a win here, and my sister can't act like an enraged banshee forever." Shit, he hoped not. "Yes," he said. "She's not inclined to reply at present."

A trace of criticism appeared in Jono's face, and it was actually a relief to see he was capable of a negative emotion. He'd been starting to make Leo feel like a grouchy, pessimistic bastard by comparison. "Are you not worried where she might be? I'm sure if she said she'd be here, she'd make every attempt."

Leo looked at him speculatively. Obviously Jono thought he was the worst brother since Scar had dropped Mufasa off a cliff, and apparently Cat's work-shirking and flirting had fallen on receptive ground. Frowning, he switched his gaze to Trix, but she was still watching him.

"Has your girlfriend just *ditched* you here?" she

asked unexpectedly, in what would have been a spectacularly tactless question if she hadn't been leaping
to conclusions again.

He cocked his head at her. There was a definite note
of…*something* in her voice. A tiny half smile turned
up one side of his mouth. "You mean, has my *baby
sister* left me out on a ledge here? Since she thought
it kicked off at eight and it's now twenty-two minutes
past, I'm going with yes."

Trix blinked. Twice. "Sister?"

"Cat Magasiva. I thought the surname might have
given it away," he said blandly. "I assume you didn't
think she was my wife."

Nice opportunity for her to get them back on their
usual footing by making a comment about the world-
wide plague and zombie apocalypse that would have
to occur before any woman would lower herself to
put a ring on it, but she remained astonishingly silent.

His text alert beeped and he pulled his phone out
of his pocket. Soz, can't make it. Fan-fucking-tastic.
"Thanks for that lengthy explanation, Cat."

"Did she say where she is?" Jono was stuck on his
own priority, and Jesus, the guy really wanted to have
his cake and eat it, too, didn't he?

Not that Trix seemed to care. "Why do you have
to drop out?" she asked him. "Is it an instant forfeit if
you have a change in model?"

"No, I'd just have to change the name on my registration. However, I don't *have*—" His voice trailed
off as he studied her with entirely fresh eyes. She was
much shorter than Cat, but that was an element of the
body effects he could alter, and her face was sculpted
with the bony angles he most liked working with.

And while she was being all uncharacteristically amenable there...

She saw his expression and caught on quickly. "Uh, no," she said. "I was going to suggest Jono."

"While Jono looks thrilled about you trying to throw him under the bus instead, Tinker Bell, I'm afraid he has an unfortunate quality that rules him out for this particular effect."

She bristled on Jono's behalf. "What quality? And don't call me that."

"He's a guy. I want a woman."

"Join the club, mate," a stranger remarked as he walked past.

"Go on, Trix," Jono said, with a sudden spark of mischief. "That'll definitely take your mind off tonight."

Trix shot him a look. "I have to be at the theatre by three."

"So do I," Leo said. "The qualifying round has a four-hour time limit. And if the judging isn't finished by the time we have to leave, I'll pull out."

She muttered something about men throughout history lying through their teeth with those infamous three words, and he grinned.

"Five minutes to start," the loudspeaker announced. "Five minutes. Would all spectators please clear the middle arena now? All spectators off the floor, please."

Leo looked at Trix.

Jono looked at Trix.

Trix looked incredibly hard done by. "Oh, *God*."

"Stop dancing," Leo said, and continued to apply rotting flesh all over Trix's face. He'd gone with the Undead Princess from *Galaxy Agent* as his qualifying entry, and so far it was the most awesomely revolting thing she had ever seen.

"I'm not dancing." She tried to remember the first-year ventriloquism module she'd taken at LIDA and not move her mouth, but those classes had been first thing on a Friday and she'd been hungover for most of them. She *was* dancing. If they wanted people to play the statue game while they were being transformed into the stuff of nightmares, they shouldn't have live bands performing. The energy and noise in the arena was buzzing.

Even though he'd been messing with her, Jono was right; for the moment, this *was* keeping her mind firmly in the present and not twirling off towards possible disaster this evening.

All around them, artists were racing against the clock at their stations, turning human beings into all manner of fantastical creatures. Some were super vocal, chatting and singing along to the music, while others were like Leo, only speaking when spoken to.

One of the other contestants, an attractive woman with the unwaveringly aggressive stare of a bull shark, pushed past their station a couple of times on her way to collect extra materials. She glared at Leo every time.

"One of your ex-girlfriends?" Trix asked, *jokingly*, but he stiffened. "Not really?"

"We went out once. And, believe me, it was only once."

Trix looked over at where the woman was standing above a semi-transformed Medusa, sneering at them.

"Wow. I wouldn't get too close to her while she's

holding those garden shears. You must really know how to show a woman a good time, Magasiva."

He didn't bother to reply this time, letting his expression speak for him.

Smiling, Trix lifted her left arm where she could see it again. "This is so cool. Your sister's missing out."

After checking about fifteen times if she had any allergies (contact dermatitis if she touched raw courgette, and a bad rash if she used products containing rosehip oil; neither of which he was planning to rub all over her today), Leo had started building up welts, lesions, and decomposing flesh with latex, putty, and whatever "pyrogenic silica" was. Bulges of latex skin were then carved into with a blunt knife, or indented with bolts and ball bearings, which he sealed with clear gel and blended into her own skin tone with the putty. She hadn't intended to pepper him with so many questions about what he was doing, but he'd answered them all, even quite patiently. When he wasn't being obnoxious, he made a decent teacher.

It was his paintwork that was most impressive. Trix watched as he made a rapid series of flickering movements with his brush, and the skin on her right arm began to crease and wither, as if she'd just knocked back the *Indiana Jones* instant-aging grail.

"I don't think Cat's at home crying with regret right now." Leo's expression was intensely focused as he moved back to her face and turned her chin slightly to get a better look. His gloved fingers were gentle on her, and she tried not to squirm at the feel of his warm skin beneath the plastic. Having someone peering at her like that, closely and impersonally, usually hit her inappropriate-giggle button, as any doctor who'd ever given her an eye exam could attest.

Having Leo's face right up in hers did not inspire laughter.

Hoping she didn't sound as short of breath as she felt, Trix cleared her throat. "Is your sister a fashion student?" she asked, semi-coherently between stiff, painted lips. It seemed like the safest, most polite response. Even if Cat had let him down today, Trix didn't think he'd appreciate it if she voiced the actual thought circling her mind: *Guess being an insufferably rude knobhead runs in the family, then.*

She was feeling *slightly* warmer towards the missing Magasiva than she had been earlier today, but she still wasn't impressed with what she'd seen of Cat's personality so far.

Leo started powdering along the silicone cap he'd placed over her hair, which was where he'd be fitting the prosthetic that would extend back over her head. It occurred to her that if the judging ran too late, she was going to have to wear this in a taxi and then walk into the theatre looking like something that had just stumbled out of a crypt.

In the extremely unlikely event that any *West End Story* viewers were hovering outside the Old Wellington, hoping she'd arrive attached to Jono at the lips, that was one way to deflect attention.

"What keeps the silicone on?" she added before he had a chance to answer the first question.

"There's adhesive under it along the line of your skin. Silicone doesn't breathe, so it traps your body heat, which warms the adhesive and keeps it sticky." Frowningly, Leo leaned right in close to her again, his eyes on her hairline. She felt the tickle of his beard against her cheek. She dug her fingers into her thigh. "And yes, Cat's studying fashion design. She just did a programme in New York. And it doesn't seem to have done her any favours."

Trix sought the tactful way to put it. "Was she... different before?"

It wasn't only Trix who'd been on the receiving end of Cat's *opinions*. Quite a lot of people had been talking about Leo's sister yesterday—it would have been helpful if one of them had referred to her by her full name—and Jono was the only person singing her praises. She was horrendously rude to anybody who didn't have direct authority to fire her. Or, evidently, anyone who didn't make it painfully obvious that they were smitten with her.

"She's never exactly been shy," Leo said drily, attaching something to her head that was heavy and itchy. "But she used to have a sense of humour, and she never had trouble making friends. Obviously something went down in New York, but she won't talk about it."

Well. It never excused taking it out on everyone else, but Trix could understand wanting to keep things to yourself when it all went balls up.

"You should keep trying," she said abruptly. "If she's hurting. You should keep trying."

There was a momentary pause, before Leo reached out and blended in a line of grease paint on her cheek, rubbing gently with his thumb. He'd removed the glove and his skin was warm and calloused.

"Yeah," he said, his voice deep and slightly strained. "I will."

Her eyes flicked up and held his.

When she was unable to bear the tension a second longer, she manufactured a cough. "Can I have a proper look yet?"

It seemed to take him an extremely long time to release a breath, lean over, and grab the mirror for her. "Not exactly red-carpet glamour."

Trix took it and examined her reflection, and discovered how difficult it was to suppress a burst of spontaneous laughter without moving her jaw. "*So* much better."

Her head was about three times larger than normal and sprouting dozens of frenetically twisting horns. Her skin appeared to be hanging from her face in rapidly decomposing shreds, and what was left of it looked wilted and shrunken.

Leo picked up another prosthetic. "I'll put the fang mouthpiece in shortly, and you'll probably find it difficult to speak while it's in."

"You could at least *try* not to sound relieved."

Chapter Five

The sound of the audience taking their seats, the mumble of voices, the rustle of clothing and bags of sweets, the smell of popcorn that pervaded even the wings, the laughter, the stray chords and violin twangs as the orchestra warmed up—usually it gave Trix a powerful buzz that lasted until the curtain call. This was when the magic happened in the theatre, when the houselights went down and the crowd brought their energy, and the exhaustion and pettiness backstage dissolved into a shared goal: to go out there and give every person in the building a bloody fantastic night.

Tonight, she had an excess of adrenaline, the bad kind. Her knees were weak, hands unsteady, stomach roiling, heart thumping, and teeth *this* close to chattering. She hadn't been anything close to this terrified on their opening night. She had *thrived* on opening night. Pre-Doralina. Pre-Dan. Pre-who-the-hell-is-this-Trix-and-could-I-have-the-old-one-back-please.

She stood in the wings, bouncing up and down, going from the balls of her feet to en pointe in a nervous tic that was going to risk injury if she didn't stop.

What a shame that would be. You could just go home then.

Shut up. You're doing this. You are not a quitter.
Even when you should have been.
Stop.

God, she was losing it.

Farther back in the wings, Jono was stretching properly, his beautiful wings feathering out behind him. He saw her looking and gave her a thumbs-up. She tried to smile back, but her mouth wasn't responding. None of her muscles were listening to her brain.

Fifteen minutes until curtain. Fifteen seconds until complete and total meltdown.

A strong arm came around her, catching her flailing arm and tugging her against a reassuringly solid body. Leo bent his head and his words tickled her ear. "You're panic-sweating through over an hour of my hard work. Deep breaths, Trix. You got this."

She put a trembling hand up to touch the pointed black crystal headdress he'd secured over her hair. All traces of pink were undercover. All evidence of this morning's Undead Princess had been picked off backstage and then washed down the shower drain. She was the Night Wraith tonight. Striking. Dangerous. Commander of shadows, figment of countless nightmares.

Ordinary woman, about to fail miserably.

She took in a deep breath and released it audibly, imitating the sound of the relaxation app, like the crash of waves breaking on the shore.

She managed a semi-normal voice. "If you're trying to shock me out of my nerves by being nice to me, Magasiva…it's working. 'Fess up. You're secretly withering away with jealousy because my comic was better than yours. The morale boost from that one should see me through to the intermission. Then you can tell me I'm cute."

Her eyes were still fixed on what she could see of the stage from here, but she could tell Leo was grinning by the way his jaw moved against her. Like his face was giving hers a little beardy hug.

"Well, I do owe you for getting me through to the SFX final. But you're going to be just fine, short stuff." His fist closed playfully around her biceps, which was fairly well-developed when her arm wasn't being swamped by giant man-fingers. "Strong as an ant."

She cut a sideways look at him. "Ant? *Ant*."

"Hey, leafcutter ants can carry stuff in their mouths that's fifty times their own body weight. They're bad-ass."

"So, big-mouthed pests prone to nicking stuff?"

"I stand by my simile."

She couldn't help smiling, but felt it shrivel when the ten-minute warning echoed forward from the loud-speaker in the backstage hallway.

A stagehand rushed past and repeated it, just to hammer it home. "Ten minutes."

"Hey." Leo gently tugged her round to face him, using his body to shield her from the view of the stage. For that one moment, as he lowered his head to a neck-cricking angle to look her dead in the eye, he created a sort of bubble around them. "Trix. Stop underestimating yourself. Everybody here has completely justified confidence in you tonight."

She made a little scoffing noise. "Marco—"

"Marco is an arsehole who's taking out his own sense of inadequacy on everyone else. Ignore him. Natalie is rooting for you every step of the way, and

Steph is a world-class aerial coach who would never
let you on that stage if she didn't think you were up
to it." He ran the tip of his thumb under the line of her
jaw, and she pressed the flat of her palm against her
bare midriff. The crystals that cupped and covered her
breasts scratched the edges of her fingers. One side of
Leo's mouth tipped up. "Whatever your myriad faults,
Tinker Bell, I've never doubted your sheer bloody-
minded dedication to your job or how much you love
it." He nodded towards the stage. "You *love* this. And
you've worked for it." His thumb tapped lightly against
her temple. "Tune out the rest of the bullshit that's ticking over in there, and remember that."

She did love this. She'd loved being onstage since
her first school play, and she'd realised from her first
circus-arts lesson that she'd found her passion.

Even when Dan had reached peak shithead mode
and tried to make her quit what he'd come to see as
hypersexualised smut with no artistic merit whatsoever, she hadn't let go of her hoop the way she'd let
dust and poisonous comments gather on her illustrative art. She'd been transfixed in the beam of his manipulation, but she had held on to that part of herself
with a death grip. She couldn't lose it now to the lingering *echo* of the bastard.

But it was all very well to have a motivating surge
of stiff-upper-lip and "soldier on, boys," but now that
she really had to start breaking out of the shell that had
carried her through that clusterfuck of a relationship
and the mess of the breakup, she was bloody *brick-
ing it*.

Leo suddenly wrapped a hand around her head
and touched his nose to hers. She stared into the dark

depths of his eyes. There was a tiny jagged splotch of silver in the left iris. Like a starburst. "Stop over-thinking it."

"Fuck off, you don't have to do it," she snapped back, and he grinned at her again. There were dimples under all that beard.

"Thank God for that," he agreed readily. "Give me a rugby ball and a weights machine any day. If I'm going to leave the ground, there better be a Boeing 777 surrounding me. But I do know performance pressure. And although I'm starting to think it'll take about seventy more years of these encounters, minimum, before I really get a grasp on what goes on under that pink hair, I know a bit about you." He held up a rock-steady hand. "See how terrified I am that you're going to bomb out there?"

"That's not always super helpful," Trix grumbled. "When people are like, 'oh, I *know* you'll pull it off; you always do.' Like, no. I do not. And shit happens."

"And if shit happens out there," Leo said, "it won't be the end of the world. We'll go home, grab a six-pack, and tune out everything beyond the lounge for a while. And then you'll nail it tomorrow. Or the night after. Or the night after that."

"Yeah. Pretty sure I'll be demoted to usher after one of those nights, Cheer Captain."

"Then you'd find another role and start over. You're young, healthy, and stubborn as hell. You'll keep going." Leo nudged her chin with his knuckle. "But since it would be better to make your next career move on your own volition, for now just do your best to go out there and not suck."

The stagehand scuttled past again. *"Five minutes."*

The noise from the audience was starting to die down; the lights would be dimming.

A camera appeared right in front of her face, attached to Pen Clicker's hand. "I got the hyperventilating," he said. "That was gold. Can we get a quick sound-bite about how you're reacting to the pressure? Not well, obviously. Haw-haw." He made a sound like a wheezy donkey. Sneezy's cold germs were spreading.

Calmly, Leo reached out and turned off the camera.

"Hey!"

"If you'd like that camera to remain on the outside of your body," Leo said pleasantly, "sod off."

Pen Clicker inflated his chest self-righteously, turned bright red, muttered something about their contract, then shrivelled under Leo's interested stare until he'd scuttled off and disappeared completely.

Trix put her hands on her hips, blew out another long, slow breath, and tipped her chin at Leo. "And you didn't even need pom-poms for that very cheering moment."

"I don't have the legs for the skirt, anyway."

The bass beat pulsed through the smoke that swirled across the stage and rose in sinuous coils towards Trix's body. She was sleek lines and compact muscles and supple skin that glittered and winked with crystals. Leo watched from the hidden west platform as she curled back, hanging from the black-jewelled straps by one hand, poised and controlled from delicate fingers to pointed toes. She performed a side split and began to spin, faster and faster, the spotlight reflecting off the crystals until she was one continuous glow.

He knew that every muscle in her body was working right now, her heart would be racing, and her mind was probably clamped down with an iron fist to get her through the routine, but she made it look effortless.

She wasn't *cute*; she was fucking beautiful.

Allie paused by his side, also snatching a moment between rapid-fire costume changes and makeup touch-ups. "God, she's good, isn't she?"

Onstage, Trix twirled the straps together and wrapped them around her waist, beginning the move he personally referred to as Give a Bloke a Frigging Heart Attack. She rolled herself up towards the roof, higher and higher, legs in a wide split, straps winding around her body. At the top, she arched, hands stretching so casually, and then as the drums reached a crescendo, she unwound, whirling like a sexy little windmill towards the ground, catching herself centimetres from the stage.

"She is," he agreed as he retrieved his heart from his throat, and hell, she *was*, light years better than she seemed to believe.

But there was something missing.

He'd been in the audience on opening night for this show. He'd been working on an independent film in London at the time, and on a whim he'd accepted an offer of tickets from a friend and taken his then girlfriend. He'd watched Trix that night, watched her flirt and play with the audience, winking cheekily, daring people *not* to laugh with her. Pierrette was a very different role to Doralina, but that spark hadn't been the character; it had been Trix. Showmanship was one of her biggest strengths onstage. She loved the audience, and they sensed it and loved her in return.

Technically, she was sailing through it out there,

but there was something…withdrawn about her performance tonight. A spark of confident joy that had somehow flickered out. It worked within the context of the new character—Doralina was meant to awe and frighten; she wasn't playful—but Leo didn't think this was entirely acting.

"What happened to her, Allie?" He didn't look away from Trix's twirling figure.

There was silence for what seemed like a very long time. And then Allie said, "If things are heading in the direction I think they are, she'll tell you herself."

He turned his head swiftly, and Allie smiled at him. "Don't let her lie to you, Mags." The alert went out for the next costume change and she turned to go. Over her shoulder, she said, "Don't lie to yourself, either."

They got a standing ovation.

Well, they always got a standing ovation, but they might not have tonight if Trix had forgotten all the choreography and just stood there flagellating herself with the aerial straps, so…yay?

She was sweating heavily under the headpiece and the adrenaline was pulsing so hard that she was going to have a serious comedown shortly. She rose from the full-cast bow and instinctively looked towards the wings and the west platform where the crew often stood to watch during performances. It was a pointless thing to do; even if there hadn't been dozens of people towering over her, she couldn't see the platform from here.

At her side, Jono squeezed her waist and spontaneously kissed her cheek. She was sure the noise from the audience rose in pitch.

"So proud of you," he shouted in her ear, and she did a nervous bounce onto her toes again.

She'd done it. Not anything close to perfectly, and she still had to work her way up to the more difficult moves they'd subbed out, but she'd done it.

Offstage, she received a few congratulatory hugs; Scott patted her on the back so hard that she stumbled. She twirled around and found herself facing Leo.

Before she had time to think about what she was doing, she flung her arms around him, too. He was radiating heat beneath his black T-shirt, and it felt so good against her shivers of reaction that she almost lost her mind and nuzzled in. She could only comfortably reach as far as his ribs, and he literally just hauled her up into the air to return the hug, leaving her feet dangling for a second before he gently set her back down.

"Nailed it." He held up his fist, and she bumped hers against it. He looked piercingly down into her face. "Have fun out there?"

There was a note in his voice that needled into her and threatened to destroy her relieved buzz if she examined it too closely, so she mumbled something and turned to hear Natalie's feedback.

Bloody Leo and his perceptive, prying little *looks*.

She was trying to wallow in temporary, limited triumph here.

"*Very* nice job, Trix, but I had no doubts." Natalie looked awfully relieved for someone who'd had no doubts. "And good news—Jennifer Carr has rejoined the cast, and she'll understudy Doralina for the next few weeks, so we're operating with a full team again, and no problems with you having time off for your friend's wedding. The board wants to see you both perform before they make a decision on permanent casting. My money's on you, kid."

Jennifer had been an understudy in the past, until she'd got a full-time role elsewhere. She was an extremely competent aerialist, not a risk-taker but level-headed and consistent. And they were going to be directly pitted against one another, like contestants in an obstacle course, waiting to see who landed face-down in the mud first.

Trix looked at her reddened palms, flexing her fingers and watching the crystals twinkle in the light—and a small echoing spark flamed to life in her belly. The first glimmer of possessiveness. Her comatose ambition starting to twitch and stir.

This role didn't belong to Jennifer Carr.

She curled her hands into fists. It didn't belong to her, either.

Yet.

She had to be better. She *would* be better.

On her way back to her dressing room, she bypassed through the hallway behind the green room and interrupted Jono and Cat Magasiva doing something semi-pornographic against the wall. He'd been onstage about ten seconds ago. From curtain call to impending wall bang in less than a minute. Impressive.

Jono put an inch of space between their lips and turned bright red. "Trix, hey. We were just—"

"Please don't feel you need to finish that sentence." She glanced at Cat. All right, it had been a bad first impression, but Cat probably had a decent reason for bailing on Leo, and Jono had wanted to meet someone he was really into for ages. It sounded like Cat might have gone through a tough time, so— "Hey, Cat. I hope you had a good first night?"

Cat flicked a shiny curl of hair away from her long lashes and looked at Trix unsmilingly. "Great, thanks. Doing up zips and helping people into their Spanx, it's every girl's dream." She let her gaze travel over Trix. "Sounds like you did a lot better than expected." Her lips turned up in a little smirk. "Guess I lose the pool." Then she laughed. "Just kidding."

Yeah, no, I don't like her.

Trix smiled tightly back and left them to it. Jono looked totally besotted and was apparently suffering a severe malfunction in his bullshit filter.

As she'd expected, the energy surging through her muscles started to drain rapidly, and by the time she'd removed the bulk of her makeup and changed into her street clothes, she just wanted to curl into a ball and sleep for a year.

She treated herself to a taxi home and practically crawled out into the street at the end of it.

The flat, and therefore the shower, was blessedly empty when she let herself in, but even standing under steaming water for almost a quarter of an hour and using generous handfuls of her most expensive bath products did nothing to help her relax. She changed into her favourite shortie pyjamas, grabbed a beer from the stash she'd hidden in the vegetable cooler, and headed out to the stairwell.

Her absolute favourite part about this flat, besides the affordable rent, was the rooftop. Some enterprising former tenant had refused to accept that the closest garden was the public park four blocks away and had worked magic on the roof. Enclosed by the towering brick sides of the neighbouring houses, they had faux grass, fairy lights, and potted trees, and Trix found it all deliciously tacky. She'd learned to accept that her taste in interior design and landscaping inclined to the irredeemably naff. If she could ever afford to buy a house, even Dolores Umbridge would look at her shelves and think "Ooh, maybe a few too many porcelain cats."

Her happy space was a little busy tonight. When she pushed open the door and stepped out into the stuffy evening air, Leo was sprawled under a tree, beer bottle and sketchpad at his side. Reggie was walking over his stomach, exploring the thick grooves of his abs.

Leo sat up, caught the hedgie and set him on the unrealistically green grass. Reaching for his discarded T-shirt, he yanked it back on, smothering that wide expanse of smooth skin and bulky muscle in well-worn cotton. And then cleared his throat. "Trix."

The bizarre shyness that had washed over her at the sight of him turned into a faint smile. "You don't have to spare my maidenly eyes, Magasiva. I have seen guys' nipples before."

"Yeah. Well." He looked uncomfortable, and Trix wrinkled her forehead.

Was he…self-conscious?

He had the same healthy ego as all the other men she worked with, most of whom would happily walk around shirtless; hell, some of them swanned around backstage with their willies out and didn't think twice about it, but…he was definitely fidgeting.

Huh.

She changed the subject. "Sorry, I didn't realise anyone was out here." Scott and Ryan weren't interested in patches of grass that were too small to set up goalposts, and nobody in the lower flats seemed to bother coming up here.

She turned to go back inside and just crank up the fan in her bedroom, but Leo said, "There's plenty of room. Sit."

With her back to him, she experienced one of those extraordinary moments that only happened at rare intervals, where an invisible crossroads opened up and she was suddenly absolutely convinced that whatever small decision she made next would impact the rest of her life.

She breathed in, and out, and went to sit in the faux-grass near him.

Crossing her legs, she leaned back on her hands, looking up at the sky. The light pollution in London was so thick that only a few stars were visible, but it was better than nothing. She couldn't wait to get out to the clear skies in Cornwall for the wedding.

"How are you feeling about tonight?"

At his seemingly casual question, she turned her head. He'd tucked one arm beneath his head and was watching her.

She was hardwired to respond to Leo's questions in a certain way, mostly because they usually contained multiple layers of him being an arsehat. A sarcastic reply tickled at her throat out of habit, but she swallowed it. His voice and expression were very steady.

"It went better than I expected," she said at last. "I still have a lot to…fix, but it'll do. For today. It'll do for today."

His lips parted as if he wanted to say something else, but after looking at her hard, he just nodded.

"You looked beautiful out there" was what he did say, unexpectedly.

She'd just taken a swallow of her beer, and almost choked. "And the punchline?" she asked warily, once she'd wiped the spit off her chin. With poise and grace like this, she'd be ready for her invitation to tea at Buckingham Palace any day now.

Those firm lips tipped up. "No punchline." Leo stretched. "It's not mutually exclusive. You can be an aggravating, sarky pain in the arse and still be pretty. It's just that the overwhelming *loudness* of the first qualities usually drowns out the last."

The follow-up sounded more like the Leo she knew, but— "Is this your new way to mess with me?"

She was fine, for the most part, with the way she looked. She'd got through her career without serious injury so far, she was healthy, and she didn't have problems pulling on a night out if she wanted to. Her body was serving her well.

However.

"Exactly how many beers have you had?"

"This was the only bottle I could find in the fridge. I assume it escaped the human garbage disposals after it rolled behind a lettuce." Leo eyed her thoughtfully. "And if you're implying that people only find you attractive under the influence, that's fucked."

"Rather changed your tune over the years, haven't you?"

He pushed up on one arm. "You want to expand on that?"

Trix put her own bottle down. "And I quote: 'She's okay to hang out with, but no one would want to *go out* with her.'" Challengingly, she raised her eyebrows.

With remembered derision, she finished reading his part in that particular scene in her history. "'Too many freckles; not enough tits.'"

Cocky, mocking words that had caused her heart and pride to shrivel to dust ten years ago. If she'd overheard any other thick-headed teenage boy spouting that rubbish about her, she'd still have been pissed off and embarrassed, but she wouldn't have been...stricken. Even now, it stung.

He looked utterly blank for the first part of the recitation, but by the time she got to the tits, a sudden wave of comprehension hit his features. "Shit," he said emphatically. He'd lost a bit of eloquence since his mouthy youth. He rubbed his fingers through his curly hair. He'd had a major haircut since his stint on *1553*. It had been long enough to tie back then. "Did you—"

"Hear you denouncing the titless wonder to the entire rugby team? Yes, I did."

He looked appalled. Unfortunately, she seemed to have outgrown the ability to take much satisfaction in that.

"Hell." He was stuck on the monosyllables. She could actually *see* things clicking into place in the changing emotions in his eyes. Suddenly, his shoulders tensed. "That was about a month before you left for boarding school."

"Yes, it was." To the delight of her foster mother, who'd been convinced that Trix was the smartest human to ever walk the earth, she'd been offered the scholarship very shortly after Leo had fallen head over arse off his pedestal. If that pleasant moment had never happened, she'd probably have been gutted about leaving Bucks just when things seemed to be developing between them.

Their arguing had been more flirty than homicidal back then. He'd done multiple things that had suggested to her, at the time, that snogging was imminent.

He'd bought her a goddamn paperback of *North and South* after she'd accidentally dropped the school library copy in a puddle. What kind of heinous cretin bought a girl her favourite book and then mocked her flat chest and face dots to his friends?

On the scale of dickbag behaviour, he paled in comparison to Dan. But, and it was a shock as she really acknowledged it for the first time, that profound disillusionment in discovering that someone she liked so very, very much just wasn't worth it—it had hurt worse with Leo.

Because she'd been so young. Her mind immediately slathered on a dollop of rationalisation. She'd been a baby, and he'd been the first. Her first real crush. Her first heartbreak. Everything was more intense at that age, before life had a chance to really swing the cynicism hammer.

Even so, it had been nose-to-nose combat with Leo after that. She hadn't shrunk away; she had come out swinging. However fiery the dynamic between them, it had always played out on equal ground.

He was visibly mulling. She wondered if he was going to come out with something profound. Like, "Why, yes, I *have* been an utter wanker." Or "Your breasts are actually jolly nice." Or "Sorry."

"Is that why you hooked up with Damon Holland?" he demanded, completely missing the memo.

And...what?

She made a noise that could not be translated into any arrangement of letters in the English alphabet. It was accompanied by a head tilt and chin jut.

He took her point, and elaborated. "That was right around the time that you started dating Holland."

At the risk of turning into a broken record: "What? I never went out with Damon Holland."

It was Leo's turn to produce incomprehensible sounds.

"I never dated Damon Holland," Trix repeated, speaking slowly and clearly for the benefit of the deluded. "He knew I overheard you that day, and I remember he was nice about it—"

"Oh, I bet he was," Leo interrupted sarcastically. "Fucker."

"But," she went on more loudly, "we did not hook up." She barely remembered what Damon Holland looked like. Big. Like Leo. Thoroughly complimentary about her face *and* figure. Unlike Leo. "Did he say we did?"

It wouldn't be that surprising. She was fuzzy on Damon's facial features, but she had a solid recollection of what most of the rugby team had been like. The scrum-half had almost incinerated the chem lab trying to set fire to his own pubic hair with a Bunsen burner. That pretty much summed up the joint mentality. Telling lies about their sex lives would have been right up their collective alley.

Damon had been very sympathetic about Leo's rank betrayal, but even at the time she'd put that down to the competition between them.

"Oh, yeah." Leo's voice was flat. "He was very…expressive on the subject. Repeatedly. At length. He was also pretty explicit about your apparent opinion of me."

"Well, it was a load of shite," Trix said bluntly.

"You used to flirt with him."

"I used to flirt with everybody."

"I noticed." His response was dry, but his expression was altering. For long, long seconds, they stared at each other.

"You never went out with him."

"No."

He looked out at the dark street and the squares of light in the seemingly endless row of houses. "Could have saved myself a bruised knuckle or two, then." He considered, then shrugged. "Although he still shot his mouth off about you to get under my skin, so on the whole, I probably didn't punch him hard enough."

"You hit him?" Trix turned that over in her mind, but it stuck out like the wrong piece in a jigsaw puzzle. "Over me. The Flat and Freckled One."

Leo winced. "I'm sorry," he said. At last. After ten years. And he even sounded sincere. "You were never meant to hear that."

"And that makes it okay?"

"No. It doesn't." He met her gaze squarely. "It was a hell of a thing to say. And it was absolutely untrue."

"Look, don't compound things now by—"

"I was embarrassed." Leo cut into her scathing rejoinder. "I was…unhappy. About things that were going on at home. I was feeling the pressure with the regional champs coming up. And I was immature and inexperienced, and I didn't have a fucking clue how to handle how I felt about—"

Her breath felt tight and stuck in her chest. "About?"

He glanced down at where Reggie was sniffing the grass. "The way I felt… It was important. It was private. I didn't want the guys talking about it, and when they hassled me, I just…lied." He said it so simply that she actually believed him.

Trix released her breath slowly. "You lied."

"I lied." Leo moved one shoulder, abruptly, jerkily. A hint of coolness returned. "Of course, right after that, you started acting like something from *The Exorcist,* and then apparently fell for a complete bastard like Holland, so in retrospect, it seemed like a wise move."

And then one biting comment had rolled into another, until there was so much antipathy between them that it barely seemed to matter how it had begun. Or what they'd once had.

"Someone I thought was—" She swallowed. "Someone I trusted tore me down in public. I was pissed."

"Yeah," he said. "I get that. So was I. Especially after Holland retaliated for that punch by crushing my knee and any chance I had at a career on the field."

Her mind was skittering about all over the place, but she registered the undercurrent in those words. She lifted her head. "You blamed me."

"I did." He admitted it readily. There was a tangle of emotions in his expression. "I knew it was unfair, but yes. I saw you as the catalyst for everything that happened then." He shook his head when she went to speak. "I regained perspective on that point a long time ago. But things between us had deteriorated so much that it was just the tip of the iceberg."

Trix had never expected to have even a civil conversation with Leo again, let alone this. This painfully raw stripping out of misunderstandings and bitterness. "Does it still bother you?" she asked quietly. "That your plans had to change?"

"If we're talking about rugby," he said with an edge of irony, "no. You know I always loved art."

She nodded. It had been the first connection between them, the initial bond. Their art classes had been the highlight of her week. Until that last month, when they had become a battleground. Many insults. Occasional throwing of clay.

"I'm good at what I do," Leo said. "Despite the unwanted opinion of the tabloids. I love what I do, and I have things I want to achieve. I have no regrets." Briefly, his gaze collided with hers again. "About my career."

Trix could hear the beeping of a truck down in the street below, and in the silence up here, the faint sound of Leo's breathing. She didn't know what to say.

She didn't know what to think.

"So." The word was low and thoughtful, and she looked over at him. "You really were into me back then."

Some of the strain left the air around them as she rolled her eyes. "It's a very *resilient* ego you have there, isn't it?"

"I knew you were looking at me at the McAllisters' christening."

"I was so drunk at the McAllisters' christening that I probably thought you were a hatstand."

Leo rolled to lie back again. "Come on, Trix. You know you looked at me and thought, 'If he wasn't such a fucking wanker, I totally would.'"

"Oh my *God*." Trix couldn't help it. She started to

giggle, and threw his charcoal pencil straight at his barrel chest, which was shaking with laughter. "You conceited prick."

He caught the pencil, grinning. "How petrified should I be about the next instalment in the comic strip?"

"Prepare to be brutalised in ink." She lowered to her back, too, the smile lingering, warmth in her chest. More stress fizzled out, and it was bliss.

She tugged her fingers through the tangles in her damp hair and cast a quick look sideways. He was still watching her, and there was a quality in his eyes that she hadn't seen for a long time. She shifted in the fake grass. "No problems with performance pressure on your end tonight."

On a personal level, Leo was provoking and unpredictable, but in his professional sphere he was calm and controlled through every manic moment. The incident on the film set was probably the first time he'd ever stumbled on the job.

"The Old Wellington is a well-oiled machine," he said. "Paige's accident aside."

She winced at the reminder—and thought she felt the brush of fingertips on her arm. When she turned her head, he was staring up at the sky. His voice was still matter-of-fact when he added, "And it's a straight-forward brief."

His passion lay in prosthetics and total body transformations, so *Masks* wouldn't be much of a challenge for him.

That thought led back to the SFX championship, and the person who should have been modelling for him. "Cat seems to have handled things well tonight, too."

With the exception of the after-show commentary.

She'd tried really, really hard to keep her feelings out of her voice, but his expression took on a shade of resignation. "What has she done now?"

Spiky territory.

"I think we just have a…personality clash," she said carefully.

"Yes. That seems to be a widespread issue the past few days." He sounded tired. "Her attitude at work is a mess. I hate that she's alienating people. She's talented, and this is a really good opportunity if she doesn't wilfully throw it away."

He looked so disturbed and angsty, she was in danger of hugging him again. Before she gave in to disastrous impulses, she said the first thing that came into her head. "Well, she seems to have made one friend, at least, in Jono."

Radio silence.

Then: "Does that bother you?"

Eye twitch. She pulled a "*Men*, right?" expression to the scanty smattering of stars, and one of them winked sympathetically. "For the last time, Jono and I are just friends. Despite what the internet fangirls would like to believe, I have never seen him naked, and I hope that state of affairs continues indefinitely. Let's just divert off this path now, shall we, before we end up in a replay of the Damon Holland situation. Jono is the closest thing I have to a brother, just like Lily is pretty much my sister."

Leo didn't look convinced, but he didn't press the issue. He seemed to be considering her last statement. "You grew up in foster care, didn't you?" Unlike Dan, who had been appalled by her lack of traceable pedigree, there wasn't even a crumb of judgment in the question.

"Yes." Trix gently held out her fingertip for Reggie to snuffle, and Leo reached over to place him on her stomach for a hedgie cuddle. "Is Cat taking Reggie back?"

Seemed a bit like giving a puppy to Cruella, but...

"That was the idea. It doesn't seem to be high on her list of priorities right now." Leo watched Reggie burrow against her tummy. Abruptly, he asked, "Was your foster home...okay?" He made an apologetic noise. "Sorry, I can't think of a way to put it that doesn't make me sound like an ignorant arsehole."

She smiled a little. "No, you're good. I don't care if people ask. Yes, it was. They both were. There were only two." Dan had made it sound like she'd been summarily handed back to the authorities about twenty-five times when people got sick of her little foibles. Her family and her job had been his two major areas of dissatisfaction. She didn't need to defend either. "My parents were never in the picture and I was put into care as a newborn. I got a permanent foster mother when I was two, and I lived with her until I won the scholarship, then went home for holidays. Her name was Marta, and she was amazing. She died six years ago."

Leo reached out and touched the loose strands of hair falling over her temple, gently, and a slight shiver shook her shoulders. She half raised her hand, then let it fall.

He started to say something else, but stopped himself. She looked at him questioningly, and he shook his head.

"Are you wondering about my birth parents?"

He rubbed his beard. Being able to lie there and

stroke your chin like a wise old Dickens must be the primary benefit to having that much hair sprouting out of your face. "I was, yeah," he admitted. "But it doesn't really seem like my business."

"It's okay. This isn't a sensitive topic for me." Unlike certain other areas of her life. "I don't know anything about my birth parents. I've really never needed to know. I lucked out; I had a great childhood. By any standards, not just the foster system. I had more love and respect from Marta than a lot of kids get from their blood relatives, and I had friends I loved like family." Reggie took exception to her invading his personal space and curled into an affronted ball. "Marta believed that as long as you have enough money to pay the bills, hugs and kisses are worth far more than pounds and pence. It's a pretty great mantra to grow up with. Useful now, too, considering what theatre pays."

That crystal-clear confidence in who and what she was, that had always been the certainty underpinning everything she did. A shadow passed over her. "I don't need to know who I might have been, in another version of my life. I choose to believe there was a good reason why my birth parents couldn't raise me themselves. Maybe there wasn't. But I don't need to know."

Leo was watching her closely, his dark gaze moving over her face. "Well," he said, "whoever your birth parents were, I think they gave you the best parts of themselves. And I'm sure Marta was very proud of the person you are."

Trix was appalled to feel unexpected tears stinging behind her eyes. In the whole debacle with Dan, he hadn't been able to bring her to tears once, and with one unbearably kind comment, Leo—

She fought desperately for a shield of humour. "I think we can safely say that at least one of them gave me their freckles, anyway."

"You suit your freckles. You always did. They're very…you."

"Whimsical and cute?"

"Haphazard and dotty."

She smacked her hand sideways, and he caught it against his chest for a second, grinning.

"I'd like to put more credence in nurture over nature, anyway." He shrugged. "My parents separated and took off when Cat was only ten. They left us with our grandparents. I'd prefer to believe that my faults, limited though they are—" he lifted a teasing eyebrow "—are all my own and that there's not much of either of them in me, where it counts. Mum definitely didn't have much in common with *her* parents."

Frowning, Trix rolled over to face him, carefully putting Reggie back on the grass. "Leo, I'm sorry. I knew your parents got a divorce, but I didn't know they just left."

"Our Nan and Pop were always our parents, really. They were the ones who made our lunches and came to our sports games. When our mum and dad took off, it just made it more official. But I was pissed off for Cat's sake as well as mine." He ran a strand of her hair through his fingers again. It was drying frizzy. They suddenly seemed to be lying very close. "The first few months after they left were…difficult."

"Do you ever see your parents now?"

"Very occasionally. Mum turned up for Nan's funeral, but took off pretty quickly when she realised there wasn't much for her in the will. Last I heard, she was in Liverpool, living with a self-proclaimed life coach, who's married, has about twelve kids he doesn't support, and needs to listen to his own podcast. No idea where Dad shot off to."

Trix touched his wrist. "I'm sorry about your Nan."

"Thank you." Leo's voice was going all deep and rough, and he sounded as if he wasn't focused on his own words. "She and my grandfather were both good people. The best." His fingertips had moved from her hair to her cheek, tracing the line of her jaw and making her stomach flutter.

Trix curled her fingers over his, halting their progress towards her earlobe. "I seem to remember you once suggesting I look for *my* people amongst *The Borrowers* and the Lilliputians."

His quickening breath fanned her mouth. "I was a bit of a dickhead."

"Was?" Her lashes were trying to flutter closed.

"And *I* seem to remember that I was picking clay out of my hair for a week after that unfortunate remark."

"I had a bit of a quick temper."

"Had?"

His strong palm slid against the side of her neck, threading through her hair and cradling the back of her head, and his mouth came down on hers.

Chapter Six

She was kissing Leo Magasiva.

Trix flattened her palms against his chest, feeling the solid strength of him. His lips moved on hers, nuzzling her, catching her bottom lip lightly between his teeth.

She was kissing Leo, and it was perfect.

He lowered to her neck, pressing open-mouthed kisses on the sensitive skin there. She rubbed her cheek against his hair as he softly kissed the hollow of her throat, curving her hands around his head when he brought his mouth back up to hers and kissed her more deeply. His tongue slid against hers, playing with her, tasting her. A low sound made its way up the back of her throat, and he shifted over her, his weight coming down on top of her.

He was hot and heavy, and unbelievably, they were doing this.

"Trix." He murmured her name, so deep and husky, his lips continuously seeking out hers, his thumb on her cheek. He couldn't seem to stop kissing her. She couldn't stop kissing him. Arousal was an insistent pulse drumming along her veins and quickening with every thumping beat of her heart.

They both kept trying to speak, but their mouths were just drawn back together. Slow and searching, and then almost frantic. Their hands were everywhere, stroking each other's faces and bodies, tracing the lines of bones and muscle, caressing scars and stretch marks, mapping moles and freckles.

Trix broke free of Leo's coaxing lips long enough to tug at his T-shirt, trying to pull it over his head, and he unmistakably tensed for a moment.

She paused, her fingers entwined in the cotton, her forehead against his cheek. She was going to have major beard rash after this, and did not care at all. "Leo?"

There was another slight hesitation before he sat up and pulled the T-shirt over his head, almost dropping it on top of Reggie when he tossed it aside. "Yes." His hand cupped her jaw again as he took her mouth in another hungry kiss. "God, yes."

He brought her hands to the wide expanse of bare, muscled flesh across his chest, pressing her right palm against his heart.

She tilted her head, evading his lips for a moment, and he kissed the corner of her mouth, and her cheekbone, and nipped her earlobe. "What was that?" She mumbled the question through the strong impulse to just throw all intellectual thought out the window and straddle him like her favourite hoop. A split pike would never have been so much fun.

"What?" He ran his thumb along her jawline, angling her head so he could suck gently beneath her ear. Hickeys: not just for the kids, apparently. Good thing he was handy with concealer.

"Are you…not comfortable having your shirt off?" she pressed, shivering. She couldn't fathom why it would bother him. He looked like the "after" shots on an extraordinarily farfetched and unattainable ad for athletic equipment.

He withdrew the suction from her neck and pressed a small kiss there. "I occasionally feel a bit...self-conscious."

"About the way you look?"

"Yes."

She stroked his upper arm, and then the thick line of his brow. "Um. Why?"

"Body grew up quicker than the rest of me." His expression briefly turned from intense lust to self-deprecation. "I was over six feet tall before my voice had even broken. I could have grown a full beard at school if I'd wanted to. You remember what I looked like at sixteen."

Yes. She most certainly did.

"When my shoulders filled out, I looked about thirty-five. Every so often, the teenager who felt awkward in the locker room resurfaces for a moment, and I have to tell that inner voice to fuck off." He bent and tugged her pyjama top up to the lower curves of her breasts and kissed the hollow of her midriff. "More important things to focus on."

Trix helped him pull her top over her head, and as he had done to her, she put her hands over his and brought them to cup what there was of her breasts. "I think if one of us should be self-conscious about their naked chest," she said, rubbing her nose into his beard, "we've established that it's me."

"You're beautiful," he said firmly, and his mouth closed over her nipple.

"So are you," she said, as coherently as she could

with her heart lodged in her throat and her blood shooting to southern regions. Her fingers fisted in his hair. "Physically," she added teasingly. "Your sense of humour could do with a little work—"

His mouth caught hers again, cutting off the dig, and one of his hands caressed her thigh and slipped up beneath the hem of her shorts to cup her butt. "God, you feel good."

Unsnapping the button of his trousers, she snuck her hand into his waistband, venturing on her own exploration. Her fingers closed around thick heat, and he groaned, a deep rumble right through his body. His erection grew even harder in her grip.

"So do—" She stopped.

"What?" he managed to rasp out, lifting his head from where he was giving renewed attention to her left breast.

She shook herself. Physically shook her head. "No, nothing. Sorry. Just had a brief moment. Of *holy shit, I'm touching Leo's penis*. Past-me was stupefied. I'm back. We're good." She tightened her clasp on him, stroking him firmly from base to tip.

"*Fuck*." With care, he pulled her hand away from him, and then with far more reckless motions, sat up to strip away the rest of their clothing.

His weight came over her again and their bare skin touched all along their bodies, raising sweat and nerve endings everywhere. Trix wriggled her hands under Leo's arms and slid them across his back, pulling him into her, settling his hips against hers. They were a much better match height-wise when they were lying down and naked. Apparently, they were a better match in a whole *number* of ways when they were like this.

Her heart was thumping against her chest wall, and his erection was slick and hard against her, but for a long time, they just kissed. Slowly and almost easily, as if they had nowhere else to be and nothing else to do.

Even when he ran the backs of his knuckles up the inside of her thigh, gently circling, stroking deep into her and making her clench down on his fingers, he kept kissing her; and she arched and made embarrassing whimpering sounds and started compulsively shaking in her thighs, but still kissed him back.

The way Leo tasted, the things he did with his tongue and hands, and the scratch of his beard were her whole world at this moment.

When he searched out a condom from his wallet, covered himself and slid inside her, they held each other closely, his nose against hers, their breath coming in jagged puffs. She cupped his cheek, looking into his eyes as they lay cuddled together, her pelvic bones rocking his in an instinctive motion.

They were both sex-talkers, she discovered as she locked her legs around him to lift her hips from the firm ground, pushing up harder to increase the friction, chasing the tingling spiral of tension.

Not dirty-talkers, as such. She loved that in books—the filthier the mouth on a fictional man, the better—but she'd discovered via extensive experience of the London club scene what happened to her when flesh-and-blood men grunted those things in her ear. On an entirely related note, she'd also discovered that people were particularly unappreciative of untimely giggling when it occurred in the bedroom.

"I think we're debauching the hedgie," she muttered at one point into the sweat-slick skin under his chin.

He braced one hand under her, gripping her leg with the other, pressing into her and keeping her lower body tilted upward as he withdrew, drove in again, power-ful, intense. Good. Really, really good.

"I came home late once," he said through gritted teeth, lowering his head back to hers and snatching a brief kiss; he thrust harder, pushed deeper, and they both hissed, "and he'd managed to walk over the TV remote enough times to turn it on and change the chan-nel to an extremely age-inappropriate film. He was a little pervert even before we corrupted him."

"Oh, sure," Trix teased breathlessly, and tugged on his earlobe, "he had to *change the channel* to find the dirty movie."

Leo slid his hand down her thigh and hitched her leg higher above his very agile hips. "There was a 48-hour *Galaxy Agent* marathon on another channel that weekend. Credit me with some taste."

She almost orgasmed right then and there.

When she did come, he rocked her through it, tuck-ing her face into his neck and murmuring gentle things in her ear. A few minutes later, when her arms and legs were still shaking, he stiffened against her, every muscle in his large body going rock-hard as he swore into her damp hair.

Then his arms tightened around her, and he rolled with her, onto his back.

They lay quietly, the night air still and stuffy around them, a few stars twinkling above and Reggie snuf-fling around in the fake grass behind them. Trix rested her cheek against his shoulder, tracing the black tat-toos that wound around his nipple and down his arm.

She was too exhausted and satisfied to really focus

on the reality that kept knocking at the edges of her brain, that this was Leo. This was *her and Leo*.

He released his breath in a sigh, turning his head lazily to kiss her forehead.

"God," he said, and she tensed. Perhaps he could offer some weighty words of wisdom that would throw some light on how they'd ended up here. "I'm starving."

Simplicity, thy name is man.

On the other hand…she could really go for some crisps right about now.

"Kitchen, then my room?" she asked, and he kissed her again and sat up, gathering their stuff.

Trix tried to move, but the stress of the day, the exertion of the performance, and the really good sex had taken their toll. Her muscles had finally gone on strike. "I can't get up," she said, flopping back down. "Just leave me here. Save yourself."

Leo zipped and buttoned the trousers he'd pulled on, and slipped his shirt over his head. "Here," he said, tossing over her discarded PJs. "Put these on, and if you can hold Reggie, I'll give you a piggy-back downstairs."

"Deal." She summoned enough energy to put her shorts and vest back on, then took Reggie, carefully avoiding the hedgie's defensive manoeuvres with the prickles, and climbed onto Leo's back. He had to practically prostrate himself facedown on the floor before she could reach. "We have a bit of a height mismatch here, Gulliver."

"We'll cope." Leo stood, his hands cupped firmly beneath her knees, and she wrapped her free arm around his neck. "Hold tight."

"Your sketchbooks?" They'd left the beer bottles under the trees, too; although he'd wrapped up the condom and was bringing it with them, because they had *some* sense of how to behave in a public space.

"I'll come up and get them in the morning. It's not going to rain."

He carried her back inside and down the stairs, and they did an awkward, leaning shuffle to get the flat door open.

"Shower?" she questioned, resting her chin on his shoulder.

"No point." A reactive jerk went through him when she rubbed her skin against his. "We're not done yet."

They made a pit stop in his room to return Reggie to his vivarium and food dish, which contained insectoid corpses that she didn't want to examine too closely, and then piggy-backed out to the kitchen to collect some crisp packets.

The foil bags were dangling from Trix's hand, her arm across his collarbone and her lips on his jaw, when the front door opened and Scott and Ryan came in, both looking a bit worse for wear.

For a moment, the four of them stood in a frozen tableau. The expressions on Scott's and Ryan's faces were ludicrous.

Then Leo tipped his chin to them and adjusted his hold on Trix. "Goodnight," he said blandly, and turned and walked into her bedroom, kicking the door shut behind him.

He lowered her to the bed, and she brought her feet up and pushed herself back on the mattress, reaching for him as he came down on top of her. He was grinning as he pressed his nose to hers. They rolled across the sheets, fatally crushing a bag of salt-and-vinegar crisps in the process.

As her vest top sailed towards the floor again, Trix heard Scott's voice from the hallway.

"I bloody *knew* it."

She was going to kill him.

It had always been a distinct possibility, but in the scenario Leo had envisioned, there had been a paint brush jutting out of his thorax; he hadn't almost had the top of his head blown off with three consecutive orgasms.

He was not complaining.

Trix lay sprawled at his side on the bed, facing him, one hand linked with his, a foot cupped around his knee. Her skin was silky soft, everywhere except her hands, which were as calloused as his. As he stroked her hip and the indent of her waist, he tried to avoid the myriad bruises from the past few days of training. Some of them had to be painful, but he'd never heard her complain about the physicality of her job.

It should feel like a solid step into *The Twilight Zone*, that they were lying here like this, but the strangest part of the whole thing was that it didn't. It felt very, and terrifyingly, right, and there was a worm of disquiet in his gut.

Tightening her grip on him, she smothered a yawn into his wrist and wriggled closer, nestling into his chest.

He spoke lightly, in sharp contrast to the dark problems flapping at the edges of his mind like ominous crows. "You realise this means that for the past decade, we've essentially been doing the adult equivalent of pulling each other's pigtails in the playground." He wound a tangled lock of pink around his thumb.

"You did look sexy with the pigtail," she said musingly, propping her chin on his pec. There was more green than brown in her impish eyes tonight. "Very space pirate. I was unable to suppress a fleeting fantasy at the *1553* party." Her hand slipped down his stomach. "Immensely impressive swordplay."

"And on that note—" He rolled her over and pressed her down into the mattress again, shoving her tangled sheet out of the way and stroking his tongue between her parted lips.

The spirit was willing, but the flesh was ready for a nap, and she obviously felt the same way, since she nudged him gently away after a few minutes.

Tucking one arm beneath his head on the pillow, he looked around her room. He'd been in here for over an hour, but the décor hadn't exactly been his priority. The walls were painted purple, there was a large abstract painting on the wall, strings of fairy lights everywhere, and clothes were falling out of the wardrobe.

There was also something suspended from a ceiling beam that looked like a sex swing, but because life was full of disappointments, he suspected it was exercise equipment.

He rubbed her thigh where it rested across his own, feeling the flex of strong muscle and the slight tickle where fine hairs were growing in. His gaze fell on a sketch portfolio beside the bed, and he leaned over to catch hold of it. "Are these your sketches? Can I see?"

She went absolutely still. Suddenly the drowsy, dare he say relaxed woman beside him was staring like a wary animal caught in a spotlight.

"Or not?" He started to put the portfolio back, but

she seemed to make a determined effort to shake off the mood that had overtaken her.

"No. No, it's okay. You can look." Her expression didn't match the words.

"If it's private—"

"It's not private. It's just—" She swallowed and retracted her leg. "You can look."

With a last glance at her, he sat up, stacked the pillows behind his back, and opened the portfolio. After turning a few pages, he slowed down and started examining each illustration in detail. "Did you write this?" She'd drawn her own graphic novel. It seemed to be a medley of space opera and romantic fantasy. Complete with space pirates. His smile grew. She *had* written the text; he could tell within a few panels. It was very tongue-in-cheek and very Trix. "It's great."

Trix sat up as well, cross-legged, and pulled the sheet around her. "You don't have to say that just because—" She gestured at the bed around them, then rubbed her nose awkwardly.

He lifted an eyebrow. "Yes, because after amazing sex, I lose all sense of judgment and perspective, and couldn't even tell the difference between stick figures and the Sistine Chapel ceiling. Don't carry modesty too far. Even back in the days when you were dumping wet clay over my head and flirting with idiots, I thought you were a good artist, and I think you're a brilliant illustrator now."

She still looked doubtful, and he frowned, too, slightly exasperated. What the hell had happened to Trix's self-confidence recently? Her ballsiness had survived his moronic behaviour all those years ago, with a vengeance. She'd been spitting fire after that.

The faltering and uncertainty was a recent shift. "Trix, I've never given a woman false compliments to get her into bed in my life, but it would be a little late now, regardless. You already slept with me. Three times. It was a legitimate opinion."

He saw some of the stiffness go out of her shoulders. "You really like them?"

"I like all of your work," he said honestly. He shot her a look. "Even the unflattering caricatures." Lifting one of the graphic novel panels, he added, "And I think there would be a market for these."

She shook her head, but without the self-doubt of earlier. "I just like doing them for me. It helps me relax. The comedown from the performance high can be brutal."

"Trix," he said, and at the seriousness in his voice, she fixed her eyes on his. "What's the matter?"

"What do you mean?" A guarded light flitted across her face.

"The self-doubt. In your art. In your performance. It's not like you. You always somehow straddled the line of wholeheartedly believing in yourself without toppling over into cockiness." He pre-empted the comment that was clearly lurking behind her brief, tip-tilted smile. "Yes, thank you, sweetheart, unlike me." He reached out and touched the pad of his thumb to her cheek, and asked, simply, "Why?"

Her movements were abstracted as she put her hand on his, stroking his fingers in return; she seemed unaware of what she was doing, lost in troubled thought. At the point when he thought she wasn't going to answer, she told him. "I had a relationship a while back that was…bad. Emotionally abusive bad."

It was a hard punch to his gut. His hand turned over and gripped hers, compulsively.

"His name was Dan St. James. He was older than I was, he was—still is—successful in the City, I met him at a party, and I fell for him hard." She wasn't making eye contact anymore; she spoke to a point at the side of his mouth. It spilled out of her as if she was afraid that if she stopped talking she wouldn't be able to start again. "He was charming, and fascinating, and good in bed, and he made me feel beautiful. I was dazzled. We went out, we had fun; it started getting serious. And then ever so slowly, one step at a time, he started to manipulate me. Little digs here and there, sneaking a bit of criticism into a surface compliment. Easy to excuse away at first. But it got worse. A lot worse." She scrunched up her face. "One day the scales started falling away and I realised I was having trouble recognising either of us as the people we'd been at that Christmas party." Her voice became brittle. "Although everyone else seems to have seen through the façade from the beginning."

Leo said nothing for a good half minute. He physically couldn't. He'd never felt such a combination of fury and helplessness; it united into something like nausea. He was running his hand repeatedly up and down her arm, with the weirdest urge to pull on it, as if he could forcibly lift her out of a situation that was already in the past. She'd dealt with it herself; she didn't need him to save her, and this wasn't about him. He was also about the last person she would have turned to if she'd needed help.

But *God*.

He couldn't help the way he felt, either, and right

now he had the irrational feeling that he'd somehow failed her by not being there.

He found some words at last, but they emerged flat and emotionless in his savage attempt to leash down his anger. "He said something about your drawings. And your performances."

With the hand that wasn't entwined with his, Trix held the sheet tightly against her naked body. Her tone was equally, carefully level. "He thought my illustrations were childish. Just a waste of time. And he wanted me to quit the show." Her smile lacked any humour. "He was really into it at first, having a girlfriend in a big fancy show, but after we'd been dating a while he decided it was basically public porn with a few sequins thrown in to jazz it up." The pseudo smile faded. "I didn't even contemplate giving up aerial for him."

"Good," Leo said emphatically.

"But I didn't touch a sketchbook again until this week." She pulled hard at a loose thread in the sheet. "I let him influence me that far. And for a moment there, I even started to believe him when he said Lily was jealous and trying to drive a wedge between us. *Lily.* Who's had my back since the day we met and she pushed some girl into the school pool for making fun of me."

He forced out the question. "Did he ever…hurt you? Physically?"

"No." A fleeting meeting of their eyes. "He had very vocal opinions on physical violence, actually. People who can't control their temper are beneath contempt. Along with foster kids. Manual labourers. People who use public transport. People who didn't get into Cambridge. And every subtle jab was to make sure I appreciated the favour he was doing me by lowering himself to date me."

"He sounds like an absolute bastard," Leo said bluntly.

"*Yes*." Trix let go of his hand. "Yes. Exactly. He *does* sound like an absolute bastard. I can sit here now and break all those months down into a few sentences, and anybody with a brain would see it was dead unhealthy and that Dan is an absolute shit. And yet back then, I completely lost my head over him. What does that say about me? I was always so sure who I was and what I wanted, and then I just fall over for his bullshit like a bloody bowling pin. I mean, how gullible am I? How…*weak*…" Her lower lip quivered and she bit it hard, and his stomach clenched again.

He took her hand back, linking his fingers through hers. "Trix, you've never been weak in your life. And you weren't *gullible*. Jesus. You met someone who went out of his way to make you feel good about yourself. You obviously had fun with him at first. You're not gullible for trusting in that. It sounds like he was a skilled liar. He'd probably been practising mind games for years."

"Yeah. That's what Lily keeps saying." All he could see was the top of Trix's head; she was looking down at their joined hands.

"Yeah, well, listen to her. And it's not *weak* to fall for that sort of manipulation. Nobody is magically immune to having their emotions messed with. It's not a question of moral strength." He hesitated, but went on, "My Nan was one of the shrewdest people I've ever met. Cat and I never got away with anything; she could spot a lie at fifty paces. But a couple of years before she died, she met a woman through her church who she thought was her friend. Both of my grandparents trusted her. And that woman manipulated them out of most of their savings." He tugged her into him. "Strong, smart people make mistakes. And if the worst thing you ever do is believe in someone who doesn't deserve to breathe the same air as you, I think you're doing okay."

She squeezed his fingers compulsively; for a minute or two, she was a gentle weight against him, her cheek cradled against his chest, one falling tear sticking her skin to his.

When she looked up, she dashed the back of her wrist against the corner of her eye and fought for a semi-believable smile. "You always make women cry after sex, Magasiva?"

"As with many things, Tinker Bell, you're the first and hopefully only." He studied the shifting nuances behind her expression. He could actually *see* her shields coming up, and his earlier worm of disquiet was now a hissing cobra.

He could still feel the touch of her skin even after she released his hand and sat back. Closing his fingers into a fist, he rubbed the left side of his chest. His skin was slightly damp from her cheek. Today had been such a continuous series of potentially life-altering curveballs that he'd given up jolting from each impact.

But they were standing in the middle of a minefield, and he didn't want it to blow up in either of their faces.

Trix pressed her thumb under her lashes and took a deep breath. Released it. "Did your grandparents get their money back?"

"Not much of it. The woman was eventually arrested after another fraud attempt, but Nan, especially, had to find her own sense of closure. But she did get through it, and the day she died she was still a happy, stubborn, cantankerous lady who took no shit from anyone, including the universe when it dealt her the odd bad hand."

She slanted him an ironic look. "And the very subtle moral of the story, Leo?"

"The moral of the story is that bad things happen to good people, but there are always better things around the corner."

"This closet philosopher in you has been buried very deep over the years."

"Well, sex brings out my inner optimist." Gently, he flicked his finger against her cheek. Her haunted expression was having an uncomfortable effect on his heart. With deliberate lightness, he said, "And the sex *was* pretty spectacular."

A reluctant smile appeared in Trix's eyes. "Spectacular, huh?"

"Until this moment, I never saw the point in having to memorise Shakespearean sonnets. I may even break out a haiku."

The smile spread to the rest of her features. "At the very least a dirty limerick."

Teasingly, he murmured, "There once was a woman from Bucks…" Then, before she could slam any more mental doors or his common sense caught up with him, he leaned forward to carefully kiss her. Tentativeness on both sides ignited into forceful mouths and grasping hands in less than ten seconds, and he'd never experienced anything like it.

The connection between them was visceral and intense and sparky, and it was either going to burn out quickly and dramatically, or—

Or it wouldn't burn out at all.

His heart was beating in hard, rapid thumps.

When they finally threw the pillows and covers around, trying to get comfortable enough to sleep in the stuffy room, Trix curled into the curve of his body and tucked her nose into his beard.

"You could stick with *Galaxy Agent* and do the Obsidian Knight for the SFX final," she murmured. "Not as much rotting flesh as you usually go for, but it's on theme. I reckon you've been hoarding a bit of chivalry with that optimism."

Leo stared up at the ceiling. A string of fairy lights on the wardrobe was casting pinpoint dots in a scattered pattern that reminded him of the freckles on her cheekbones.

The SFX final.

The championship he needed to win, for the sake of the career that he was soul-deep invested in.

The career that was currently following the same path as hers, but could soon diverge in a completely different direction. To a different continent.

He cupped the side of Trix's head, stroking the tangled mess of her hair. Her breaths were warm puffs against his cheek. Beneath the muskiness and sweat of the sex, her scent was sweet and floral and intensely familiar, as if his body had stored the memory for years.

They could have *had* this for years. If he could go back into the past and stop himself from spouting that utter crap about her, they might not have spent a decade at each other's throats. She might never have met her ex; he might never have fought with Damon, and—

And things could have unravelled in a completely different way. He'd have busted his arse trying for a career on the field, which would have been a worse professional mistake than the one that had landed him in the tabloids, and he'd still have struggled to cope with his feelings for Trix. His grandmother had once described him as an emotional late-bloomer in front of her entire church group, which was just embarrassing, but—not inaccurate.

Trix's own words slipped into his mind and came to rest with heavy significance: *I don't need to know who I might have been, in another version of my life.*

"Leo?" Her voice was quiet.

"Mmm?"

"Is this going to be a problem? What happened tonight?"

His hand tightened on her. At last, he said, "Do you regret it?"

Her breath, still faint and ticklish against his skin. "No. But I don't… I can't—"

He closed his eyes. "It doesn't have to be complicated, Trix." It was the only thing he could say.

It was also a total bloody lie.

It was them.

It was going to be completely fucking complicated.

Chapter Seven

Trix's second outing as Doralina made the first night look like an unqualified triumph. The performance started unravelling before the curtain even rose. By the end of the night, they were all frantically grabbing at loose threads and trying to patch the holes before it fell apart.

To be fair, it wasn't all on her. A third of the cast and crew were battling a bad cold, and decongestants and antihistamines were being passed around like sweets. Whenever the Moon Princess's four-poster bed wasn't being used as an active prop, poorly people collapsed on top of it backstage, coughing piteously and sweating off their makeup.

Leo and the rest of his team were working at double their usual pace, trying to make sure that the Night Creatures were the only ones who looked like they were recently deceased. They were running so late in the afternoon that Trix attempted to start her own makeup, painstakingly copying the photos on the mirror. She'd always done her own face as Pierrette, but Doralina was a being of trompe l'oeil shadows and mirrors, and about three million individually glued crystals.

Leo found her peering into the mirror with a kohl pencil in her hand, and observed her progress for about two seconds before he cracked. "It hurts. It physically hurts me," he said, and plucked the pencil from her hand. With his thumb beneath her jaw, he did her eyes in a few expert strokes, then interfered with her attempt to put mascara on as well.

"I can do *normal* makeup." She studied her reflection. "And it would take me at least half an hour to get anything close to that. I begin to see the benefits of having you around, Magasiva."

"Look up." Leo swept mascara over her ridiculously long falsies, blending them with her natural lashes, and planted a stealth kiss beneath her ear where there was nothing to smudge. "I'm supplying the eyeliner skills. What talents are you bringing to the table?"

She considered the matter while slipping her hand under his shirt to trace a circle around his navel. "Trapeze sex?"

His hand lurched and he almost poked her in the eye with the wand. "All right. You win."

If Marco had stalked in even five seconds later, he'd have caught them doing something extremely unprofessional against the autoclave that was used to sterilise brushes.

As it was, they retrieved wandering hands just in time, and for lack of anything else to complain about, Marco was reduced to a finicky dig about her song solo the night before. She recognised that it wasn't a valid criticism, so she tried to ignore it, although Leo went all tense with testosterone and second-hand annoyance; but it came back to bite her onstage when she actually *forgot a line* in the second verse. She had to ad-lib something nonsensical while her brain did its best to freeze in place and scramble the rest of the lyrics. The usually raucously loud theatre had never felt so endlessly quiet; her heartbeat drowned out the orchestra. The crowds behind the halo of the spotlight seemed to press in around her.

It made her hands shake for a good half hour afterwards, and that in turn threw off her most complicated aerial routine, forcing her to sub in a couple of placeholder moves while she tried to get her composure back.

Things peaked into one of the most stressful performances of her life when she rushed backstage for her major costume change in the second act and Cat tore a seam in her leotard. Trix hesitated to say that it was *absolutely on fucking purpose*, but the younger girl did a bad job of hiding a smirk and then said loudly: "Oops. Are you a bit wobbly tonight? I hope you're not coming down with the bug, too?"

Allie employed a few hasty stitches and a safety pin as a makeshift fix, but Trix came very close to missing her cue.

The final straw was when somebody was unable to suppress a sneeze during the Doralina and Oscurito kiss, and the nasal explosion through the microphone was so loud that Jono jumped and accidentally bit Trix's lip. If they'd been using tongues rather than mashing their closed mouths together in the best sexless black-and-white film tradition, she'd have had trouble swallowing for a week. His dark eyes expressed an apology, and she tried not to feel for blood.

After the curtain call, Jono caught up with her backstage. "Are you okay? I'm really sorry. It was like a car backfiring. David needs to see an ENT. That can't be normal."

"I'm fine." She smiled at him, tentatively touching her lip. It was slightly swollen, but she didn't think his teeth had actually severed anything. Although— "You picked up some of my black lipstick. It looks like you knocked your front teeth out."

Jono let out a tired breath. "What a night."

"Tell me about it." Trix strove desperately for a bit of Leo's so-called optimism, but it side-eyed the echoing memory of her fucked-up solo and scuttled out of her grasp. Perhaps optimism was like thigh quivers and only appeared after orgasms. "At least we seem to be avoiding Sneezy's germs. All that ducking and running away from the film crew has fringe benefits."

"I actually called him that to his face the other day, thanks to you."

"Well, until they stop editing footage to look like I'm trying to get in your pants, I refuse to address them correctly. It's a small, petty rebellion that gives me joy."

Jono grimaced. "Yeah. That's not exactly blowing over, is it? There was an article about us online yesterday."

"What?"

"Apparently we're one of the internet's hot new couples to watch. Literally watch."

"Unbelievable."

"My mother saw it."

"Oh, God."

"She's into it. She added a hashtag-Jinx to all her social media profiles. She likes the idea of pink-haired grandchildren."

"She does realise I didn't come out of the womb like this."

"She thinks that the power of your personality is such that if you want naturally bubblegum-haired babies, you'll get bubblegum-haired babies."

"I *do* like your mother." Trix sighed and adjusted the crystal headpiece that was digging into the back of her skull. "Do we have any recourse against this?"

"Short of breaking our contracts and immediately quitting, I don't think so. Even if we kept twenty feet apart at all times, they'd still cut and paste a shot of my longing glance at the cupcake table and make it look like I'm hot for your body."

Trix shifted her gaze to the left. "And they're literally filming us right now."

Without moving his head, Jono held up his arm, did a twirling flourish with his hand like a really sassy conductor, and raised a finger.

A much-needed giggle bubbled out of Trix. "Such style, Watanabe."

"Hey, there's a lot to embrace right now, despite all the annoying shit." Jono turned his back to block the shot, and tweaked her nose. "For both of us, I reckon." He wiggled his eyebrows at her and headed off towards the dressing rooms.

Trix watched him go, a frown on her face and her mind on somebody else entirely, until she realised that Coffee Stealer was still filming and she was giving them a lingering clip of her apparently ogling Jono's arse.

She was about to follow him to get changed when Marco caught sight of her. "Pinky! We need to discuss your solo."

Odds that she would be fired and blacklisted from all current and future musical theatre if she employed Jono's jaunty little gesture?

Unfortunately high.

Leo rested his hand on Trix's thigh, watching her.

She was taking advantage of their otherwise empty carriage to practice her song solo on the Tube ride home. She wasn't actually making any noise, but sat sideways with her legs over his lap, earbuds in, eyes fixed on the screen of her phone as she lip-synched to the lyrics.

He put his head back against the seat, listening to the rattle of the rails. It was artificially bright in here, the sort of harsh lighting usually embraced by dental rooms, and he could see their reflection in the solid blackness of the windows, distorted by safety lights as they flashed by.

He was tired. Tonight's show hadn't been an unmitigated disaster, but he doubted it was going down as a career highlight for any of them. When people were filled with cold germs, they tended to be short-tempered and sweat a lot, neither of which made his job easier. There had been a few hiccups for Trix as well, which was unfortunate since her confidence seemed wafer-thin even without Marco's skewed idea of constructive criticism.

He circled his fingers over her bare knee. There were dark smudges under her eyes that hadn't come from a palette. She was pushing herself too hard, and that was probably half the problem.

When she moved her thumb against the screen and started the song over—he knew every word of the bloody thing; she'd been singing it in the flat all week—he tugged on her earbuds.

She looked up. "What?" she asked, too loudly.

He tapped his own ear, and she took her buds out. "Trix, maybe give yourself a break, yeah? It's late, and you just did a full show." He ran his hand back up her leg. "And I'd really rather you didn't work yourself into a splitting head-cold. I have imminent plans and they'll be a lot more fun with properly functioning sinuses."

"I clearly need the practise." Trix scowled, yanking on the end of her ponytail. "I don't want to give Marco any more legitimate reasons to slam my performance."

"Marco is an obnoxious prick, and I doubt if he'll be in his job for the long haul. For one thing, it'll be a miracle if we make it to September without one of the Shadows shanking him with a juggling baton." Leo stroked under her skirt, and she caught his sneaking fingers. "I don't think tonight is going on anyone's top ten, but you recovered pretty damn well. I'm not sure anyone would be able to transcribe that exact lyric you invented," he risked teasing her, "but you pulled it off and you kept going. No stage manager worth his salt could ask for more. And it was a lot less notice-able than the second-act sneeze. Somewhere, several astronauts looked up at that point to see if the shuttle engines just exploded."

He'd been taking his single eight-second break of the night then, watching from the backstage platform as Jono jumped about three feet in fright and almost head-butted Trix out of their kiss.

He'd never blinked an eye at stage or screen kisses before. Even if the actors in question *were* shagging off-set, which seemed to happen almost as frequently as the tabloids claimed, nobody found scripted love-making remotely sexy.

For the first time, with this production, he was having to remind himself of that fact.

He pulled her fully into his lap, and she turned to straddle him with an exhausted sigh, winding her arms around his neck.

There was no hesitation in the way they touched each other. They had moved from raised hackles to cuddles with barely a hitch. He could question it, but he didn't feel like being that introspective when she was nestled against his groin.

"Even way back in art class, you were always singing and dancing." He had a very clear memory of her, full-on club dancing to rap music as she worked on her tenth painting of plastic grapes and empty milk bottles. Their teacher's ideas of interesting still life subjects had been limited. "Just because you were having fun."

"Yes," she said into his throat. She was warm and soft, her breath touching his skin. "I recall being asked if I could strangle my cat elsewhere, because it was ruining your vibe."

"I'd apologise for that," he said, tugging her face back to drop a whisper of a kiss on her wry mouth, careful not to put pressure on the mark of Angel Boy's teeth. "But at this point, the tally on both sides is so long that we'd be sending abject gifts and performing remorseful sexual favours for the next three decades to even the score." Which didn't really sound all that arduous. "My *point* is that you're a natural performer. You sing when you're happy. You dance because when you're enjoying yourself you can't sit still. Having to get up on a stage and belt out a show tune to a packed theatre would sound like hell on earth to some peo-ple—probably *most* people—but the stage is a com-fort zone for you."

Trix eased back to perch on the edge of his lap. He couldn't read the expression in her eyes. "And?"

"And I think you're putting too much pressure on yourself to meet some sort of invisible standard that, Marco Ross's arsehattery aside, exists partly in your own head, and you've forgotten how to actually have fun out there."

She slid off his lap and stood up. "I am not *invent-ing* nonexistent pressure."

"Not what I said," he returned mildly.

She walked a few paces away, catching herself against a seat as the train jerked. He could hear her grumbling over the hiss and rattle. Something about "thick-headed male" was swallowed up when they clat-tered into a station.

Under the inadequate cover of the voice on the loud-speaker announcing that they weren't home yet, he mur-mured something, and saw every muscle in her body freeze. From flesh-and-blood woman to human ice sculpture in one very dangerous jibe. She would make a good portrait of Judith, about five seconds before she hacked off Holofernes's head and threw it in a basket.

Trix turned around and gave him a look that could have shrivelled at least three of his vital appendages to the respective size of peppermints and a jellybean, a tragedy for all concerned. "Did you just say *Short Person Syndrome*?"

The amusement tugging at Leo's mouth widened into a full grin, and he watched her fight between jus-tifiable wrath and her sense of humour.

She angled her hip and hooked her elbow around the nearest pole when the doors closed again. "Fuck, you're annoying."

"But am I that far off-track?"

She leaned her head against her arm, bracing as the train picked up speed. "Apparently there are two incontrovertible laws of the universe." She lifted one finger against her cheek. Probably not the one she felt like raising. "One, you have a vile habit of being right all the time." A second finger joined the first. "And two, cocky know-it-alls do not get laid nearly as often as they'd probably like."

"I could handle my impending celibacy better if you weren't standing there hugging that pole."

She studied the pole thoughtfully, then suddenly slid her grip up and swung on it, doing a seductive, shimmying little bump and grind. When she shifted her weight and did a lightning-quick side split, slanting him a provocative look, he was already moving.

Catching her behind her knees, he wrapped her legs around his waist, and she pulled him into her, her feet crossed at the small of his back. Her arms were above her head, hands still circling the pole. She was breathing more quickly than the short sequence warranted. Her chest rose and fell against him.

Leo hesitated with his mouth hovering millimetres from hers. He looked down into her eyes, which were hazing into darkness. "Your lip is swollen." He barely recognised his own voice in the husky rasp.

She tore her gaze from his long enough to glance at his own mouth. Then, deliberately, she reached up and bit his lower lip, a sexy pinch of pressure.

He took the hint and took her mouth, kissing her

hard. Her lips were slightly dry, and she tasted of the strawberry chewing gum she liked. It was a taste he'd found completely rank the one time he'd tried a piece himself, but addictive when it was part of her. Her thighs tightened around his hips as she thrust her tongue against his, and he made a muffled sound and dug his fingers into her bare skin.

The blast of the loudspeaker brought them both back from an intense precipice. He took a deep breath, leaning his forehead against hers, and kissed her one last time, a brief, gentle, close-mouthed nudge. "That's our stop."

Trix sounded as fuzzy on reality as he felt. "Thank you, London Underground, for that stellar piece of timing."

He pressed his nose against her cheek. "If that was a preview of your skills at acrobatic sex, it's probably safer if you demonstrate it in places that aren't monitored by security cameras."

"Yeah." Trix released him from the clasp of her legs. Unfortunately. She tilted her head and looked up at the bar. "Also, I've just realised how many germy hands have touched this pole in the past twenty-four hours alone, and I just rubbed myself all over it. I may need an antibacterial wipe."

"I think you may have misinterpreted the meaning of 'dirty talk.'"

Trix turned on the shower and reached for her phone to start her Doralina music. There was a text from Lily on the screen. An unsubtle reminder that Trix still hadn't provided any interesting details about her date for the wedding, including but not limited to a name.

Turning off the water again, she slid her thumb across the screen and hit the call button.

"I told you, I don't need a plus-one," she said as she trekked back to her room to get her robe. "This is a really important day, and I'm planning to take approximately two thousand photos. I don't want to look back and reminisce about the time when I had amazing triceps and could drink eight glasses of champagne without falling into a creaky-jointed coma, and not remember the name of the guy standing next to me."

Slinging the robe over her shoulder, she walked back out into the hallway and almost bumped into Leo, who was heading for his own room. He'd clearly overheard her, and he didn't look impressed.

Obviously, that remark hadn't been directed at him. He was invited to the wedding himself, so they'd both be attending by default. And as he hadn't mentioned taking a date and they'd spent most of last night bouncing each other into her mattress, she assumed they would probably join forces on the dance floor.

She was putting off mentioning that fact to Lily, however, since she could anticipate the commentary that would follow.

Leo slipped past her into his bedroom, stripping his shirt off—and it really was criminal that he ever felt self-conscious about blessing people's eyeballs with that sight—but there was a definite flicker in his eyes.

Trix stood, scuffing her bare foot against the floor, half listening to Lily teasing her about not wanting to endanger her budding love story with Jono by showing up with a new bloke.

When she ended the call, she tapped the phone

against her chin, then followed him into his room. "I wasn't talking about you."

He was pulling clean clothes out of a drawer. "Right," he said, without raising his head. The very calm syllable was somehow more provoking than if the word had dripped scepticism.

"Lily's been nagging me to bring someone. And even though we're not— Even though this isn't—" She stuttered to a halt a second time. Situations like this weren't usually so awkward. Of course, they didn't usually involve a man living across the corridor, and they never involved *him*. And he wasn't helping by just *standing* there, admiring his underwear selection. "We're both going anyway, so I figured…"

He finally looked at her. "Trix. I get it."

Good.

She was glad that at least one of them understood what they were doing here.

Her darting gaze landed on a familiar-looking leaflet he'd left on his dresser. She picked it up, snatching at the distraction. "Are you going to the festival?"

A new graphic novel in the *Galaxy Agent* series was coming out and there was going to be a three-day festival on the South Bank to celebrate the launch. The artists, writers, and some actors from the TV series were going to be there, and the leaflet promised food, a street carnival, and loads of nutty-looking activities, and yes please.

"I thought I'd stop by on Sunday. Take advantage of the day off. Allie was coming as well, but she has to go back to Bucks for a family thing."

Trix played with the edge of the paper. Her internal warning system was twanging hard, but if Marta was watching over her right now, she'd expect to see a demonstration of the manners she'd taught by example. "We're going on Sunday, too. Jono and I. You should come with us."

His expression was a little quizzical, and she swallowed.

It wasn't only politeness that had prompted the offer. She might not want another relationship right now, but she was enjoying spending time with him. A little too much for her comfort.

Leo stared at her hard for a moment, then shrugged. "All right. Sounds good." He nodded towards the door. "Are you still having a shower? I'll go in after you."

She didn't answer immediately. "What? No, you take it. I might do some yoga first."

Her muscles felt like they were about to snap from tension. The answer to her problems wasn't likely to be found in Child's Pose, but it was worth a shot.

He touched his palm lightly to the small of her back as he went out.

Thirty minutes, multiple King Pigeon Poses and a hot shower later, she was still restless, and was forced to the last resort of Lapsang souchong. When in doubt, pick tea.

Leo was in the lounge, watching a film with Scott and Ryan. He gave her another unreadable look as she walked past him into the kitchen.

While the kettle bubbled away and she filled a strainer with a loose-leaf blend, she found herself singing her solo under her breath. She reached for a teaspoon, and her mind went blank and she forgot a line again. Not the same line this time, and it was obviously less catastrophic when her only audience was three men who were more interested in the bombshell on the TV screen and her cascading tits, but *Jesus*.

It didn't help when Scott and Ryan suddenly broke into song and filled in the elusive gap. Even Tweedledum and Tweedledee knew all the words. She was *useless*.

A hand came down on hers and removed the teaspoon from her grasp. "Right," Leo said. "Upstairs. Roof. I've got an idea."

"I can't. I need tea. And talent. And a new brain."

And an entire jar of chocolate-hazelnut butter to go with the teaspoon he'd just nicked.

"You need a holiday, and barring that, a flick of the mental re-set button."

"I'm in my robe."

"I noticed. I don't think the moon will care."

He caught her hand as they went upstairs to the roof, and she looked at their entwined fingers in the dim light and shut her mind to the continued stirring of apprehension low in her belly.

Their empty beer bottles from last night were still under a potted tree. He bent to turn on the fairy lights, and she put her hands on the balustrade and looked over. Someone down the street was having a party, and the music and screams of laughter were spilling out into the night, fighting to drown out the sirens a few blocks over.

London. Always a haven of tranquillity.

Turning, she met the glint in his eyes. "Well?"

"Right." Leo tested the sturdiness of an old wooden crate with his foot, then sat on the edge of it. He gestured at the space around them. "Stage." He nodded towards the expanse of city lights beyond. "Audience." He raised the familiar brow. "Sing."

"What?"

"You have a gorgeous voice, years of training, and a mind that's unfortunately riddled with sarcasm but otherwise whip-sharp. The only thing holding you back in your vocal performance is self-doubt and avoidance. You're getting the words out just to get the moment over with. You're not investing yourself."

Trix folded her arms. "You know, you're a microphone, a studio audience, and one upbeat catchphrase away from your own chat show."

"Lunch in the West End next week," Leo said, ignoring that interjection. "Do it and I'll pay. Cop out and you pay."

"What, like I'm going to respond to blatant coercive bullying just because you phrase it as a dare and throw in the possibility of free food?"

"Are you?"

"Yes." Reluctantly, Trix looked out at the anonymous lights and dark of the night. "You seriously want me to stand here and belt out Doralina's anthem of despair and vengeance in public? People are trying to sleep."

"If anyone is sleeping through the rave down the street," Leo pointed out, "I don't think a few extra decibels are going to make a difference. And no, that song is seeping into the walls of the flat. I've started humming it in the shower. Sing something fun."

"Fun," Trix repeated, turning the word over in her mind and coming up blank.

"Channel teenage Trix, who played the song from *Ghost* on an empty milk bottle every time I got a turn at the pottery wheel, and just sing something for the hell of it."

"Such as?" She ran her hand up the back of her neck, gathering her hair into a loose knot, and shifted her uncertain gaze from her fidgeting feet to his calm face.

He looked at her star tattoos. "The theme song from *Galaxy Agent*."

A smile started quivering to life behind her voice. "You want me to sing the theme song from *Galaxy Agent*. Out here. At this time of night. Without even a triangle for accompaniment."

"Tell you what." Leo reached over and snagged their discarded bottles and tipped the dregs of the beer into a plant pot. "I'll even accompany you on your instrument of choice."

Trix's smile grew as he put his thumb on the rim of one bottle and blew experimentally across the top of the other, before he proceeded to produce a decent facsimile of the first notes, like some kind of bottle-whistling savant.

Over the bottles, he coughed pointedly.

She cringed, looking behind her, then back at him. His dark eyes were sparkling with almost…affectionate wryness.

And she sang. The theme song from *Galaxy Agent*. On the roof of her flat.

And it was as embarrassing and utterly ridiculous as she'd imagined. But about sixty shaky seconds in, when she increased in pitch and started belting it out, because in for a penny, in for a pound, and things really couldn't get any more awkward, somebody down on the street joined in.

Then another person, from the opposite direction. And another. And finally, what sounded like the entire flat party started shouting out quotes from the TV series.

Trix struggled to keep going as laughter shivered right through her body and weakened her voice, and Leo abandoned the bottles completely and sat with his head in his hands.

She couldn't keep it up anymore and left it to the street choir to finish out the performance, and Leo lifted his head, grinning, and opened his arms to her.

She went into them, sitting on one of his heavily muscled thighs, her robe falling open over her knees. He rubbed his cheek against hers as giggles continued to spill out of her in a release of strain that rivalled a full-body massage. "You know, Magasiva," she said, butting him with her nose, "behind that smart mouth and very pretty exterior, you are a *massive* geek."

He gave her an admonishing bounce on his leg and she had to grip the sides of his neck to stay balanced. "Should I be insulted?"

"No." She smoothed her hands against his dark hair, feeling it spring back under her fingers. "That's one of my highest compliments."

He raised a brow. "Well?"

Wrapping one arm about his head, she curved her palm against his forehead, and hummed. "You were right. It was fun." A hell of a lot more fun than she'd been having onstage recently. Whether she could translate any part of that into the performance she was being paid for remained to be seen.

"If you could just repeat the first part of that into my phone," he said thoughtfully, running the side of his thumb along her knee, "I'd like to add percussion and turn it into my text alert."

She tugged hard on a short curl of hair, and propped her chin on him while the sound of alarm sirens grew louder and louder.

In the street.

Not just in the back of her mind.

Chapter Eight

When Trix woke up in Leo's bed on Saturday morning, she felt oddly…sticky.

And not in a "morning after the fun" sort of way. In a "what the hell is on my face?" sort of way.

She knew Leo was up even before the sleep fog cleared. He was an extreme cuddler, and there was currently a nice wide expanse of space around her legs. Summer nights were the only time that she wasn't a physically affectionate person, for the sole reason that sleeping pressed up against a large naked man tended to generate enough body heat to power a small car. However, every time she'd tried to edge away, he'd followed her in his sleep, until she'd ended up clinging to the edge of the mattress while he flung all limbs about her and snored into her neck.

Something furry touched her face.

Their flat might not be Versailles, but it wasn't a complete hole. There was very little reason for her brain to jump to the conclusion of sewer rat.

Her eyes popped open, her hand jerked up to rip Rizzo the Rat away, and Leo's paintbrush went flying across the room.

Her scream ended in a dry cough.

Leo, seated on the edge of the mattress, watched his brush roll along the wooden floorboards, leaving a snail trail of black drips, then looked back at her.

She pushed up to sit, the sheet falling away, and his interested gaze dropped to consider her bare breasts. He was fully dressed and showered, and he'd set up a little table of makeup by the bed.

Gingerly, Trix touched the patch of her cheek that was tight and tacky, and turned her forearm from side to side. Interesting. She appeared to be decomposing into a delicate pile of bones. He was painting a section of her arm in black and grey shadows that receded around the three-dimensional illusion of a skeleton.

She cleared her throat. "This gives whole new meaning to the phrase 'boning.'"

"I was wondering if you were actually going to wake up." After retrieving his brush, Leo sat down and picked up a squeezy tube of goop, which he started smearing on her face. Her eyes slid left to peek at the clock. Eight in the morning. Slightly unexpected hazard of dating—*sleeping*—with a makeup artist. "I got much further in than I expected. You barely stirred. Which was admittedly useful from my perspective, but I'm not sure that the way you sleep is medically normal. I had to hold a hand mirror under your nose a couple of times to check you were breathing. It was like something out of a vampire film."

Obligingly, Trix turned her cheek so he could blend. After he'd been working quietly for some minutes, she spoke. "I don't mean to sound *overly* inquisitive, but what the hell are you doing?"

He studied her with a critical eye. "Now that you're vertical, I can see where I used too much shadow."

"You *painted* me while I was asleep."

"And all you did was roll over a couple of times."

She turned her arm again, examining the details. "Total violation of all rules of bedroom etiquette, which dictate *not* drawing on someone's face after sex, but artistically impressive. Is this for the championship final?"

"Now that I see it from a better angle, no." He bent his head and kissed her mouth, which he'd left free of paint. "Back to the drawing board. At least I've still got a few days to decide."

Her stomach grumbled and she rubbed it with her non-skeletal hand. "So, are we scrapping this idea in favour of breakfast or do you want to completely putrefy me?"

Leo looked at his handiwork with a frown. "Eggs?"

"Yes, please."

He gave her hair a playful tug and headed for the kitchen. Trix swung her legs out of bed and walked across to his dresser to peer in the mirror.

He'd rotted the skin around her cheekbones. And there was something about the juxtaposition of Death-Face and the messy hair sticking straight out of her head that reminded her of a decaying coconut, which was not fortunate.

As she slipped into her robe, she bent to look into Reggie's vivarium. He was asleep in a little ball, and she wouldn't mind going back to bed and following his example, but she had training at ten and was now going to have to take an extensive shower. "You're very cute," she hummed into the tank. "And Uncle Leo is a bit of an opportunistic pillock, isn't he, Reginald? Yes, he is."

When she got out of the shower and walked into the

lounge, zipping up her gym hoodie, Leo was dividing scrambled eggs between two plates of toast.

"Thank you." Trix took the one he handed her, but ducked away from his attempt to pull her in. "Sorry, if you wanted snogging, you shouldn't have waved a plate of food under my nose."

Opening a drawer, she dug out cutlery for them with one hand, while Leo stood at the table and held up a piece of paper.

"Apparently I wasn't the only one who was feeling creatively inspired in the night." He studied the illustration. "Are you purposely receding my hairline with each instalment?"

"No," she said, forking in a mouthful of eggs. "I'm just ennobling your forehead. Eggs are good."

"Are you referring to the breakfast or the shape of my head?" Leo's gaze narrowed. "Should I be reading something sinister into the fact that we're both hanging from a cliff by our fingertips?"

"There are multiple levels to my art, Magasiva." She bit into a corner of toast. "One of which is literal. I want to try rock climbing tomorrow."

He lowered the drawing. "Rock climbing."

"Calm down. I'm not talking Everest. There's going to be a climbing wall at the fan festival, so you can pretend you're scrambling up Mount Melancholy. I saw a picture of people hanging upside down like bats, and this is clearly what I've been training for my entire working life."

"Don't you have some kind of clause in your contract that prohibits extracurricular activities that might cause physical injury?"

"I wasn't intending to tap management on the shoulder and ask permission. And if that clause exists, you weren't too concerned about it last night, Speedy Gonzales."

After a decade of deliberate provocation bouncing off obstinately thick skin, she finally managed to outrage him completely.

When she saw his expression, she realised what she'd said and started to giggle, her own preoccupations temporarily doused. "Sorry. I was thinking of fictional characters that just keep going, and that was the first one that popped into my head. The more obvious implication temporarily escaped me. I take it back. No speed. You're painstakingly slow. You're a veritable tortoise in the sack."

"You can stop any time." Leo gestured at her with the drawing. "Fine. If this is something you've been wanting to do, we'll do it."

It was something she'd been wanting to do. She'd had plans to try out a climbing wall gym before she'd met Dan, and then she just…hadn't made it happen.

"Thanks." She ate another mouthful of eggs. Stress eating for the win. "Pity the fan festival isn't today. It might help me burn off some nervous energy before the show."

"Last night's solo was better."

"Guess the rooftop operetta helped." *Fractionally.* "What are you doing this morning?"

"Well, I was supposed to be taking Cat to stock up on new makeup so she can use my industry discount," Leo said, "so basically, I'm going to attempt to ignore everything she says, fail and rise to the bait, engage in a few insults in public, and further erode our long-term sibling relationship. Just your average relaxing weekend."

Trix put down her fork and looked at him. Behind the levity, his eyes were genuinely, deeply troubled. "This is really getting to you."

His jaw moved once, jerkily, before he lifted a broad shoulder. "She's my little sister. Family-wise, when it comes to a question of daily support, we're pretty much it for each other."

Trix didn't have a biological sister, as far as she knew, but she had Lily, and she remembered how badly it had hurt when their relationship had become strained. And regardless of her growing apprehension about Leo and this whole situation, it was difficult at a visceral level to hear that note in his voice. She sucked her lower lip between her teeth. "Do you think Cat would be interested in the fan festival? We could ask her to come with us tomorrow." She drew heavily on the memory of her acting module for "believable enthusiasm." "I mean, Jono's coming, so…"

The words hung in the air around them and started to reform themselves into the phrase *double date*, which was not what the manufacturer intended.

"It could be a good way for everyone to blow off some steam," she added quickly. "It won't be all fan stuff. Who doesn't like a day out on the South Bank?"

Leo looked sceptical. "You want to spend a whole afternoon with my sister, who apparently referred to you yesterday as the lost Womble."

She'd momentarily blocked the memory of that from her mind.

She forced a smile. "Why not?"

He looked as if he could supply several answers,

but restricted himself to: "Well, she does watch the show. Occasionally."

"Cat likes *Galaxy Agent*?" It was difficult to imagine, but Trix hoped the query had come out as polite interest. Not as doubtful, judgmental shrew.

"Cat likes Tarik Khan."

Tarik Khan played the Ice King, whose costumes pretty much consisted of blue paint and silver spangles. "Well, sure." She and his sister had at least *one* shared interest, then. How bad could it be?

Now you're just asking for trouble.

The heatwave seemed to be on its way out. The Sunday sky over the South Bank was heavy and grey, and Trix actually had to wear a cardigan and it was brilliant. She had always been more of an autumn person and started to check the calendar at this point in the summer to see how many weeks to go.

Even if it rained today, a lot of the fan festival was taking place under a seemingly endless series of massive, conjoined marquees. The only downside was that the acoustics inside the tents echoed. It was similar to being at an indoor pool.

Which meant getting the full audio experience of Cat Magasiva and the Complaints, live in 360-degree surround sound. She was somehow managing to drown out the actual band. There was no escaping it, no matter how fast and how far Trix clambered up the climbing wall.

"Oh my *God*, now I broke a nail," Cat snapped from her position really damn high up the wall, and women all over the world face-palmed at that ultimate cliché of feminine disaster, usually employed in fictional scripts written by men.

To be fair, Trix wasn't thrilled about what the climb was doing to her manicure, either, but that was picky comment number ten-thousand in the space of an hour, and she was getting crabby.

"I'm getting down. Whose idea was this, anyway?" Cat started descending the wall rapidly. She'd just completed the blue-level footholds, the third most difficult route, without fumbling a single step.

Feeling the stretch in her hamstring, Trix climbed to the next purple foothold. The third *easiest* level. She'd cockily thought she'd be really good at this, given that she built up her upper-body and leg strength for a living, but it turned out they were very different exercises. It was still fun, if she tuned out the commentary to the right.

Leo was climbing quietly to her left, making it look even easier than his sister had. For a big guy, he really was incredibly fluid when he moved; she noticed it frequently, when he was playing rugby, or lifting weights, or dancing at a party. Or pushing her into a mattress.

She swallowed that thought and kept moving. Beside her, Jono did a perfect dyno, jumping from one red hold to another at an almost impossible angle, and Trix stopped to rest for a moment. "Show-off," she teased, and he swung into the awesome bat hang, suspending himself upside down to adjust his position, before he grinned at her.

"Not doing too bad yourself there, Spiderwoman."

Below them, thunderclouds overtook Cat's impressive bone structure, and Trix's smile faded when she saw Leo's mouth tighten as well.

So far, as outings went, this was not a raging success.

"Um, maybe we should finish up and move on," she suggested. "Find some coffee. I could do with a caffeine boost. I haven't slept that well the past few nights."

That was not code for "I've got the yawns because I've been riding your brother like a mechanical bull," but Cat clearly interpreted it that way and looked more revolted than ever with her company, surroundings, and general existence.

Trix *had* been having a lot of sex with Leo, but she wouldn't *announce* that to his little sister.

She looked down to check the best descent route, her foot slipped, and she floundered gracelessly in the air before she managed to find a hold again.

"Careful." Leo let go of his own hold and caught another one with enviable ease, lowering down to her side. "Here." He reached out a hand to help her.

"No, I'm good." She measured the distance to the next stepping point. "I've got it." She wouldn't be capable of scaling an actual rock face or the outside of a building any time soon, so hopefully no cartoon supervillains were in imminent danger of taking over London, but she could at least get herself back to the ground.

His jaw shifted, and she pressed in close to the wall to stabilise herself and frowned. He was holding himself very still.

"What?" she said warily.

"It's all right to accept help sometimes," he said, after what seemed like an extensive internal debate.

"Yes. I know that." She could feel herself stiffening. "But I can get down myself. I don't *need* help. Thank you."

"I don't just mean now." Leo swung himself the remaining distance to the ground. Landing solidly on his feet, he straightened and stood close enough to catch her if she slipped, but didn't attempt to reach for her again as she finished the descent. "I'm just putting it out there. As a general observation."

Trix dropped to the padded floor and dusted her chalky hands off against her butt. "I appreciate that piece of wisdom, Aristotle, but I know how to accept help, when I need it." Even she could hear the defensiveness. It wove around her words like a thorny vine.

Leo lifted his head and stabbed her through the chest with one piercing look. "Do you?"

She took a deep breath, but Jono interrupted before she had to scramble for the right reply. "I need sustenance." He tore his attention from Cat's arse long enough to point through the crowd. "There's a caravan selling muffins and espresso next door."

She held Leo's gaze, then shook her head slightly and followed Jono.

An army of cosplayers tumbled through the entrance as they reached it, splitting up their group as they all dodged around laser swords and shields. Jono ended up walking at Trix's side, and said to her in a low voice, "How great is it about you and Leo? *Huge* improvement over your last relationship."

Trix darted a look over her shoulder. Leo and Cat had been waylaid by a giggling girl dressed as a Zero Agent who seemed to know them.

An Obsidian Knight with a longsword pushed past her as they headed into the food tent. "It's not a relationship. We're just—"

There were several phrases she would usually bring out here: "Having fun."

"Messing around."

"Friends."

None of them would form on her tongue.

Jono looked sceptical. "You're *just*, huh? And yet, curiously, you look so very, very *not just*. He seems like a decent bloke to me. Sharp, sarcastic, and a wide streak of geek. He's essentially you with a Y-chromosome."

Not that long ago, she would have been *so* annoyed by that comment. Now she could recognise the comparison as a compliment, and the speed with which her thinking had shifted only added to her growing disquiet.

She took an interest in the menu board in front of the Muffin Van. Which, if she could afford to, she would pay to drive beside her at all hours of the day, because *hello gorgeous*. "I'm trying to get my life back on track, and I don't do serious relationships anymore. Been there, done that. I'm not…temperamentally suited to it."

Jono ordered them a couple of coffees, and held up a blueberry muffin and a chocolate cupcake that was ninety-percent icing. "Do you want healthy for the body or healthy for the soul?"

Trix took the cupcake. "By 'healthy for the body,' are you referring to that football-sized muffin?"

"It's fruit. There are at least four blueberries in here."

They leaned against a makeshift catwalk while they waited for their coffee. There was no hope of getting a seat. There was barely room to breathe.

"Trix," Jono said, peeling the paper off his muffin, "I hope you don't think Leo is anything like Dan. Because there's no comparison."

"No." She looked down at the cupcake, suddenly not hungry at all. "I know there isn't." The words tumbled out before her brain had a chance to catch up. "Although Dan and Cat would probably get along great."

Jono's expression changed. He stood straighter and accidentally squished his muffin. "Cat's nothing like Dan, either. She's a nice girl."

It had been an unfair comment on Trix's part; Cat wasn't her favourite person, but she wasn't at Dan's level. But "nice"? *Nice*? "I think we have different definitions of that word."

"I know she's having difficulties at work, but she's still settling in. And she's an amazingly talented designer."

That was true. Allie had showed her some of Cat's concept sketches. She was a brilliant designer. Total brat, but great designer.

"I guess if she's treating you well, that's all that matters."

The barista gestured to them with a couple of cups, and he stood up to grab them. Trix looked through the crowd, but she'd lost sight of Leo completely now.

She thanked Jono as he handed her the coffee. "Can you see the others?"

"I think they're still talking to the girl in the catsuit." Jono finished his muffin and she passed him the cupcake she'd barely touched.

There was a burst of commotion near the front of the tent, and she tracked the pointing fingers and fangirl shrieks to where Tarik Khan was signing autographs and posing for selfies. He was smiling, and gracious, and clothed in nothing but leather trousers and a shining aura of otherworldly beauty. Seeing him in person was a bit like seeing the stained-glass windows at Sainte-Chapelle for the first time.

"Oh my God!" A girl who had been clutching her Tarik-signed leaflet and just about rubbing it against her face turned around and caught sight of Trix. Her avid gaze moved to fix on Jono. "You're Trix and Jono from *West End Story*. Oh my God." She came up and held out the leaflet, pulling a pen from her pocket. "Could you sign, too, please?"

"Uh…" Trix looked down at the pen and paper, slightly dumbfounded. "I don't think—"

—that there was any logical reason why any person on the planet would want her autograph.

And more people were turning and coming over, a sudden diversion in the surge of fangirls, like a little stream of interest breaking away from the whirlpool around Tarik.

"Can we have a picture?" Hands stole their coffee and shoved Trix to stand next to Jono, who looked at her with equal bewilderment.

"You guys are *so* hot together."

Another teenage girl giggled. "I don't suppose you want to update the photo for me." She held up her phone, and she'd actually put a screenshot of them kissing onstage as her background image.

Trix was currently at a fandom event, and the romantic sub-plots were always her favourite parts of books and shows. She got the fascination. It was just a little different and a lot more creepy when she had somehow *become* a character having a made-up romance.

"Sorry," she said. "The snogging requires a stroppy stage manager and a pay cheque waiting in the wings."

"But you're together, right?"

"No, we're not—" She was cut off as somebody else pushed against her, knocking her into Jono, who caught her arm to steady her, setting off an entire chorus of "*Awww.*"

They're just kids. This is not awkward.

Leo and Cat appeared at the edge of the madness. They were watching the self-proclaimed Jinx shippers with an identical expression.

All right. It was a *little* awkward.

"Excuse me." Cat pushed forward, just about knocking over a skinny girl with plaits who looked about seven and should really be watching cartoon pigs on YouTube, not faux-sexual melodrama. She seized hold of Jono's arm and forcibly dragged him away. "We're a little busy right now."

If her eyes were actually lasers and not just giving a good impression of it, hundreds of thousands of pieces of Trix would be drifting into the breeze.

Another *Galaxy Agent* actor joined Tarik, inciting a fresh round of squeals. Trix took advantage of the renewed commotion, hastily signed a ticket that was shoved under her nose, and excused herself to go to Leo.

"Want to get some air? It's getting a bit nuts in here."

After a delay in which she accidentally fiddled a button on her cardigan right off, he said shortly, "Yeah. Good idea."

The tent was so crowded that it was difficult to get to the exit, but Leo made himself useful by being built like a human steamroller, and he caught her hand to tug her along in the wake of his extremely wide shoulders and impatient demeanour. People just dove straight out of their way.

Outside, the air was blessedly fresh and clear, and free of the widespread smell of popcorn that kept reminding her of work, which in turn reminded her of everything she'd done wrong in training yesterday. The sky was still thick and heavy with clouds, and a few scattered raindrops fell on her cheeks.

"It's going to rain," she said, with sheer brilliance, and Leo didn't bother confirming the obvious. She put her hands on her hips and looked to the horizon. She could see part of the London Eye, looking like the discarded wheel of a giant Cinderella carriage from this angle, and beyond that would be the river, flowing rhythmically—there was a nice, calming thought to fix on—and somewhere beyond *that* would be Big Ben, standing tall on the skyline, observing the relentless passage of time, watching as all the feeble little humans failed to ever learn from their mistakes.

Trix squeezed her lashes shut, trying to clamp down on the shadows of old anxiety as they crept out of the memory vault where she *knew* they belonged and began to twine cold arms around her again.

"This is bothering you," she said. "This stupid thing about me and Jono."

She heard Leo exhale, thought she might have felt his breath against her hair, and opened her eyes to see that he was mirroring her own stance exactly: hands on his waist, head lowered, frustration radiating.

"Yes." He shoved his fingers impatiently through his hair. "It does bother me when I see people calling you a couple, even if it's just silly kids. I'm not that keen on you kissing him every day, either."

Her heart was beating too quickly. "We kiss because we're paid to play a part. Not because we want to rip each other's clothes off and are about to embark on a torrid affair."

Leo lifted his head. "I'm fully aware of that, and when excess testosterone isn't shrivelling my brain to the size of a gumball, I can recognise that the way you care about Jono is no different than the way I care about Allie. I don't think there's anything going on. I don't think there ever *will* be anything going on. But when it comes to you, there are times when I find it a little difficult to think rationally."

Trix pressed her hand against her stomach, feeling for the loose thread where she'd pulled off the button. She was having a horrifying impulse right now, to literally start crying with frustration. This was an ingrained reaction. She no longer found jealousy in men sexy or flattering; it sent a warning shock right along the wire that connected to her self-protective instincts. But she had a brain that was supposed to be in reasonable working order, too, and functioning eyes and ears. She could see this was Leo, and hear the rueful note in his voice, and it was *not* the same situation it had been in the past.

And she needed to breathe now. Preferably without having to pull out her phone and open the anxiety app.

"Look, Trix, I realise this is *my* problem. I have a jealous personality, and like with every other emotional response I've ever had, apparently you can smack your hand down on that button harder and faster than anyone I've ever met. I'm not sure if there's much I can do about that, but I can control how I react to it. And I bloody well will. Especially if it puts that look on your face."

With a huge effort, she relaxed her expression. It was more of a shifting of her cheek muscles than a smile, but it wasn't a quivering lip and impending melodramatic tears, so she'd take it. "What look?" she asked quietly.

He reached out and tucked a strand of hair behind her ear, his fingertips lingering against her temple. His thumb traced very slow circles on her cheekbone, and she got the feeling that the response in his head was very different to the one he voiced aloud. "Like you're about to channel Angel Boy and lose your lunch."

"Angel Boy?" she repeated, wrinkling her nose at him, and he tweaked the end of it.

"Sorry. Knee-jerk response. I'm working on it."

Trix could smell the popcorn again, and somebody was barbequing sausages somewhere. "Leo. You and me…"

It wasn't just a flicker in his eyes this time; it was a hard, sharp flash of something, and his face seemed to close off. "Yeah?" he said after a moment when she was still trying to separate out the right phrase from a jumble of possible words. Pour a can of alphabet spaghetti into a tumble dryer and that was the state of her brain right now.

She didn't even know what she wanted to say. Did she want things to go back to the way they'd been before? Absolutely not. Was she feeling this whole situation gathering in size with every passing day and rolling out of her control like James's giant peach? Yes. Yes, she was. "We're…"

"We're fine, Trix." Leo sounded perfectly calm, totally *casual*. But he'd stopped touching her. "We're having fun, right?"

Not right this second, they weren't, no. But in general, that was the idea, yes.

"Right," she said, and wondered if that sounded as half-hearted to him as it did to her.

It was warm enough outside, but the odd scattering of raindrops was fast turning into a steady fall. Normal for the usual English summer. Symbolic for this conversation and increasingly fraught silence.

Suddenly, Leo took a stride forward. Ignoring the crowds of people around them, most of whom were speed-walking to get out of the rain, he slipped his hands under her hair, brought her up on her tiptoes and lowered his head to press his mouth to hers. Her nose rubbed against his, and his lips parted hers, his skin soft and his intent firm, beard prickling her chin.

Trix slid her hands up between them to clutch his shirt, twining her fingers into the faded cotton. His body was big and warm, bending over her, curving around her, and it could have felt claustrophobic, but it didn't. He was sheltering and gentle, one hand moving to span her back and slip down over her arse before he returned it to the more festival-friendly location of her hip, where he kneaded lightly.

She felt the tendons tautening in his neck, his Adam's apple moving under her fingertips as she kissed him, her tongue delving to meet his.

At last, he tipped his head and let his lips slide from hers, resting them against her cheek. They were both breathing too quickly now, but Trix would take a head rush of knee-weakening lust over anxiety any day. Rain continued to trickle down, wetting their hair and plastering fabric to skin.

"We have to institute a three-feet-apart rule in public," she muttered, rubbing the heel of her hand against his chest. She flattened her palm over his heart, spreading her fingers and feeling the strength there. "Marco hates me enough that my chances of getting the permanent casting are already low without adding an arrest for indecency to the score sheet."

And with every passing performance, she was feeling more covetous about Doralina.

She wanted the role.

For over a year, she'd been hiding on a ledge where nothing and no one could reach her, afraid to want *anything*, and now she was trying to edge forward. But it was hard.

"Marco is one member of the casting panel. You're going to be fine. And nothing we do is indecent," Leo murmured into her ear. He kissed her once more, on the throat. "Although I'd be prepared to test the limits of that."

Wisely, however, given that there were young families in the vicinity and they'd already publicly groped one another, he stepped back and nodded towards one of the tents they hadn't been into yet. "There's a display of original illustrations and storyboards from the books in there. Want to check it out?"

Trix made an effort to shake off the stranglehold of uncertainty. "Uh, *yeah*." She suddenly remembered that they weren't alone here. "What happened to Jono and Cat?"

"Cat was tearing strips off Jono, so if he's still with her, I'll give the guy full credit, he's a saint." The grand plan to reconcile Leo and Cat in the light-hearted atmosphere had collapsed faster than a poorly made soufflé. "I'll let them know where we are."

As they walked and he texted, a lot of the strangers they passed gave him second glances. To most of those people, he probably looked completely relaxed. Just a really hot guy enjoying a damp summer day out.

Trix could see the lines of strain around his mouth and eyes.

Inside the tent, they moved around the displays, looking at twenty years of original *Galaxy Agent* art, and she was happy to avoid reality and geek out for a while.

"Your graphic novel is as good as this," Leo said as they studied one of the latest incarnations.

"Oh, sure. They should fire the illustrators immediately and queue up on my doorstep." She was dismissive, but a small flicker of pleasure unfurled between her ribs at his obvious sincerity.

"Seriously. It's not as good as *this* one," he teased, moving on to the next case, "but definitely better than that one."

Trix leaned in close to the glass. "Do you think if you stare at something long enough, you can absorb someone else's talent through sheer willpower?"

"The number of hours I spent watching old Rugby World Cup matches would suggest no. And while we're on the subject, I've got a concept in mind for the SFX final."

"You're not going to turn me into some famous rugby player, are you? Because I just don't think I'd suit cauliflower ears and no neck."

"Actually, I was thinking of the Warrior Fairy."

She turned around. "My Warrior Fairy? From the book? Have you been reading it again?"

"Yes. She's perfect. The rainbow scales on her skin will boost the technical score, and I wanted to incorporate beaten silver into the design, so the wings are ideal." Leo propped one arm against the wall and leaned over her, looking down into her eyes. "I think the Warrior Fairy," he said slowly, "might be exactly what I need."

Trix's heartbeat was quick and heavy. The marquee seemed very small suddenly, and it was as if threads of anticipation and apprehension stitched the air around them, tugging them closer together, one millimetre at a time. "I—"

"Sorry to interrupt." Cat, not sounding all that sorry, marched up to them with Jono in tow.

Wrenching her gaze painfully from Leo, Trix tried to focus on them; and Jono stopped looking like a preoccupied blur and crystallised into a familiar man, with an unusually wooden expression.

Cat cast a critical eye over the displays, then over Trix. "As fun as this has been, I'm going to get going." She flicked a glance at Jono. "You're coming with me, right?"

"Yeah," he said, but the infatuation-glow didn't seem to be shining quite as bright.

Cat sifted through the contents of her handbag and frowned. She touched her hand to her head, and swore. "Shit. I've lost my sunglasses."

Trix had noticed her sunglasses earlier, and the designer insignia on the side, and they would not have been cheap. "Are you sure they're not in your bag?"

"I'm not blind." Cat continued to ferret through the contents. "They're not here. Shit," she snapped again. "Those sunglasses cost three hundred pounds, and I've only had them for a week."

"Three—" Leo just about choked on his own tongue. "You spent *three hundred quid* on a pair of sunglasses? Have you completely lost your fucking mind?"

Not totally unwarranted, but also not a mastery of tact.

"You can literally buy them on the high street for a pound," Jono said, equally unhelpfully, and compounded the issue by adding, "It doesn't really make sense to buy designer on something you're going to lose or break easily."

Trix thought she'd better jump in before Cat beat them both to death with her even more expensive handbag. "Do you remember when you last had them for sure?"

Cat shrugged, scowling. "No." She hesitated. "I definitely had them when we were climbing."

"Well, we'll go check there. Thrifty and Hindsight here can search back at the muffin van. Should we meet back at the gates in fifteen minutes?"

Leo opened his mouth, and Trix looked at him. "Fine," he said with suspicious meekness, and slapped her lightly on the arse before he went off with Jono.

Trix followed Cat outside and the two of them darted for the climbing-wall marquee. The rain-snogging had already frizzed her hair beyond redemption, but Cat was still managing to look defined and glossy in that department, a feat of supernatural proportions given her thick curls, and she obviously intended to keep things that way.

There was a long queue at the climbing wall now that more people had been driven inside, and they squeezed around damp bodies, murmuring apologies. Trix did a clockwise circle of the marquee, Cat went anti-clockwise, and they met with empty hands in the middle.

Trix shook her head. "No luck. Sorry. There's probably a lost and found. We'll ask."

"I bet someone's nicked them," Cat said coldly.

Trix would lay heavy odds on that, too.

One of the guys setting up a bandstand told them where to find the lost property box, but it was as they'd suspected. A bottle of sunscreen had been handed in, some baby paraphernalia, one sandal, a lace thong— she didn't really want to know how someone had mislaid that without noticing—but no super-pricey sunglasses.

"Great," Cat said as they emerged back into the daylight. The sun was coming out again, at least, and the rain was easing back to a light spattering. "Perfectly in keeping with the rest of my life lately."

Trix looked sideways at her. Cat was singing a very familiar anthem with that one. She debated whether to stick her head in the firing line or not, but she couldn't ignore that distinctive chord of pain. "Are you…okay?"

For just a second, Cat's face flickered with uncertainty, and Trix thought she was going to answer properly. Then a wall came slamming down. "They're just sunglasses. It's a waste of money, but I'm not going to cry about it." She cut Trix an unreadable glance. "Although if I do, Jono would probably buy me a new pair. He's very generous. Who needs a guy you can trust when you can date a trust *fund*?"

Trix stopped walking, her concern rapidly taking on a much sharper edge. "Seriously, what the hell is wrong with you?"

"Sorry, was that crass? Well, we can't all be cute little poppets like you, Rainbow Brite." Cat turned to face Trix from a few paces away. "You know, there's something particularly irritating about the sweet-wee-me girls. Men lap it up, and you obviously have to have every guy you meet wrapped around your little finger, but it's really transparent."

"*Excuse me*?" Frankly, Trix was surprised she managed to find any words at all over the wash of sheer wrath. Apparently all Magasivas in her life had the uncanny ability to find the fuse to her temper, and knew exactly where to hold the lighter. And among the many things she took issue with in that villain-monologue—*sweet*? In what far-off parallel universe had she ever been *sweet*?

"It's not enough to make a play for my brother, you have to have Jono on the hook as a backup."

"For the last time," Trix said, striving for a last unravelling skein of patience, "there is nothing going on between me and Jono. Is it just a family trait to believe everything you read on the internet? Because I have some information about those emails from foreign princes who want to share their millions with your bank account that's going to blow your mind."

Cat ignored her. "It's a little difficult to start something with a guy who's already involved elsewhere. I'm surprised he doesn't say your name during sex."

Every cell in her body cringing, Trix held up

her hand. "If you and Jono are having trouble get-ting something going, it's probably because you're being—"

Cat's eyes flashed. "Being what?"

"A little abrasive, shall we say? To both Jono and Leo, neither of whom deserve it."

"I know what my brother deserves, thanks. And it's much more than a superficial flirt who has no prob-lem poking her nose into my business, even though she obviously has no idea what she's doing with her own life."

"And we're done. At least now we know where we are." Trix started to walk away, then spun on her heel. "My nose is out of your business, but do yourself a favour. Drop the attitude and tell your brother what's up. He cares."

Not waiting for another acid response, she turned in the direction of the gates, where the guys should be waiting for them.

She tried to leave the imprint of Cat's last observa-tion behind her.

Chapter Nine

"Hi, this is Cat. I can't take your call right—"

Leo ended the call when his sister's voicemail picked up for the third time. He'd see her at the theatre for tonight's performance. She was more polite in a recorded message, but she'd find it harder to ignore him in person.

In theory.

She'd managed it well enough this week, after leaving the festival on Sunday in a much worse mood than was warranted even by losing a piece of extortionately expensive plastic. Jono, who apparently had a lot more patience than Leo, had invited Cat as his date to Luc and Lily's wedding, and the trip to Cornwall next weekend couldn't come too soon. Everybody needed to get out of London for a day or two and get some clearer air, hopefully in more ways than one. He was rapidly reaching the end of his rope with Cat, but he was still worried about her.

He was also worried about Trix, who wasn't ignoring him in the physical sense but whose mind had been shut away behind a barrier this week. She actually had been polite to him, and it had been both chilling and unnatural.

The sound of high heels tapping on the paving behind him was followed by Allie's cheerful, "Hey, Mags." She caught him up and hooked her arm through his, practically skipping along, although he wasn't sure how she could even walk in those shoes.

"You're in a good mood." He wasn't.

"One more week of the daily grind before Cornwall. Then the sea. A gorgeous historical estate. Pasties of the edible variety, rather than ones I have to attach to people's tits. And the wedding of the best director I've ever worked with, who's probably never bought anything but the toppest of the top-shelf champagne in his life. I am flying high, my friend."

"How are you getting out to the estate?"

"That would be in your car, Jeeves. Didn't Trix tell you? She said you guys are driving down together and offered me a lift. That's okay, isn't it?"

"Yes." He shook himself out of his preoccupation. "Yeah, of course it is. Trix has to be there to get ready with the bridal party, so we'll pick you up about seven."

"In which case I will be asleep for at least half the drive." Allie lifted her hair from her neck, fanning herself. "How's it going? With Trix?"

Leo grimaced.

He wasn't going to discuss that with anyone *but* Trix.

Although that would be difficult, when they were dodging every serious subject like they were jumping obstacles in a video game.

"Things between us have always been..." *Complicated.*

"Like two feral cats in a bag. I bet the sex is *great*."

He shot her a look, and she grinned. "Oh, come on. Keep the salacious details to yourself if you must, but give me something. You two have been a powder keg waiting for the right spark since the beginning. All that sexual tension—it's been like sitting through ten seasons of my favourite TV show, waiting for the hook-up."

"Most of the tension was located in my neck. She was a walking headache."

And now, she was…what?

Still a pain in the neck. Still prickly, and sarcastic, and overly inclined to flirt with people who were not him.

Still the smartest person he knew.

Owner of usefully bendy arms and legs, and what was fast becoming his favourite face.

Happiness. She was, still unbelievably, happiness.

All the other shit of these past couple of months seemed bearable now because of her.

And it was looking increasingly likely that he could have a hell of a problem on his hands.

In more than one respect.

"Shame she met the douchecanoe before you two could retract your heads from your arses," Allie said, her mind on the same wavelength. Although he would have worded it differently. "I'm not surprised if she's a bit anti-relationship right now?" She looked at him questioningly, but he kept his face blank. "Fine. Be all respectful of her privacy, then." She patted his arm. "Even if she hadn't got tangled up with that prick, Trix would always have been the trickier one. No pun intended. She's more complex than you are."

"Just to be clear, Trix may have held back on the

cutting personal comments this week, but that's hopefully a temporary ceasefire and I don't need anyone else to step into the breach."

She twisted her hair back and stuck a clip in it. "Are you all set for the SFX final on Tuesday night?"

He would be more relieved about that rapid change of subject if he didn't suspect where it was leading. "Mostly. Just final touches on the concept sketch and a few materials still to pick up."

"Going to be a bit of an issue if you win, isn't it?"

Allie had always had an irritating ability to hone in on thorny facts.

Leo leaned his palm against the theatre door, keeping it closed in case somebody came out suddenly and caught part of this conversation. And by "somebody," he meant Trix, who had an established track record of unexpected appearances and already had one foot out the metaphorical door. "It's going to be a close final. There's a good chance I *won't* win."

Allie was touching up her red lipstick. At his words and tone, she lowered the hand mirror. "Does Trix actually know what the prize of this competition is? Since she's trying to win a role that will keep her well and truly tied to London, and is sleeping with a guy who might be upping sticks and heading across the pond?"

He set his jaw, and she snapped her lipstick closed. "You haven't told her."

A thread of Leo's patience snapped. "Trix is looking for any excuse to cut me loose right now. If I tell her I might be moving to the States for two years, she'll be gone. There's no point in making an issue of it yet. It could come to nothing. I have to win the championship first, and even then, it's only a meeting. Not a guaranteed job offer."

"But you want it." Allie looked at him directly.

He wanted what it represented. He wanted what it could do for his future.

He also wanted Trix, and it was becoming very clear that they were nowhere near to being on the same page. She was clinging with both hands to a much uglier chapter.

"We're not even in a relationship." God, that was such shit. "Trix isn't looking for anything more than casual. So it probably doesn't matter anyway."

Footsteps echoed down the alley. A bunch of the lighting crew were heading back with coffee cups in hand.

He straightened and pulled the door open for Allie to pass through. "By the way, that lipstick is the wrong colour for your skin tone."

Allie tapped the pointed toe of her shoe into the floorboards, as an alternative to kicking it upward into a much more sensitive area. "You know, Trix may have been dead on the money when she called you an incurably insufferable knob."

When he cut down the passageway behind the green room, Leo crossed straight into the path of Trix and Marco, who were having a one-sided argument. Trix stood with her face set into concrete lines and her mouth still strangely zipped. For some reason, she was persistently patient with Marco's behaviour, which had now crossed over authority and landed on bullying, but Leo wasn't.

"What the hell is going on?"

Trix shook her head. "Nothing. It's fine. I was just

explaining to Marco that I did *not* use the gym without permission last night. Natalie signed it off."

"Natalie is not in charge around here," their own personal dictator retorted, "and I'd appreciate it if you wouldn't participate in underhand behaviour when my back is turned."

"And I'd appreciate it," Leo said, equally coolly, "if you wouldn't speak to her like that."

Marco bristled, and Trix surreptitiously put her hand behind Leo's back and poked him with a pointy knuckle. It was not an affectionate nudge. It was Morse Code for *Shut the hell up before I get fired, you pillock*.

"At least you're putting in the extra work," Marco snapped before he turned and stalked off, "because your performance for the board is coming up fast. Tick-tock."

Relaxing the hand he'd once more curled into a fist, because he couldn't actually slam the guy into a wall without ending up with assault charges and an extremely irate…whatever Trix was prepared to call herself in relation to him, Leo looked down at her. "Performance for the board?"

She puffed out her freckled cheeks. "More of the overly complicated casting processes this management team gets off on. Jennifer and I both have to do the second-act straps routine for the casting panel, after they've seen her mainstage performance next weekend, so they can make a final call going forward. Like it's a frigging reality show. Although with the single-celled organisms still wandering around with their cameras, I suppose the lines are getting blurred."

Trix played with the zipper on her hooded sweatshirt, pulling it up and down in a nervous tic, and scowled at him. It was better than her distracted Stepford smile of the past couple of days. "Hopefully if they give Doralina to Jennifer, I can at least have Pierrette back and am not bumped down to permanent understudy, but if you knock Marco's teeth out, I rate my chances even less."

"I can't understand how *you've* kept your fists to yourself." He curled his hand around her short ponytail, running his fingers through the silky strands, because apparently he was now incapable of standing with her and not touching her. "History and your ingrained temperament suggest you should have delivered at least a verbal knockout by now. Manager or not, the guy's being a bullying arsehole. And you're being uncharacteristically—"

"Yes?" she asked, not looking at all docile, which was the reckless word his brain had pounced on.

"All I'm saying," he said, playing that one a bit smarter, "is you can stand up for yourself without crossing any professional lines. And if you keep booking training space after performances, you're going to exhaust yourself."

"And you." Trix rubbed her hands over her face. "Sorry. I didn't expect you to wait for me."

"I'm not leaving you alone in a deserted gym at midnight."

Trix opened her mouth to reply, then shut it again. Finally, she said in a quiet voice, "I really want this role."

"Yeah. I know you do." He looked at the walls around them. The whole building was invested with so much history that the ghosts of past performances were probably infused into the stones. The oldest West

End theatres were such a fundamental part of London's social tapestry—and Trix belonged here. She was an actress to her fingertips and this was where she needed to be. "And you deserve it. Just—don't push yourself too hard."

She sighed and brought her arms up to stretch. "It's only one o'clock and I'm ready for this day to be over now."

He rested his back against the wall. "Hang in there. One more week and you'll be in Cornwall, smelling sea air, drinking too much champagne, and surrounded by furniture nobody will be allowed to sit on."

Trix dropped one forearm to rest on her head, and when his hand came up, their fingertips dovetailed at the first knuckles. "I can't wait. I do enjoy a good glass of bubbly and a roped-off chaise longue." A note of breathlessness overtook the words as he leaned down to touch his lips to her neck in a gentle nuzzle. "What about you? Are you nervous about Tuesday?"

Not for the reason she probably thought. "With you as a model? It's in the bag."

"No pressure, then." She turned her head to catch his mouth with hers, teasingly light and flirty, dusting him with one butterfly kiss after another. She was cuddly and affectionate and sexy—and at the core, where it mattered most, where he was currently standing on a precipice by himself, she was as distant from him as she was in her performances.

When they'd ducked out to the corner coffee shop during the break yesterday, and the barista had said the words "your boyfriend," she had flinched. Physically recoiled.

Still holding her hand, Leo deepened the kiss, ignoring the crick in his neck and rapidly losing all desire to do anything with his mouth that didn't involve her lips and body.

But at some point, they were going to have to start being honest with each other.

Grosvenor Arena was usually quiet on weekday afternoons. By two o'clock on Tuesday, it was all but rocking on its foundations. Trix was lost in a mental run-through of her second-act choreography when her taxi found a space to stop outside, but the utter chaos inside the building dragged her mind back into the present with a bang. Literally a bang. Some tiny woman was wielding a giant hammer and whacking the hell out of a sheet of metal, like a medieval blacksmith. The guy at the workstation next to her was using power tools. Fortunately not on his model, who stood on a wooden block, wearing nothing but a thong and a few splashes of paint so far. More semi-naked people danced around, some already sporting odd headpieces and extra limbs. Leo had explained that things amped up for the finals, but all they needed was a few barrels of wine and things would be looking very bacchanalian.

She signed in at the registration desk and edged around the perimeter of the madness, looking for Leo. He'd told her two-thirty, but a lot of people had started their designs already. Skirting past a man carrying two long pieces of plywood, she locked eyes with a woman who looked familiar. It wasn't until the snooty-looking blonde sneered at her that she remembered Leo's erstwhile girlfriend with the chip on her shoulder. Little Miss Sunshine was currently holding an electric drill up in the air. She chose that moment to turn it on, and Trix did not think that was coincidental timing.

She spotted Leo's head above a cluster of average-sized people then, and made a thankful beeline towards him. He was frowning down at a palette as he mixed a violent shade of red. When she reached out to touch the hard bulge of his arm beneath the sleeve of his T-shirt, his muscles contracted and his brush slipped forward in the paint.

She tucked her hand into her armpit. "Hi," she said lamely. She thought she saw something in his eyes that left her breathless.

"Hey," he said quietly. "How was training?"

"I think I made some progress." With a jerky motion, she nodded to the crowds. "I hope I'm not late. People seem to have started already."

"They stagger start times so that people who need to use the heavy machinery aren't standing around in queues." He checked his watch. "Ten more minutes and I'm allowed to touch you. Professionally speaking."

"Is there anything I can help with? Am I allowed to help?"

"The rules allow you to take the lids off jars and fetch extra brushes, and that's about it."

"Finally, all that triceps work pays off."

A man with an official-looking lanyard around his neck bustled past and thrust a pile of papers at Leo, who took them and glanced down at them. "Actually, you can double-check these and sign them." He passed them over. "Consent forms, confirming you won't sue the venue or the administration if I accidentally poison you or nail one of these silver feathers directly into your skull."

Trix scanned through the top form. "I don't know, Leo. I've seen what you can do to someone's head with just a bottle of lotion. Seems like tempting fate, bringing a hammer into the equation."

He lightly rapped his knuckles against her hairline. "With this hard head? The nails would snap in half. I'm going to get the rest of my supplies. When you've signed that, just stick it in that folder, would you?"

Trix read through to the last page of the consent form, which detailed many alarming and hopefully unlikely scenarios, including the release of noxious gases into the atmosphere if one of the contestants turned out to be a halfwit who would mix dangerous chemicals in an enclosed space. There was a flash of movement in her peripheral vision, and she turned around in time to see the departing back of Leo's unpleasant blonde as she slunk back into the crowd.

She frowned.

"If you've reached the part about the mass asphyxiation," Leo said, appearing back at the workstation with an armful of leather, "that almost never happens."

"What did you say your friend's name is?" Trix turned in a semi-circle, studying all the materials scattered around them. For someone who focused so intently while he was working, he was very messy with his stuff. She couldn't see if anything looked different. "The homicidal-looking blonde?"

"If you're referring to Zoe Mitchell, we're not friends." He laid out the straps of leather. "I'm maxed out on befriending women who harbour murderous fantasies about me."

"She was just here. Zoe." Trix looked around again

suspiciously as she signed the forms and stuffed them into his neat little folder.

Leo just shrugged, all his attention devoted to the mass of beaten silver feathers he was lining up against the leather. "It tends to be a bit chaotic in the first couple of hours while people are still going back and forth between stations. The closer we get to the prep deadlines, it quietens down and nobody looks up from their own work."

Another official with a clipboard stopped at their station and gave Leo a significant nod before marking off something on his paper.

Leo straightened and tossed her a small bundle of black vinyl. "We're off. Changing rooms are over there."

Between her finger and thumb, Trix held up the very shiny strapless bra and hotpants. "I'm beginning to understand your inexplicable enthusiasm for the Warrior Fairy concept."

"You drew it, gorgeous."

"I didn't envision myself wearing it, however."

"Our imaginations clearly work on very different levels."

However light they tried to keep things, the atmosphere between them was like one of those plasma globes; as soon as they got near one another, lines of electricity stretched from her skin to his.

In the small changing cubicle, she got undressed as quickly as possible and wriggled into the hotpants. The bra was a little trickier. It was so narrow and tight that she could sew elastic into it and use it as a hair scrunchie. She made a face at her reflection in the mirror. The current lighting in the arena was a real treat: super bright and harsh to show up every line, spot and bloat. A boon for the artists and their accurate execution of minute details; not so much for the models' premature wrinkles.

Time constraints or not, she took a slightly circuitous route back to Leo, to avoid the artist who was working five stations over. The middle-aged man was transforming his willing victim into a manic-looking clown with oversized jaws of steel teeth. There was no music this afternoon, since all the show elements were reserved for the public runway performance tonight, and she could hear every creak and clash of the hinges as the escapee from the nightmare circus gnashed his fangs. Most artists had opted for the spectacularly gross over the cute and fluffy, so the room was shortly going to be full of zombies, creepy-crawlies, and mythological villains. For those fantastical beings, she felt nothing but admiration and fascination. For the clown, nothing but fear and loathing.

It was an unfortunate phobia for a person who'd trained in the circus arts. If *The Festival of Masks* had clowns instead of the Masked Fools, she'd have quit after the first rehearsal.

Leo's back was towards her as he sewed metal to leather, so he didn't see her approaching. Nor did he see Zoe Mitchell when she walked past his station and casually set a small bottle on his supplies table.

With narrowed eyes, Trix watched Blondie saunter back towards her own station, her hand playing with something in her pocket.

She returned to Leo's side and watched heat spring into his eyes when he saw what she was—or wasn't—

wearing, but she had other priorities. "Do you have spare plastic bags and gloves?"

"What?" He finally raised his gaze above her neck. "Yes. Why?"

"Can I borrow a couple, please?"

He raised an eyebrow as he handed her a couple of small resealable bags and a pair of gloves. It continued to arch higher when she snapped on the gloves with an admittedly dramatic flourish, picked up the bottle that Zoe had snuck onto the table and dropped it into the bag. "Why are you making a forensic specimen out of my castor oil?"

"This is yours?"

Leo reached over and turned the bag to take a closer look at the bottle. "It does appear to be my castor oil, yes, Poirot. What do we deduce from that?"

"And what would you be doing with it?"

Amusement came into his expression. "I use a few drops to lubricate the latex putty I'll be putting on your face shortly to give you a cute little pointy nose. Why?"

"I'll be right back."

She left him staring after her. Zoe's workstation was on the other side of the room. The designs and photos the woman had pinned to a board indicated that she was attempting a centaur. So far, it looked nothing like the sketches. No wonder the nutjob needed to cheat.

Years of being paid to do sleight of hand tricks made the next ten seconds a walk in the park. Trix waited until Zoe moved around the station again, presumably to collect something, or possibly to sabotage yet another man who'd taken her out and then never called her.

Then she collided with her. She immediately apologised, reaching to help the other woman regain her footing. "I'm sorry. Are you okay?"

"I'm fine," Zoe said coldly. "Just watch where you're going. You could have broken something." She pointed, to make it clear that she meant one of her possessions, not one of Trix's bones. "Could you get away from my station, please? I have a lot of delicate materials here."

"Yes, you do," Trix said, looking over the assembled items. "Including—" she held up the little glass vessel she'd just lifted from Zoe's pocket and turned it in the light "—an empty bottle of rosehip oil. You seem to have run out. Perhaps I can offer you a refill." She opened her other hand to reveal the "castor oil" from Leo's station, and watched Zoe blanch under her makeup. For a pro makeup artist, she used an extraordinary amount of blush.

Zoe automatically put her hand to her pocket. "How did you—" A rush of red returned to her cheeks, clashing with the pink blush. "You *picked my pocket*—"

"Moral outrage from the saboteur," Trix said thoughtfully. "The irony." When Zoe made a grab for the rosehip oil, she did a lightning switch to her other hand, then dropped the empty bottle into the second plastic bag and resealed it. "I have to say, I admire the level of commitment. I assume you were eavesdropping during the qualifying round to find out that Leo's model has a strong allergy to rosehip oil, and decided to boost your otherwise slim chance of beating him in the final by swapping out some of his oil. End result: Leo has yet another client expand like a balloon into a swollen rash, finishes bottom of the board, and his professional reputation takes a serious hit. And you get a few petty chuckles and finish one rank higher than you otherwise will with your overly ambitious and poorly executed design."

Zoe was opening and closing her mouth like an outraged cod.

"I wonder if it's a criminal offense," Trix mused, "purposely aggravating a serious allergy."

The other woman swallowed, but immediately tried to brazen it out with the good old method of deny everything. "I don't know what you're talking about."

"Yeah," Trix said sympathetically. "I suspect that's often the case when you're having a conversation, but I think you're fairly clued in this time. I wouldn't bother to deny it. I've been standing around with nothing much to do while Leo gets ready, other than film the action on my phone."

Not that she'd been hovering around taking pictures; she only took her Harriet the Spy routine so far. Fortunately, Zoe didn't seem too well-endowed in the brains department.

"You—" Zoe stumbled over her words. "I—"

Trix slipped the plastic bags out of reach again when Zoe made another lunge. "I don't want to disrupt Leo when he's a few hours away from winning, so I'm not going to take these to the judges and have you disqualified." Although it wouldn't hurt to let Zoe sweat on that point. "At least, not yet. But you're going to give me a bottle of untainted castor oil, right now, and then you're never going to attempt anything like this ever again, and I highly recommend you speak to someone. Like a therapist. Or a priest."

She kept the bottles behind her back, and held out her free hand expectantly.

If looks could kill…

Zoe breathed like an angry minotaur a few times, then finally spun around and stomped to her table, where she snatched up a bottle and thrust it at Trix. "Castor oil," she said between her teeth.

Trix checked to make sure it was still sealed. "Thank you." She took a final look at the centaur preparations. "My commiserations in advance."

As she turned away, Zoe snapped, "You're exactly what he deserves."

Trix's hands were shaking only slightly as she returned to Leo's station.

He'd done a huge amount of work during the past few minutes, but he set his tools down and looked at her, then over the crowds towards Zoe's station. He let his eyebrows speak for him.

Trix handed him the fresh bottle of castor oil. "Castor oil for my fake nose."

He took the two plastic bags from her other hand and looked at the labels on the bottles. "Rosehip oil." The surge of fury made his features snap taut. He turned in Zoe's direction again. "That nasty little—"

Hastily, Trix caught his arm. "Come on. Clock is ticking. Wings to make. Incompetent saboteurs to beat soundly."

"If I'd put that on your face, you—"

"Wouldn't have been able to leave the flat for a week in case people thought the Bubonic Plague was rife once more. But you didn't put it on my face, and it's our word against hers. I don't want you to be disqualified for making a scene when it would be so much more fun to walk down the runway tonight beside her so-called centaur, which so far looks like a poorly goat, and watch you kick her nasty little arse."

Leo was still scowling over her head, but she saw a reluctant smile twitch at his lips. His eyes cut back to meet hers. "You watching out for me, sweetheart?"

Little ribbons of warmth and unease were uncurling inside her, twining together into a complex emotion. "You know me. Tough as an ant."

He touched her hair. "Preaching to the choir, Tinker Bell."

Trix walked the runway at exactly nine o'clock that night, extending her currently webbed arms to show off the full expanse of her metal plumage. The silver wings arched and fluttered under the swirling spotlights. The thumping beat of the band was energising the crowd and putting an extra bounce in her steps, and when she stepped up to the podium for the judges, the beams of light caught every individual, iridescent scale Leo had painted on her skin and turned her into a flickering column of rainbows.

From the raised platform where the artists were witnessing their creations in motion, Leo watched her cock her hip and move so that the wings snapped back behind her. She turned to pose for the head judge, and winked, in a flash of coquetry that was pure Pierrette. Trix, the performer of old. He felt a grin spreading across his face.

He stood at her side while the judges did their final deliberations. They drew out the suspense for the audience with an extended drum roll, and Trix's small, sweat-slicked fingers slipped into his. He lowered his gaze to hers. They stood there, ignoring the applause and cameras and hundreds of spectators, and just looked at each other.

Somehow, it was as if every encounter they'd had over the past decade seemed to swirl around and come together into this moment.

The gut-punch of pride and apprehension when he won was almost anticlimactic in comparison to that heartbeat of time under the lights with her.

He shook hands with Sylvia George when she handed him the trophy and a bunch of roses, which he put in Trix's arms. "Fantastic," she said, studying the expanse of Trix's wingspan. She gave him a nod. "I'd like to speak with you in a less noisy location. Someone from my office will be in touch tomorrow to arrange a suitable time."

Trix rubbed his back and gave an excited little hop for him, and he tightened his grip compulsively on the trophy.

Backstage, he helped her to detach the wings and webbing and anything that could poke an eye out in a taxi. She shivered when his hands moved over her body. She couldn't shower until she got home, but she changed back into her T-shirt and jeans, and put on a light coat even though it was a warm, clear night.

"Without the wings, I bear a faint resemblance to a rainbow trout," she said in response to his glance at the coat. "This'll cover enough that it should be safe to walk past the fish and chip shop next door without someone filleting me and adding me to the menu."

She did up one button, and then threw her arms around him again. "I'm really proud of you." Her words were muffled against his chest.

He put his arm around her, holding her to him, and

lowered his cheek to rest on her hair. It was stiff with glitter spray and smelled like acetone. He didn't care. "Thanks," he said softly.

Outside in the foyer, Scott and Ryan gave him enthusiastic smacks on the back, and Allie squeezed him. Over her head, he saw Cat standing at Jono's side, chewing her lip.

In an abrupt movement, she came forward and slipped her arms around him in a quick hug. "Congratulations, bro." Before she stepped back, she muttered, "Sorry I flaked on you in the qualifying round."

"It's okay." He glanced at Trix, who was fending off Ryan's attempt to touch her remaining facial scales. "It may have worked out the way it was meant to." His eyes returned to his sister. "Things usually do."

He wanted to believe that.

The weight of the trophy was heavy in the crook of his arm.

"Decisions to make?" Allie asked quietly.

Possibly one of the most important of his life.

Chapter Ten

Sylvia George was another early riser. Her assistant had offered Leo a choice of either eight or eight-thirty on Friday morning. He was awake by six as usual and lay on his side, watching Trix sleep. She was curled in a ball, facing him, her hair falling over her face, making little snuffling noises that he could barely hear over the snoring that rattled the wall between his room and Ryan's room.

When there was a moment of comparative calm like this, it really hit him. That they were here. In each other's beds, in each other's lives.

They'd made such an art form of provoking one another that it was probably completely perverse that he felt like this.

As if he had a proper home for the first time since his grandparents had died.

And it had nothing to do with this overcrowded, poorly soundproofed flat.

He smoothed the hair away from her closed lashes and bent forward to touch his lips to hers, very lightly, although he could play the national anthem on a saucepan and she still wouldn't wake up until she was ready.

He breathed in the scent of her warm skin.

Then he got out of bed and went in search of a tie.

* * *

Sylvia George's London offices were on the top floor of an old stone building not far from the Palace of Westminster. The morning sunlight flooded the large loft room and reflected off her enormous glass desk, where illustration boards were propped up against stacks of paperwork.

She nodded as she examined one of the sketches. "You're very good."

Simple words in a very modulated tone, but from one of the top names in the business—

"Thank you." Leo eased his stance slightly where he stood, waiting for the verdict.

"I understand you've had a few difficulties recently." She produced a magazine from beneath a file, and he managed to suppress a groan when he saw the image on the cover. The person who had snapped that photo at the peak stage of the allergic reaction was sitting on a tabloid goldmine.

"There was a lack of disclosure on the client's part," he said evenly. "But yes. I do take responsibility for that incident."

"From what I've ascertained, it was beyond your control." She looked at the photo, and for the first time, her impassive demeanour cracked into a tiny smile. "And frankly, it couldn't have happened to a nicer person."

She resumed her seat behind the desk and nodded him towards one of the leather guest chairs.

The silence stretched as she studied him over her steepled fingers.

Finally, she spoke. "How do you feel about Los Angeles?"

* * *

With Trix's performance for the board looming, every session in the gym was taking on a new sense of urgency. After another two hours of training with Steph, she emerged with a fresh batch of bruises, a bleeding blister between her left thumb and forefinger, and the thumbs-up to add another move back into the most difficult routine.

Also, another lecture about believing in herself and "finding the joy." Between the two of them, Steph and Leo were a walking motivational audiobook.

He had his meeting with the studio exec this morning. She checked the time, wondering if he was out yet and how it was going.

He came to find her in the gym at twelve to fulfil his promise for her rooftop karaoke and cough up the cash for her bribery pizza. She was sitting on a pile of crash mats, doctoring her hand. "Hey. How did it go?" Not wildly successfully, if the body language was an indication.

He just looked at her, until she started to get seriously worried. Then he shook his head. "It went fine. She's a force to be reckoned with, but she knows what she wants." He rubbed at his beard. "And usually gets it."

Maybe she could give Trix some pointers, then.

"So?" She pushed up from the mats and tugged down the skirt she'd changed into. "Any good news? Job-wise?"

Again, there seemed to be a strange beat of tension. "Not yet. But…things might come of it."

"That's great."

Leo looked at her hand. "You okay?"

"Jury's still out on that one."

They went for their extortion lunch at Tragicomedy,

her favourite restaurant in the theatre district. Most of the seating was outside, under a winding labyrinth of trellising, threaded with lights and very *A Midsummer Night's Dream*-esque.

Apparently, on certain days of the week, it even came complete with West End royalty.

Lily and Luc were sitting at a table set for two, that was unfortunately large enough to accommodate four. They were smiling at one another, and from the way Luc was sitting and Lily was squirming, Trix suspected that either his foot or his hand was doing something under the tablecloth. She resisted her first impulse to hide behind a topiary; but when Lily caught sight of them and her brows shot sky-high, Trix came very close to imitating a spooked Reggie and curling into a ball with her prickles out.

"Hey!" Lily recovered enough composure to call out a greeting and wave them over, and Luc retrieved his wandering limb and politely got to his feet. "That's convenient. I was going to call you soon about the plan for tomorrow." Her eyes slid from Trix to Leo, and then back again, with an expression that would have been comical if it hadn't been so incredibly uncomfortable. "Hi, Leo, how are you?"

"Lily, hi. Luc." Leo shook hands with Luc. "Are we crashing your last date before the wedding?"

"We're just enjoying the calm before the storm that is my mother and her clipboard," Luc said. "Good to see you. Both. Together."

Luc was one of the heavyweight directors. He was very charismatic and Old Hollywood handsome with smooth dark hair and silver temples, and Trix had always found him on the cool side. Extremely business-like. A little stern. Dare she say, intimidating. Now, he was glancing between her and Leo like an amused, mischief-eyed schoolboy, and Lily was clearly rubbing off on him *way* too much.

"Please, join us," Luc added, pulling out one of the spare chairs for Trix.

She balked. "No, really, we're not going to intrude on—"

"You're not intruding." Lily yanked Trix into the chair so fast that the hem of her top was dragged out from under the waistband of her skirt. "Absolutely, sit with us. We haven't ordered yet." She rested her chin on her folded hands and stared straight at Trix. "And we're well overdue for a catch-up."

Trix cleared her throat and reached for the drinks menu as the men sat down opposite them. With a night of straps-dancing ahead, her options were water or one of sixteen varieties of juice. "We had dinner last week." She fixed the back of her top with pointed movements, and half listened as Leo and Luc started talking about Luc's new production.

"Yes. And yet evidently there is so much news."

If Trix took out her phone and snapped a photo of the blushing bride-to-be at this moment, it would be a textbook example of "What the actual fuck?" face.

She ducked her head on a pretence of sharing the menu with Lily. Trix was fervently grateful that they had chosen to sit near the classical pianist, and she'd be leaving the noisy young girl an enormous tip on the way out. "Whatever you're thinking," she murmured under cover of a slightly plinking-plonking version of *Clair de Lune*, "stop."

Deliberately casual, Lily turned a page of the menu.

"What the fuck is up with the cosy lunch date?" She inclined her head towards Trix as if they were debating the relative merits of pineapple and cranberry juice. "If this is the first act of a revenge thriller that ends with Leo's body washing up on a beach, hold off until after the wedding. In case any guest is stupid enough to get legless at the reception and fall into the sea, Célie's got boats patrolling the coast. So if you shove him off the cliff, you'll probably be caught. And not to be crass, but I'd prefer to spend my wedding night on top of my husband rather than trying to break you out of a cell." She paused. "Although I would do it."

Trix tapped her finger against something on the page. "I'm not going to murder him at your wedding." She considered. "Well, the odds have lowered."

"*Have* they?" Lily asked meaningfully. "Could it be that you've come to a mature truce and decided to set your differences aside for the duration of the show?"

"Yes. Exactly."

"Or could it be that the rough shag in your flat no longer refers solely to that hideous '70s carpet in the loo?"

A waiter appeared at their table. "Can I get anybody a drink?"

Trix snapped the menu closed and straightened up. "Oh, God, yes."

What a joyous time to be booze-free.

As casual lunches went, this one felt more like the subtle tension and underlying subtext of a Hitchcock film. Lily kept looking at him and then at Trix, almost vibrating with interest. Even Luc looked intrigued, and Leo would have considered him the last person to care about sex lives that were not his own.

Trix appeared to be mentally mapping the fastest route to the exit.

He tapped his fingers on the table. Sylvia George's contract was resting on his shoulders like a barbell. She'd given him a couple of days to think it over.

A month ago, he probably wouldn't have needed more than two *seconds* of mental debate. Now...

"How's your castmate doing?" Luc asked Trix. "The one you've taken over from?"

"I've been to see her a couple of times this week, but she's pretty withdrawn. Not that I blame her. I'm probably the last person she wants to see right now."

"Well, somebody had to step into the role," Lily pointed out reasonably. "It's not like you did some sort of arch-villain plotting and sabotaged her performance. You're just doing your job."

"It's business, it's not a personal slight to her," Luc agreed. "Things can't grind to a halt. If the strength of your show rests solely on one performer, then you've just launched a disastrous money-pit. It sounds like you stepped up to the plate and did your job superbly."

"Do you know what's happening with the role long-term?" Lily asked, and Trix wound a lock of hair around her finger.

"Jennifer Carr's filling in for me while I'm in Cornwall, and they want to see us both before they make a final decision."

"Please. As if it's even a question."

Trix found a passing smile, but she looked as if one more loyal word would shatter her composure like brittle glass. Leo reached across the table and touched her hand. Her lashes fluttered and her posture became even more stiff, but her fingers stroked his palm before she pulled away.

Lily cleared her throat and pushed at the remains of the pizzas on the table. "Well, we should probably get going," she said to Luc. "We have to be on the road by five if we're going to beat your mother to the estate and tip the staff generously enough that nobody quits when the clipboard arrives."

Luc took the unsubtle hint and pushed his chair back. He reached for his wallet, and Leo shook his head.

"I've got it," he said. "You can't buy your own lunch this close to your wedding." Ignoring the protests from the other couple, and trying to ignore Trix's twitchy silence, he stood and pulled his card case from his pocket. His keys came out with it.

Lily, who had been wiping up the ring of water from her glass with a napkin, suddenly went very still.

When he returned to the table, folding the receipt into his pocket, Trix and Luc had disappeared.

"Luc spotted a director he knows out front," Lily said, with an oddly searching expression. "I suggested he introduce Trix. You never know when contacts like that will come in handy."

"No, you don't." Since she was making no move to get up, Leo sat back down and coolly returned her stare. "Problem, Lily?"

She didn't bother to deny it, but he wasn't expecting her return question. "Do you mind if I look at your keys for a sec?"

"You want to look at my keys."

"Please."

He shifted in his seat and snagged the keys out of his pocket again. Lily took them, turning them over in her hands, and singled out the keychain. It was an old, now defunct miniature game console, of a type that had been popular—and expensive—when he'd been at school, mostly because they'd fit easily into a pocket and could be hidden in one hand during class.

"Interesting choice of key ring," she said, and flipped it over to look at the reverse side. With a fingertip, she played with the curly edge of the sticker that someone had stuck on the back, a small, faded picture of a cartoon wasp. He'd always assumed it was a sports emblem.

"Old memento."

She tilted her head, and he shrugged. "I fucked up my knee at school. Completely blew my chance to play in the rugby champs in front of a talent scout. I was in hospital for a while. My parents had just split up, and it wasn't a great time." Understatement. "When I woke up from the second surgery, someone had left that on my bedside table. Saved my sanity that week."

"You don't know where it came from?"

"No." He spoke slowly, studying her. "I don't. I asked around my friends, and I checked it didn't belong to the hospital, but no one had seen it before."

"I have," Lily said, holding it up. "Seen this before. I remember it very well. I frequently borrowed it, in fact, to take to an incredibly boring physics class. Trix tutored people in maths for months to buy this. Cleaned their dorm rooms. Drew portraits of prized puppies and horses and boyfriends."

Leo reached out and took the keys from her, laying the game console on the palm of his hand. His stomach felt hollow as he looked down at it. "This was Trix's." Turning it over, he ran his thumb over the sticker. "Why the wasp?" His voice sounded odd.

"Not wasp. Bee." Lily's voice was steady. "Beatrix. Her foster mother called her Honey Bee. Every time Trix went back to Buckinghamshire for the holidays, Marta would put one of those stickers on something for her to find when she came back to school. To make her smile."

He could feel a muscle clench in his jaw.

"I asked her what happened to that," Lily said. "She told me she left it on the train, coming back to school after a weekend at home, but after I suggested we ring up the rail line and check their lost and found, she said she'd given it away. To someone she thought needed it more than she did. I asked her which friend. And I remember very clearly what her response was. She said, 'Not a friend. But sometimes that doesn't matter.'" She held his gaze levelly. "That's the sort of person Trix is. She's taken some hard knocks recently, and I know she has regrets, but that's Trix in a nutshell. She would give up her prized possession to her worst enemy if she thought it was the right thing to do."

Leo remained silent as she stood up and picked up her bag, glancing over her shoulder. "Here they come." She looked at him again. "I cannot *begin* to tell you how much I hated Dan St. James and what he did to Trix. She's been fighting so hard to get back on her feet, and she's succeeding *way* better than she thinks she is. I like everything I've seen of you so far, Leo, and if you're going to be good for her, I will continue to like everything about you. But if you do anything to make her hurt any worse, I will skewer you like a barbeque shrimp." She smiled sweetly and shouldered her bag. "See you in Cornwall. We're so happy you're coming."

She walked over to Luc and he slipped his arm around her, cuddling her against him.

Leo's fingers closed tightly around the game console.

Chapter Eleven

As a first experience of Cornwall, this one was pretty damn spectacular.

Lily and Luc were getting married in the incredible clifftop estate of a Savage family friend, a massive stone mansion sitting dark and imposing in the sunshine. Trix was relieved about the beautiful weather for their sake, but the entire dramatic aspect of the house would be more suited to thunder and lightning.

She stood at a bevelled window, looking down at the sprawling lawns where a rose-flanked path led between row after row of white padded seats to the altar, the huge marquee beyond, and then the sea.

According to the antique clock on the mantelpiece, they were due to walk down the aisle in ten minutes. Guests were gathering in large groups on the grass, and she thought she recognised Allie's hat, so Leo was probably somewhere nearby. He'd dropped her off a few hours ago and gone to find his hotel in the nearby town, and the afternoon had disappeared in a blur of makeup, hairspray, and booze.

In fact, time in general seemed to have sped up into a confusing whir of spiralling minutes, in which she'd gone from loathing the very thought of him to craving his company and knowing his touch and his taste and smell and expressions with incredible intimacy. He'd gone from years-long antagonist to—

Her fingers curled against the glass.

"Here you go, darling." Célie Verne held a fresh flute of champagne in front of her face, and Trix turned around and found a smile for Luc's mother.

"*Merci, madame.* And may I say, you look *spectacularly* hot today."

Célie threw back her head and laughed. "You just became my favourite person at this wedding, petite." Célie gestured with her own glass out the window. "How's the view?"

"Staggering. From every window. It looks like the Jolly Roger should be appearing through a wall of mist."

"It does have a rather piratical aspect, does it not? I was thinking more about ghosts and smugglers, myself. The first time Luc's father and I stayed here, I was reading a dreadfully delicious Gothic novel and fancied myself as the lovelorn heroine. Our hosts made the mistake of giving us the room with the widow's walk and I indulged myself shamelessly." Célie inclined her head. "Although when I asked after the view, I was referring to the human element. The masculine element. I saw you arrive with a startlingly attractive young man. He is yours?"

Wordlessly, Trix looked from Célie's enquiring face back to the window.

"I see," Célie said softly, and her smile grew.

In Leo's experience, the ceremony was the part of the wedding that you sat through politely before the reception, at which point the day became worthwhile. Well, that, and the privilege of being present to support good friends as they symbolically joined their lives together and began a new chapter. But in general he'd take the band, booze, and catered salmon over the lengthy vows.

However, as he stood on the sprawling lawn of an incredible clifftop estate in Cornwall, watching Luc watch Lily as she walked down the aisle, he really—he *got* it for the first time. A classical pianist and a violinist were playing Canon in D Major, and Luc's face when he saw his fiancée was so intimate that Leo had the uncomfortable feeling of prying into a moment that was meant to be private between two people.

He'd expected Luc to be as easy and confident at the altar as he was in front of a theatre full of critics, but the other man stood tensely, and swallowed hard, and the look in his eyes was…

Something you would only ever recognise, fully, if you were very lucky.

Leo was nowhere near ready to be standing up there himself; this was as close as he wanted to get to a celebrant for the foreseeable future, but he recognised what was in Luc's face right now, because it was a hard, steady pulse of awareness throughout his own body, from head to heart to groin. All the way to his fucking feet, he just—knew.

He didn't look away from Trix as she reached the front of the aisle. Sunlight gleamed on pink hair and purple lace. A thin strip of skin showed between the high waist of her skirt and a little top that did interesting things for her breasts. She looked sassy and sexy, and like she'd just ducked out for a brief break between routines at the Moulin Rouge. If Lily was a Michelangelo sculpture today, serene and fluid and slightly otherworldly, Trix was a Tamara de Lempicka painting, bright, gorgeous, and edgy, with shadows in her eyes.

He was only half aware of Allie at his side, her skirt rustling, and Cat and Jono farther back. As Trix took Lily's bouquet for safekeeping, her gaze moved over the guests, and eventually found him.

They maintained that connection, neither of them smiling, as Lily took Luc's hands and he bent to touch his forehead to hers, murmuring something in her ear.

For a moment, Leo's ears blocked out the music, the celebrant's voice, the screech of gulls overhead, the crash of waves on the shore below, and every sound except an exaggerated one-two drumming, the imaginary beats of their hearts. *Thud-thud. Hisheart-herheart.*

And—yeah.

He was in love with her. Head over fucking heels for her. It was as simple and as huge as that. He loved Trix. In a way and to an extent that his younger self could never have envisioned.

"Aww," Allie whispered, hugging his arm. "Look at them. I'm never going to have someone look at me like that." She looked up at him from under the angled brim of her hat, glancing between his face and Trix's. "Or like that. Man. I'm going to die alone. I should get a puppy." Nudging him, she murmured, "Bet you're grateful to past-you for exploding that dude's face now, huh?"

"Key word: *accidentally.*"

But, as he returned his gaze to Trix, he was. Despite all the many, *many* obstacles he saw in his immediate future, he was grateful that he'd ended up here.

* * *

The last dying rays of the sun cast pink and orange streaks across the wide expanse of sea, echoing the dancing searchlight beams that crossed the side of the stone mansion in time to the pulse of music. Everywhere, people were on the dance floor, or milling around drinking and laughing, or still gathered at their tables over the remains of dessert. Trix lifted her cocktail glass above the head of a seated person as she wove back towards her table. Slightly unsteadily. The pre-ceremony champagne was catching up with the post-ceremony tequila.

Jono and Cat were on the dance floor, joining in with the cast of the recently ended run of *42nd Street*. Best thing about a theatre wedding: plenty of people who were used to partying hard and without shame to show tunes.

Trix set her glass down on the white linen tablecloth and slipped back into her seat next to Leo. He'd shed the jacket of his suit, rolled up his sleeves and yanked the top of his shirt open. His bowtie was hanging loose at each side of his brown throat, and he was brooding. Full-on Heathcliff-level brooding, although hopefully the comparison ended there.

"Are you okay?" she asked him, trying to pitch her voice loud enough to be heard over the music but not by anyone else at the table.

He reached for his own glass and tossed back the contents of it, then set it down next to hers and touched the back of his index finger to her hand. "All good."

She turned her hand over, catching his fingers with hers. He leaned forward to kiss the skin over her collarbone, where she was sparkling like a unicorn after

Lily's makeup artist had dusted highlighter across her chest.

"Oh, you two. So sweet. So soon to be in need of a room." Allie set her clutch down on the table and dropped into the seat on Leo's other side. "Good thing the *West End Story* crew aren't loitering about with their cameras tonight," she remarked. "All the little Trix/Jono fangirls would be crushed."

She pulled the toothpick from her drink and scraped off the cherry with her teeth. "Have you checked out the other side of the house yet? They're opening up gelato and pizza vans, I assume to help soak up the booze. There's also a photo booth and a temporary-tattoo artist. Ink guaranteed to last for at least a week."

"Shower-resistant ink and a field full of completely trolleyed people," Leo said drily. "What could possibly go wrong?"

Trix propped her chin on her hand. "That's a very unadventurous attitude for someone with a tattoo on his butt cheek."

"Exactly. Learn from my mistakes. No ink of any kind unless completely sober."

The band played the first beats of a song that had been popular when Trix was at school, and Lily appeared at the table, bubbling over with happiness and champagne. "Sorry," she said to Leo, "I'm nicking your date. This is our song."

On the dance floor, they almost collided with Cat and Jono, who were red-faced and appeared to have been arguing again. Cat glared at Trix and walked off with a very definite flounce.

"Wow," Lily said. "If you keep seeing Leo, I foresee some very awkward family dinners in your future."

Trix watched Cat stalking away. "I'd better steer clear of the cliff tonight." She wobbled on her heels and grabbed hold of Lily to steady herself. It was going to be a hell of a hangover tomorrow. "Or there may be a body washing up on the shore after all."

"Yours or Cat's?"

"Depends who has the best reflexes after eighty-five mojitos." Trix eyed Lily's moves. "I wouldn't audition for *Footloose* any time soon, Ginger Rogers."

"Hey," Lily said indignantly. "Who was the best dancer in our year at LIDA?"

"Me."

"Oh. Yeah." Lily suddenly swung her into a twirl, almost knocking both of them off their feet. They ended up in an uncoordinated slow dance that did no credit to their very expensive tuition. "I'm glad you're acknowledging your own talents at last. Now if you could just do it sober."

She wriggled her hips to move the hem of her dress, which was in danger of getting stiletto-spiked by their terrible footwork. It was a sleek, simple cascade of white satin, falling with the fluidity of liquid mercury.

"By the way," Trix said, "if I didn't make it clear enough earlier—most gorgeous bride ever." An unexpected sting wet her lashes. "I'm so happy for you, Lily. I hope you have the *best* night, and the best life. You deserve it."

Lily squeezed Trix's hand where she held it in a mock-formal waltz. "So do you, T." She blinked to stave off her own mascara-ruining tears. "And you will. We're all going to be great."

Trix smoothed back a strand of her meticulously straightened hair. It was like candy-pink satin today, all dark roots gone, thanks to a miracle-worker stylist from a salon in Westminster that usually had an eight-month waitlist. "You think?"

Lily smiled at her. "I've got a good feeling."

Trix danced with Jono after that, who was silent and preoccupied, and then Leo pulled her into his arms. She turned into the sheltering warmth of his chest.

"Where did Cat go?" she asked, watching Jono flag down a waiter with a champagne tray.

Hopefully not to lurk around the clifftop, waiting for an opportune moment.

Leo traced the line of her spine with his fingertips, his skin tickling hers when he reached the gap between her skirt and bralette. "Last time I saw her, she was talking to a guy from Lily's old TV show."

As the sky outside turned completely black, scattered everywhere with pinpoints of light, as if someone above had looked down on the festivities with a tolerant eye and thrown an entire fistful of stars over them, they danced.

The music became an intoxicating, heavy pulse, the lights low and moving lazily over entwined bodies. Trix swayed slowly, barely moving, her head resting between Leo's ribs, his body curved down around hers. It couldn't be comfortable, but he wasn't complaining. His thumb rubbed slow circles on the dip at the base of her spine.

She looked up, watching the purple and blue lights dapple his cheek. His eyes were just opaque pools of black in the shadows, the expression in them impossible to read, but the lines of his face grew taut when he reached down to touch his lips to hers.

Trix inhaled against the scratch of his beard and

reached up to cup his head. Her nails dug in as he
deepened the kiss, scraping against his skin under his
thick hair.

A large hand slid down over her butt, hauling her
up against him, and she felt the groan echo through
his chest.

"Want to go for a walk?" It was a husky murmur
directly into her ear.

They barely made it out of the marquee and past the
people sitting in the fairy-light glow outside before they
were kissing again, hands sliding and stroking. Trix was
hardly aware of time passing or even where they were
as they weaved towards darker areas of the property, her
walking backward and then him; they backed each other
into a tree at one point. Her high heel caught in a paving stone, almost turning her ankle, and Leo scooped
her up against him, his forearm a steel bar against her
back. She wrapped her legs around his hips, crossing
her feet in the lethal heels against his arse, and felt the
warm night air dangerously high on her thighs as the
lace skirt rode up.

Framing the sides of his neck with her palms, her
thumbs rubbing along his jaw, Trix snatched rapid
breaths between kisses. The designer hadn't factored
violent snogging into the measurements for this crop
top. Serious oversight; she was one deep inhale away
from a literal bodice-ripper.

The momentum of her climbing him like a ladder
drove them back against a stone wall, but Leo held her
easily in his arms. It was dark wherever they were now,
the only real light from a slice of moon, and the music
from the marquee was a distant bass beat. Trix shifted

her grip, her left hand flattening on the stone behind his head. It was cool and damp with moss.

With an effort, Leo dragged his mouth from hers long enough to speak. "Bridesmaid."

"Honoured guest."

"What?"

"I don't know. I thought we were doing annoying nicknames again."

"You're a bridesmaid. You have a room upstairs. I'm assuming it has a bed in it."

"It does." Trix touched her nose to his. "Four posts, a canopy, and an alarming headboard carving of Charon ferrying souls across the river Styx. Pretty sure it's to dissuade anybody from getting carnal and banging up against it."

"So it's the Bed of Judgment or—" He nudged her hair out of the way with his chin, so he could try to see in the darkness. "Where the hell are we?"

Trix craned her neck to look over her shoulder. There was another stone wall a couple of metres behind them. And a third to their left. "I think we're in the labyrinth."

Under the influence of excellent champagne, Leo accepted that without further question. "How long do you think it would take to get to your room?" His lips were back on her neck. She felt the light scrape of his teeth and shivered.

"About five minutes." Her fingers ran an exploratory path down his abdomen, and he jerked. "However, we'll have to pass at least fifty people to get there, and even if someone doesn't interrupt us before we reach the beady eye of Charon, I will be forced to keep my hands to myself the entire time, because public shagging at the reception is probably really frowned upon."

"Then we're sticking with the labyrinth." Leo loosened his grip so she could slip back to the ground, and caught her when she stumbled on her heels again.

One arm circling his neck, she held his mouth to hers as she reached down without looking to yank the shoe straps open. She unbuttoned his shirt and kicked her heels into the darkness, which lost her about five inches of height. His bare stomach tensed under her fingers, and she looked up. "What?"

His head lowered the extra distance. "You suddenly disappeared."

Grinning, she closed her teeth over his full lower lip. "Sorry to crush your hopes there, but this is as low as I'm going right now. These are very sharp stones. It would be like kneeling in a pile of broken glass."

He nipped her back, his chest moving with a laugh. "I said nothing."

She hummed in her throat, pushing her hips against him as she tugged his shirt off his shoulders. "Even under a quarter-moon, I recognise that expression."

He swept her hair aside again, kissing the tip of her nose as he tried to find the fastening on her top. "Did they sew you into this?"

"Just about." Trix had spent years training herself to multi-task in the air, perfecting moves that required all four limbs to perform independent tasks. She utilised that skill now, hooking her bare foot around his calf while she simultaneously opened his buckle and reached behind her back to fumble for the hidden zip in the lace.

He took over, dragging it the rest of the way, and

pulled the top down her arms to toss it into the dim shadows. In some far-off corner of her mind that wasn't fogged with lust, she hoped she would be able to find all these items of clothing before they did have to reappear at the reception, or that was going to be a picture that would liven up the wedding album for the grandkids. Her hands went back to Leo's head, twining into his hair as he kissed down her chest and closed his mouth over her nipple. His palms were warm and strong as they shaped her bare back, then caressed downwards and opened the zip of her skirt. She turned in the circle of his arms, thousands of nerve endings prickling to life, and his shoulders flexed forward to cradle her back against him, his kisses increasingly urgent along the curve of her neck.

The little sounds she was making seemed to echo in the still air around them, diffusing their heady bubble to mingle with the muted throb of music. The band had sped up into a rock song. The beats penetrated the darkness to join with the rhythm of their skin sliding slickly together when he pushed into her from behind. His forearm braced against the wall, and she pressed her forehead into his wrist. His other arm held her waist; she wrapped her own across it, their fingers locking.

She was on her tiptoes, but the rough pebbles stabbed into her feet, dragging her senses from building pleasure to nagging pain. She solved the problem by letting him take her full weight, and bent her knees to hook her ankles back around his thighs.

His breath was coming fast and rough against her neck. His voice was a rasp. "Are you seriously comfortable like this? I feel like I'm about to snap something."

She turned her head; her hair was sweaty and catching on his beard as he moved against her. "I *hope* not. Considering what I'm balancing on right now."

She felt the breathless laugh against the nape of her neck, and then his lips pressed there, and through a haze of arousal and the lingering buzz of mojitos, she somehow felt that kiss in her heart.

Her fingers tightened over his.

Chapter Twelve

Trix was being slowly pecked to death by a giant bird. Its beak struck her temple and ripped in, drilling into her skull as the ominous sound of squawking spiraled, and—

She could smell the sea. Slowly, painfully, she cracked one eyelid open, and immediately slammed it shut again when the sun smacked her in the face. With the universal moan of morning-after regret, she dropped one arm over her eyes and flung the other to the side, where her fingers encountered warm, silky skin.

Someone else groaned, and she risked vision again, pushing herself up on one elbow. A couple of feet away, Leo rolled over and sat up. He was shirtless and every muscle in his torso rippled. Unfortunately, she was too nauseous to fully appreciate it.

A wave crashed nearby. Very nearby. She extended her awareness beyond his abs and looked over her shoulder. "Oh, hell. How did we get down here?"

They were curled up on the cliff-side path down to the beach. She wasn't sure if they'd been the idiots Célie had feared would go for a drunken swim and had collapsed halfway back up to the house, or if they'd just given up on the idea halfway down.

Leo scrubbed his hand through his hair. "I have no idea." He looked down. "To be honest, I'm just relieved I'm wearing trousers right now."

Trix ran her hand down her midriff. She was wearing her bridesmaid skirt, and—she shifted in the grass—hopefully underwear, and his missing shirt, done up by three buttons, none of them in the right holes. "I have your shirt," she said lamely, and the corner of his mouth turned up.

"Keep it," he said, spreading his palm against his bare chest. "It's a bit late to be self-conscious about getting my kit off right now. Anyway, you've made it pretty clear that you're hot for me."

She rolled her eyes and managed to work her way up to a kneel. Hesitantly, she ran her tongue over the inside of her cheek. Desert-dry. It felt like she'd been getting intimate with the suction tube at the dentist for about two years straight. "I'm going to take a wild guess that at some point last night there were more mojitos." She swallowed hard. "And possibly champagne. And martinis." Another swell of nausea overtook her. "There was definitely gelato. And if the image of licking sprinkles off you is a legit memory and not a really inspired dream, I hope we at least moved away from the ice cream truck first."

Leo leaned over and kissed her shoulder. She didn't blame him for falling short of her lips. She'd avoid her own dragon breath if she could. There were mints in her clutch. Wherever that was. She looked around again. Below them, the rhythmic wash of the waves against the rocks ought to be soothing, but the seaside soundtrack didn't stand much chance against the trombone players in each of her temples.

"We didn't actually go swimming, did we?" She felt her hair, but it was dry. Sticking straight out from her head like that poor doll from *Rugrats*, but dry. "Because that seems—"

"Unbelievably dangerous?" He stretched his arms above his head, then rubbed his own temple with another sigh. "No. I don't think so. The last thing I remember was looking up at the sky and listening to you tell some extremely unlikely constellation legend. I don't think we got as far as the beach."

"Thank God." Trix scratched her chin and winced when her fingers came away stained with lipstick. She probably looked like the Joker right now. Even on normal nights, things started to degenerate the moment she fell asleep; the concept of repairing, refreshing sleep was slightly undermined by what happened to her appearance in the space of a few hours. After a night when she'd collapsed into unconsciousness in the open air, with a full face of makeup and a body comprised of ninety-five percent alcohol and five percent gelato, the situation was likely dire.

When she lowered her arm, the rolled-up sleeve of her borrowed shirt shifted. Shoving the rest of it out of the way, she examined her inner forearm with a groan. "Before that last memory of what I'm sure was a fascinating and accurate lecture on astronomy—" although off the top of her head, she couldn't recall *knowing* any constellation legends "—do you remember paying a visit to the temporary tattooist?" Turning her arm, she tried to work out which way the design went. "What even is this? A fishhook? A hieroglyphic?"

Leo reached forward and held her wrist, moving her arm where he could see it. He frowned, and then his expression slowly cleared. A smile appeared in his tired eyes.

Even through the bloodshot fatigue, she knew that wise-arse glint. "What?"

He ran his thumb over the tattoo. "Apparently you're as clued up on astrology as you are on astronomy."

"Astrology? What astrological sym—" Realisation dawned. "It's *not*."

"It's the symbol for Leo." He pinched her chin. He was openly grinning now, the tosser. As a side-effect of losing her mind, she at least seemed to have distracted him from his hangover. Nice to be useful. "Trix. That's so…sweet."

The word choice reminded Trix of his sister, and she grimaced and rubbed the ink hard with her finger, but it didn't budge. It would be invaluable as smudge-proof liquid eyeliner, but as an enormous drunken *brand* on her arm, not ideal. "This has your name written all over it, Magasiva."

"Drawn all over it, more accurately. And if it'd been my idea, it would have been on a more interesting location than your arm." Complacently, lips twitching, he stood up. "I did warn you about mixing alcohol and any sort of ink. You really have no one to blame but yourself."

Trix's brain was finally starting to function, and she found her own short-lived spark of amusement when he bent his arm to rotate the muscles in his shoulder. "Because you're so full of maturity and wisdom these days that you're above these little errors in judgment?"

He patted her condescendingly on the head. "Exactly."

"Check your ribs, Einstein." On the smooth expanse

of skin, there was an ink mark that hadn't been there the last time she'd kissed down his side. She could see fluttering wings. "Nice butterfly."

"Butterfly?" All she could really see was the top of his head and his nose as he examined his own little boozy fail, but his body started to quiver, and growing suspicion gave her enough momentum to push all the way up to her feet.

She leaned forward to take a proper look. "You—" Words failed her.

His eyes were alive and bright with laughter now, the morning sun reflecting off that little silver star in his left iris. "Incurably insufferable knob?" he suggested helpfully.

"Apparently even under the influence of that much alcohol, your more annoying side prevails."

He lowered his head so he could pull her graffitied arm around his neck. They were both smiling, so his attempt to kiss her almost resulted in clashing teeth. "On the bright side—and I say this not to undermine what I bet twenty quid was *your* grand gesture, but as a person with a smudged sketch of Tinker Bell on his body—there's no way this ink will last a week or more. I have a solvent at home that will take it off in about ten seconds."

Trix closed her hand against the nape of his neck, her fingertips lightly brushing the hairs there. Her smile faded as she looked up at him. He'd turned them around so that the sun wasn't directly taunting her hungover face, and in the light she could see the very faint laughter lines beside his eyes. It was going to be a hot day, but there was a breeze and it ruffled around his ears and temples. She watched the quiet rise and fall of his chest.

And as she looked back at him, the emotions that were tickling against her consciousness sparked into full life, and for a moment she couldn't breathe. It was like when Doralina raised her hand and snapped her fingers in the first act and the spotlight came on, bright, relentless, and emphatic. Everything lit up and under scrutiny. The impact of it skittered across her nerve endings and wound in a fluttering coil in her abdomen.

She loosened her hold so she wasn't digging her knuckles into his spinal cord.

The reaction wasn't panic.

Fear. It was fear.

Not—never—of him. Not even because of what she thought she saw mirrored in his eyes.

She was afraid because—

Her hands slid down his bare chest and fell away, and she shifted her stance. The grass was soft under her feet; she didn't have her shoes. Another thread of memory supplied their probable abandonment in the sex labyrinth.

A small frown appeared between Leo's brows, and his hand came up to cup her cheek. His head bent to hers, his lashes brushing her cheekbone as they stood toe to toe, both silent, both of their minds probably working overtime.

Her eyes lifted back to his, and that *something* passed between them again: thought-shifting, life-twisting, almost tangible.

She was suddenly *so* afraid, and it was because of the part of her that *wasn't* gripping her lungs with cold hands right now. The part of her that wanted to ignore that other voice of caution and distress, and just reach out.

Reach for *him* and not let go for a long time.

Maybe ever.

Too soon. *Too much.*

Her breath hitched in a tiny squeak, and *no*. She was *not* going to do this again. Not here, not now, and what kind of fucked-up person ended up on the verge of a panic attack because unexpected, fun, *casual* sex with her long-time enemy turned out to be, possibly…

The best thing that ever happened to you, you absolute tit?

She took a step back and stumbled where grass met rock on the cliff path. Leo shot out an arm, but she steadied herself and lifted a hand.

"No," she said automatically. "I'm fine."

How many people uttered that particular phrase and really meant it?

"No. You're not." His expression took on a sliver of wariness beneath the concern, but his voice was blunt. "Your mind just propelled itself miles away."

She shook her head, but he went on a little roughly, "In every way except physically, you're shoving me away as hard as you can. Not just now, either." Somehow she couldn't look away from him. For a fraction of a second, his features softened, and her fingers flexed into the crumpled lace of her skirt. "Given our history, I know the irony is resounding, but I wouldn't do anything to hurt you, Trix. Ever."

As quickly as the breeze had picked up, scattering dust around her ankles, the mood between them had gone as taut as an overstretched wire. And if she didn't get away from it, and give herself some time to just… process—*hide*, taunted the pervasive little voice—she was going to end up either saying something she would regret, or hyperventilating and humiliating herself.

With jerky movements, she unbuttoned the borrowed shirt and refastened it correctly, knotting the tails at her waist so it didn't hang loose to her knees. It was going to be obvious enough what they'd been doing all night without looking like she was completely naked underneath.

Another breath. Deep and slow. Fleetingly, she touched his hand. "I know. I know you wouldn't. I'm just…tired. And hungover."

The silence was weighty, and she sensed the very deliberate, difficult attempt he made to step away from the weight hanging over them, the reality that was going to come crashing down on the temporary bubble they were living in.

"We should get back," he said, finally. "Hopefully the rest of the wedding party is still sleeping it off. We might be able to slip inside without being seen by anyone who's likely to bring it up at every other event from now until retirement."

With Célie's mania for organisation, Trix wasn't surprised to see that most of the wedding aftermath had been cleared away overnight. The gardens were neat and clean, alive with birdsong and smelling strongly of the rose bushes. It was almost surreally serene and pretty. She found her clutch on a stone wall, but there was no sign of her missing top, and her shoes were no longer in the labyrinth. It was probably too much to hope there was a well-shod poltergeist floating about.

Their attempt to sneak into the house was thwarted

when they rounded the corner to the back entrance and found Jono sitting outside on a bench. He still wore his suit, and he looked about as well-rested as they did—and he was smoking. Jono was a professional performer; he'd kicked the habit years ago for his health and his career, and he very rarely lit up these days. It was his last resort in times of extreme stress.

Trix had been planning to dash up to her room before he had a chance to smirk, but she stopped dead at the sight of the cigarette. "Uh-oh. What happened?"

Jono flicked a bit of ash away and rubbed his other hand over his shaved head. His eyes moved between them, before his gaze returned to rest on Leo. "Your sister's upstairs. When we realised we'd missed the bus, we were too knackered and skint to call taxis all the way out here after midnight, so Luc's brother offered his room to Cat. Which was chivalrous, but I think his hangover was kicking in by that point and he just wanted her out of hearing distance so he didn't have to listen to her anymore."

Leo groaned. "What happened? Is she okay?"

Trix had never heard Jono sound so sarcastic and exasperated. "Highly debatable point. And not really my concern anymore."

"She broke things off?" Trix asked warily. Honestly, she thought it was about time, given the way Cat had been treating Jono. He deserved better than to be messed about while Cat worked off her current grudge against the world.

A flash of uncertainty had her glancing at Leo.

It's not remotely the same thing.

Was it?

She'd preferred to take a breather from the drama

and keep things mutually casual in her dating life, which she wasn't apologising for, and it wasn't because she blamed all possessors of a penis for the fact that one of them had turned out to be a fuckhead. But it was only uncomplicated fun if there were no deeper emotions and needs on either side and nobody was getting hurt—

The tension knotted tighter in her stomach.

"No. I did." Jono stubbed out the cigarette against the sole of his shoe. "Sorry," he said to Leo. "I like Cat, a lot, but I'm not a total masochist, and I'm not an idiot. She didn't really want to start something with me. She threw a fit last night about me flirting with Trix while we were dancing, with a few equally ridiculous accusations thrown in, but I don't believe for a second she's really jealous. Whatever's going on with her, it's not about me." He flipped the cigarette butt around his fingers like it was the dagger he juggled with in the show. Mouth puckering, he looked down at it. "I'm suddenly remembering one of the many reasons I gave these up. The aftertaste is vile."

"To be honest, mate," Leo said, equally fed-up, "I'm surprised you put up with it for longer than five minutes. I suppose I'd better go and see her." He didn't sound enthusiastic, and Trix didn't blame him. In her current form, Cat was more likely to slam the door on his foot than actually have a conversation with him.

"You'll probably need your shirt back first," she murmured, and he pressed his palm against his ribs.

"Yes, I will."

Jono shook himself out of his preoccupation. "I'd suggest you get Luc to lend you a clean one, but you're bigger in the shoulders than he is, and you'd probably end up looking like the Incredible Hulk losing his temper."

"With the way I'm feeling right now," Leo said, "not a bad comparison."

Trix swallowed on another wave of nausea.

Upstairs, Leo took a lightning-fast shower and went to find his sister, while Trix stood under the water for a few minutes longer before she combed out her hair, put on her most comfortable dress, and sought out Lily.

The newlywed was outside on the front terrace, knocking back coffee. She was also rocking the nicked-my-man's-clothes look this morning, although the shirt she had tucked into her shorts looked freshly ironed and had probably been taken from Luc's side of the wardrobe rather than directly from his back. She lowered her mug. "Good morning."

"Morning." Trix tried to ignore the penetrating observation coming her way. "I'd ask if you slept well, but I'll spare your blushes."

Lily snorted. "*My* blushes? According to the gossip circulating since someone found your shoes and top last night, you boinked your boyfriend in the labyrinth."

Trix rubbed her nose in a fruitless attempt at covering her blush. "Um. Nobody actually witnessed the… shoe removal, did they?"

"No, although I gather some eerie moans and groans and a lot of enthusiastic 'yeses' scared the hell out of Luc's aunt, who is now convinced that the labyrinth is haunted by a monotonous ghost. She suspects pirates, and is never coming back." Lily cleared her throat. "So, we're not throwing down against the use of the term 'boyfriend,' then?"

Trix just shook her head, more in bewilderment than agreement, and Lily's frown deepened.

Fortunately Jono chose that moment to interrupt, appearing through the folding glass doors to inform them that Cat was refusing to drive back to London with him, so she'd have to carpool with Leo, Trix, and Allie, and wasn't that going to be a bloody laugh and a half.

Lily tracked her down before a van arrived to ferry them all back to the hotel to collect the cars. "Are you all right?"

To quote Jono, that was a debatable point. But she wasn't going to offload on Lily the day after her wedding.

"Because you look a bit...odd," Lily added bluntly.

"Thank you. That's probably because I'm exuding tequila fumes from my pores and I have an imprint of the stone wall in the labyrinth on my kneecap."

She'd spilled her heart out to Lily too many times to be convincing now. Her best friend looked more concerned than ever. "Trix—"

"It's all okay, Lily. Really."

If she repeated it enough times, she might even believe it herself.

Chapter Thirteen

Trix didn't notice until Monday morning that someone at the wedding had changed her standard text message alert to the ice cream truck jingle, which could mean that she actually *had* sucked gelato off Leo's pulse-points in plain sight.

She put down her cereal bowl and went to retrieve her phone from the table. It was currently being used as a paperweight for the note Leo had left her. Usually his pre-gym notes were borderline insulting caricatures, which she was keeping in a scrapbook. This was a few scrawled, ominous words: *Gone with the guys. We need to talk later. Hope you slept well.*

Yesterday, when they'd finally got back to London after the most awkward road trip in the history of automobiles, things had been so weird between them that they'd circled each other warily for the rest of the day. They'd ended up agreeing to watch a film with Ryan and Scott. Leo had stared blankly at the screen, while Trix held a silent conversation with Reggie on the floor. The voice that her imagination supplied for the hedgie was irritatingly judgmental.

Then they'd had bad sex because she couldn't get out of her own head and suspected he was having the same problem. Not even mediocre, "well, the kissing was good and the closeness was nice and nipples are fun" sex. She didn't equate a mutual non-orgasm with bad sex, if everyone had a good time anyway. However, if they were excruciatingly aware of every sound and movement, continually jabbed elbows and knees into vulnerable places, and then eventually gave up mid-thrust and lay there without looking at each other until they finally dropped into an exhausted and headachy doze, it was not the stuff of fairy-tales and fireworks.

Rubbing her hand over her face, Trix set the note aside carefully and picked up her phone to read the message. It was from Natalie. Morning texts from the assistant stage manager were always news she'd rather not hear.

Hey, T. See weekend went well. ;) Just a heads-up that Marco's not super impressed with the new developments online, but all publicity is good publicity, & Leo's smoking hot, so go you. Casting board have confirmed they want to see you & Jennifer perform the Act 2 straps routine tomorrow before they make a final decision on the role going forward, so see if you & Steph can add back the last side planche transition sequence today. Training space open in gym this morn if you need it. Rooting for you, kiddo.

Her attention was so caught by the short deadline to get her shit together onstage that it took a moment for the more obscure part of the message to register.

What new developments online?

With a sinking feeling, she sat down and opened one of her social media apps—and was immediately hit by a helpful pop-up informing her that she'd been tagged in so many comments that her phone suggested a notification filter.

She had to scroll past four posts from outraged tweens, two of which expressed sympathy to poor, betrayed Jono and used cry-face emojis, and one that basically called her the whore of the West End, before she found the photo that user Cat Magasiva had uploaded late last night. Cat had tagged it as Lily Lamprey's wedding, which would have gained most of the initial attention, and then whacked on an additional hashtag for *West End Story*, just to make sure all the web-series fans didn't miss it.

It wasn't an especially scandalous picture—and thank God, because (a) the few strips of sequins and mesh she'd worn as Pierrette was as naked as Trix wanted to get in public, and (b) Leo's sister had taken that photograph.

But it was intimate.

It was obviously a wider shot of the dance floor and band, but it had been cropped so they were the main subject. Technically, they'd been dancing at the time, but copy and paste them backing towards a bed and it would be seamless. They were kissing, although that word suggested something a bit tamer than this. There ought to be a full scale of terms for each heat-level of a kiss. This was about an eight out of ten, more than a snog but unlikely to get them censored unless the intensity went up and hands went down.

When she scrolled to a comment about the look on Jono's face, she belatedly realised that he was in the photo, too, standing a metre or so behind them. She groaned out loud when she saw the expression the camera had captured. Both devastated and furious, his mouth drawn up into a pouting sneer.

It was his stomach-pain face, which he always got when his IBS was playing up. Another reason he shouldn't have been smoking yesterday. And on closer inspection, he definitely wasn't looking at them. His gaze was directed somewhere to their right. Probably, not to be indelicate, towards the bathrooms.

Another text message popped up on the screen. Lily. I seem to have been tagged in a post about a cheating scandal at my wedding. WTF?

She texted back. Sorry. Leo & I just paid price for Jono dumping Cat. I'll try to get it taken down ASAP.

L: Not worried about me! If you're reading the comments, stop right now. Take advice from a seasoned pro on internet abuse and just log out. There's no way to respond to it without opening a whole other can of worms, and you'll just drive yourself nuts.

T: Shutting down apps now.

L: Call if you need anything.

T: Thanks. X

L: Hot kiss, though, T.

L: Why does Jono look like he just swallowed battery acid? Crush on you?

T: Intestinal difficulties.

L: Say no more.

Trix read a few more comments that criticised her personality, hair, freckles, and "figure of a twelve-year-old boy," before she took Lily's advice and closed the app, but made the mistake of giving in to dark curiosity and opening another one. Her crossed leg bounced compulsively.

She forced herself to get up and start gathering her stuff for training. Might as well make some use of the excess adrenaline.

When she went out into the overcast day, the streets in her neighbourhood were quiet. Nothing to distract her busy brain, which was stuck in a continuous loop of the same thoughts. On the Tube, it was standing room only in her carriage, and as she stood holding one of the centre poles, she tried not to think about Leo pushing her up against a similar one.

At Oxford Circus, Trix followed the flow of traffic to street level, then diverted off towards her favourite café on Regent Street. She bought a herbal tea in the hope that it would soothe the nervous restlessness in her arms and legs. The constant fluttering in her stomach was having a knock-on effect on the rest of her body.

Smiling at the guy who held the door open for her as she stepped back out into the street, she ducked out of the way of a businessman who was barrelling down the pavement, barking into his phone and ignoring anyone in his path, and turned in time to see another tall man in a suit holding a newspaper.

She froze.

Fuck. Fucking fuckety fuck fuck.

London: why so vast when it came to navigating and paying for public transport, and so very, very small when it came to avoiding people she secretly hoped had fallen into a sinkhole somewhere?

The heat of the tea burned through the paper cup, stinging the straps-callouses on her palm, as Dan St. James tucked the paper under his arm and looked up.

Surprise wiped his handsome features clear of expression, then a glint appeared in his green eyes. His gait was familiar and confident as he came to a stop in front of her, brushing her with a head-to-toe survey. The last time she'd seen him, when the spur of outrage over his treatment of Lily had supplied her with all manner of satisfyingly cutting things to say to him, his face had been ugly with frustration and irritation.

Like the proverbial rubber ball, he bounced back. Or, more aptly: like some sort of stubborn fungal growth, he just re-established his position and continued sliming about.

She saw the smooth change that swept over his face. Apparently, he was going to go with the charm offensive. It was the attitude that bothered her far more than when he was openly being a dick. It was mortifying that she'd ever been fooled by it.

"Trix." His mouth smiled, but his eyes were still calculating. "It's been a while. Nice to see you." As if they'd parted on such cordial terms. "How are you?"

She debated responding. But there were a lot of people within earshot, and this day had already taken a turn into the trash heap before she'd even woken up. She didn't fancy a public scene. She moved to just leave, and stiffened when he caught her elbow.

"Not even a hello, darling? Not very friendly after everything we had."

She turned her head, because she wasn't giving him

the higher ground by refusing to make eye contact. He didn't intimidate her; he disgusted her. And he made her disgusted with herself. "I'm not really inclined to chat, no. I think we said everything that needed to be said months ago."

That considering gaze travelled over her body again. Dan was outwardly a gentleman, sophisticated and charismatic, but the days were long gone when she could find anything attractive in him, physically or cerebrally. The residual flicker of lust in his eyes made her skin crawl.

"You look well," he said. "Still working at the Old Wellington?"

She lifted one eyebrow.

"I ran into Liz Shaw the other day," he went on, unperturbed by her silence. "You know Liz? Her office handles the financial investments for your...show."

And there was the implication of flagrant immorality, all neatly couched into an inflection on one word. Quite a master of the subtle shade, was Dan. He was also a blatant hypocrite. Behind closed doors, and as long as he wasn't stewing with irrational jealousy, he wasn't so puritanical in the sex department. More skin-crawling thoughts, that she'd actually orgasmed with this snake.

"She said that you've been promoted to a better role." Dan smiled again, another meaningless stretch of his lips that went no further. "Temporarily."

Her hand closed more tightly around the cup of tea. Somehow, she didn't think it was going to be up to the task of soothing her into a good mood.

"I understand you're seeing someone," Dan added coolly, and she looked at him sharply. "An acrobat."

He made no attempt to disguise his opinion of that, but she was just relieved that his knowledge of her social life was only the public sham version, and didn't think it was worth rising up in defence of Jono. Dan was trying to be provocative, and Jono wouldn't give a rat's arse what he thought. "Well, I never did believe in the opposites-attract theory when it comes to lasting relationships. I suppose, in the end, like turns to like."

With a calmness she didn't feel, Trix nodded. "I actually think that, too." She saluted him with her cup. "And if you ever find your soul mate amongst your own kind, I wish you two all the best. Your odds are decent. There's no shortage of maggots in the world; I'm sure there's at least one that isn't too choosy."

Dan didn't lose even a scrap of the faux-gent façade. "Classy as ever, Trix."

"Not quite up to your standards? Literally the only good news I've had all day." She looked straight at him. "Goodbye, Dan."

She turned her back on him and walked away, and he made no attempt to stop her this time, but his final words followed her: "Give my congratulations to Lily, by the way. I see she's fallen on her feet. Obviously appearances are deceptive and she's one of life's winners. They say that people often pick friends who possess the qualities they lack, don't they?"

Trix didn't bother to look back as she turned the corner and left him behind.

She tried to go straight to the gym when she arrived at the theatre, hoping she didn't run into anyone who wanted to chat. She didn't particularly want to discuss her upcoming audition for a show she'd already been working in for years, and she definitely didn't want to talk about the imaginary love triangle with Leo and Jono.

However, because the universe was a cackling bitch right now, Marco hailed her when she was within arm's reach of the door.

"I hate to put you out," he began, and oh the sarcasm, "but I'd appreciate it if you wouldn't drag my show into your social life. The documentary crew have been very vocal about the number of comments on the latest episode."

Yes, and she'd bet a month's salary that they were bloody *stoked* about it. Any hint of sex drama increased views. In fact, she'd go double or nothing that they'd ramp up their attempts to drag footage of Leo into the next episode. He was the stuff of fangirl fantasies anyway, and had only been spared so far because he wasn't contractually obliged to participate in "promotional activities," the blanket clause that had tied the hands of everyone in the cast where the webseries was concerned.

"Since the documentary crew manufactured half of it," she said, battling to suppress a surge of temper, "they really have only themselves to blame. And whatever negligible impact my social life has on the show, I highly doubt it'll hurt ticket sales."

Marco's eyes narrowed. "Have you reserved the gym space this morning?"

She adjusted the strap of her training bag and did a bit of silent meditation. "Yes." She was patient; she was professional. She could not pour tepid herbal tea over her SM's silver head. "I rang and cleared it with the office. I have it until twelve."

He glared at her for a moment longer, then snapped,

"You need more speed and a lot more power in the death spin. Friday night's performance, it was about as suspenseful as watching clothes flapping about on a washing line. Doralina is not a role that covers weaknesses. I need more."

She didn't roll her eyes until he'd marched off to critique someone else, but before she could let herself into the gym, another voice called her name. Natalie. After the text message earlier, Trix suspected more commentary on the wedding shenanigans, but Natalie just handed her a piece of paper.

"Good timing. I was going to give this to Leo, but I can just pass it along to you directly."

"Thanks." Trix took the note and glanced at it. It was a name she didn't recognise and contact details. "What is it?"

"It's the contact information for my agent friend." When that clearly enlightened nothing, Natalie added, "The one who might be interested in taking a look at your illustrative work?"

Trix lowered the piece of paper. "I'm sorry?"

"Leo was telling me about your graphic novel— which I'd love to read, you talented little sausage—and I told him I'd grab my friend's contact details for him to give you, so here you go, and you should definitely give her a buzz about it. She *loves* stuff like that."

The edge of the note crinkled between her fingers. "Did Leo—tell you that I wanted to publish my novel?"

"We were talking about illustrative fiction, and he—" Natalie's attention drifted over Trix's shoulder. "Oh, hell, there's Marco. I'd better give him the schedule changes before he gets on my case. Happy training. Paige'll be in this week, by the way, to sort out her pay and pick up her stuff. I'm sure she'd like to see you."

Trix stood looking at the crumpled paper in her hand, then shook herself off and went into the gym before anyone else could talk to her. Three unsettling conversations seemed like enough for one morning.

She dropped her stuff to one side and turned on the sound system. She could hear footsteps above, in the offices on the second floor, but the training space itself was empty.

After a few restless bounces, she launched right into a warm-up, almost daring the restless quivers in her joints to let her down as she slammed through a series of back handsprings. *Bam—bam—BAM.* Each thump of her hands and feet into the mats formed a satisfyingly hard rhythm. The tumbling parts of her floor choreography were a lot more cathartic than the balletic side. She didn't feel like being the graceful, melancholic Doralina right now; she wanted to be the powerful, fists-up-and-kick-hard Doralina.

An hour later, she was up on the straps, working on the most difficult transition sequence, when her concentration fractured enough to see Leo. He was standing against the wall, watching her. She saw the heavy flex of muscle in his arms, and her brain tried to register the expression on his face, but the complex timing of the routine required so much attention that she couldn't seem to piece together his individual features into a recognisable whole. A flash of dark eyes as she spun, a blurred glimpse of beard and full lips. Gritting her teeth, she forced her full focus back to the routine, the muscles in her own arms burning as she lowered into a straddle back lever, her eyes fixed on the floor below as she hung from the straps, her body in a horizontal plank and her legs scissoring to balance her weight.

Then she saw him change position, crossing one booted foot over the other, and her attempt to transition into the side planche wobbled. The moment her concentration was shot and her alignment changed, that was it. She swung herself back to a vertical hold, but before she could dismount, her left hand slipped from the straps, jerking her right shoulder as her weight distribution shifted, and she had to let go.

It was a short distance onto a highly sprung floor, and she automatically hit the ground rolling, her limbs loose and moving with the impact.

"You hurt?" Leo was suddenly there, crouching in front of her, and she heard the rough concern in his voice. He'd seen her take tumbles at practice before, and he'd worked with plenty of stunt artists; he knew when a fall wasn't serious, but apparently he had a protective instinct for her that overrode common sense.

Pity that protective impulses often came in a package with unwanted interference.

She wasn't hurt at all, but as she pushed up on her elbow to get her breath back, it seemed like the last straw.

"No," she said, and disliked the abruptness in her own voice. "I'm fine."

He rose to his expansive height, and jumbled emotions were putting her in such a strop that she found herself resenting how tall he was. Like he was being purposely smug and superior, choosing to stand there in the body that genetics had given him, rather than hunching over like an old man with a bad back to appease her irrational mood.

This was ridiculous. She was ridiculous. She loved however tall he was. She loved his body, his face, the *huge* hands that were extended to help her up. Even that stupid beard. She loved—

Sharply, she ran her hand over her hair, closing her fist around her ponytail and pulling on it. Then she scrambled to her feet, pretending she hadn't seen his offer of assistance.

His face suggested that she hadn't been too subtle about it. In fact, it was just thunderclouds brewing there in general.

Tired and crabby, party of two.

"I sent you a text a while ago to see where you were at," he said, "but you were probably busy spinning upside down."

It was a distracted comment, not a criticism, but her spine went a little straighter. "I've been working."

The slight sharpness of her tone drew his full attention back to the space between them. "Yes, I see that." There was an echoing edge in his response.

His probably justified irritation acted on her simmering temper like a cat having its fur stroked in the wrong direction. Spikes, prickles, and instant claws. "And I'm a grown woman. I don't have to justify my whereabouts to anyone."

He rolled his eyes, which only annoyed her more. "I wasn't implying that I'm entitled to know where you are at all times." With an insufferable air of "Calm yourself, woman," the prat added, "Don't overreact."

You can't pour cold tea over him, either. It would make a mess. A puddle on the floor is an accident waiting to happen.

She would recognise this later as the crossroads mo-

ment when the situation could have been defused. Deep
breaths taken, weapons lowered, a mutual acknowledg-
ment of a not-great night and a so far shitty day. Instead,
she chose the path that was piled knee-deep with in-
flammatory topics and struck a match. "She tagged your
social accounts in the picture, too, so I assume you've
seen what your super-fun sister has done now."

Leo was blatantly striving to keep his own temper
in check. "I did regret checking my messages, yeah."

"I doubt if Lily and Luc wanted that *particular*
photo of their wedding uploaded online, and, you
know, just ideally, I prefer to start my day without
being called a hundred variations of a thoughtless,
cheating slapper, but at least it made Marco's morning.
Something new to complain about. The weaknesses
in my performance are such old news."

"The only *weakness* in your performance is self-
doubt," Leo retorted, his own patience snapping. "Your
skill level is second to none; there's no technical reason why you couldn't have done the most advanced
choreography from the moment you took over this
role. No matter how much you second-guess yourself
before a show, you nail every trick out there. If you
could just get out of your head and throw yourself fully
into the performance, you'd be an even better artist
now than you were before you got involved with that
fucking douchebag and he kicked your confidence in
the teeth. Which, incidentally, is exactly what I'd like
to do to him."

The encounter with Dan was still too fresh in her
mind for this. "None of which addresses the issue of
Cat, who's one more nasty comment and scheming plot
away from Shakespearean villain territory."

"Look, I'm not happy that you're having to deal with this shit." Leo's jaw clenched so hard that it moved his beard. "And I'm not exactly thrilled about it myself, but I'll get it sorted. I've already texted Cat to tell her to take the photo down, and I'll deal with her in person later."

"Right, because that's worked so well so far." Trix was having a slightly out-of-body experience. She wasn't sure how things in the past few weeks had escalated to this, where they were standing here, facing off on a crash mat, with an intensity that was far beyond even the most heated of their past spats. Her fingers were shaking.

The pervasive reality of who they were to each other was skewing everything, shifting the horizon line in every direction she looked.

Past Leo would have offered sarcasm in exchange for her snide comment—which she *knew* was out of line; he wasn't responsible for Cat's behaviour and he was trying really hard with his sister. Trix had always been the more quick-tempered one. He had an infuriating ability to let barbs roll off his back. Usually down into his hand, where he fired them straight back at her. But this Leo was pissed off in a way that put a deep bite into his words. "I know exactly how obnoxious Cat's being. She's obviously hurting over something, and newsflash, sometimes people act out of character when everything goes to hell. But I'm not excusing the way she's been acting."

"If that was a dig at me, I don't recall trying to trash anyone's reputation when everything went to hell."

"No, your sabotage attempts are all directed at yourself."

She jerked her chin up and chose not to directly address that remark. "This isn't exactly fair on Jono, either."

"What, you mean people are being forced to acknowledge who you're actually with instead of the fake fuck? What a shame." *There* was the sarcasm. Leo's shoulders flexed as he stood there, all towering and acerbic like a warlord in a film. "And there's no way you're this pissed because of that photo. You've never taken that bullshit seriously. You don't care that much what a bunch of strangers think of you."

"It's a little different when every second word from those strangers would have to be bleeped out of live TV." He wasn't wrong, though. He didn't just presume to know how she would think. He really did know her pretty damn well.

"This isn't about the photo," Leo said coolly. "This is about you and me."

That skitter of panic was speeding through her body, and her heart began to hop and skip like a manic rabbit. "You and me. All right, let's talk about you and me. We could start with this." She walked over to unearth the note that Natalie had given her, holding it up for him to see.

"And what is that?"

"It's from Natalie. Contact details for the agent who might be interested in my graphic novel? The graphic novel that I specifically told you is just something I do for myself? You didn't think that maybe if I had wanted to publish it, I would have looked into possible avenues *myself*, without needing you to sneak around behind my back?"

"Sneak around?" Leo shook his head once, dismissively. "Yes, I mentioned how good your work is to

Natalie. We were talking about commercial art, and shock, a mention of graphic novels makes me think of you. She said she knew someone who might be interested in a new voice in graphic illustration, and offered to pass along the agent's details. And I agreed, in case you might be interested after all if it was an actual option. I didn't *sneak around* behind your back. If you don't want to put your work out into the public domain, fine. I wasn't trying to push you, it just came up in conversation. Because I'm proud of how talented you are." He bit off the last words, exhaling in a sharp burst of frustration. "Seriously? *That's* what this is about?"

Trix closed her eyes against a sudden burn in the back of her throat. She pressed her hand to her forehead, then wiped her damp palm against her thigh. The wicking fabric of her yoga shorts caught on her rough, scraped-up skin. "This was meant to be just sex." She was grasping at the last tumbling pillars of stability around her, watching them crumble into dust and slip between her fingers. "*You* said it was just casual. At the festival."

"Well, I fucking lied, didn't I?" Leo snapped, reaching up to clasp his hands behind his head, his movements abrupt and jerky.

"It's too…intense." The words spilled out of her almost accusingly.

"Of course it's intense," he said impatiently. "Jesus, Trix, when has it ever been *casual* between us? At what point during the past ten years were your feelings ever that lukewarm? We've slammed up against each other from the moment we met. We resented each other that single-mindedly—that *intensely*…" His eyes cut back to hers, deep and dark and—yes—angry. "And I think we're going to love each other just as hard."

Her breath caught, but the emotion that instantly flamed to life was swamped in the next instant by apprehension. "You're not in love with me." The automatic denial came from the part of her that was still trying desperately to retreat to safe ground.

"Don't tell me how I feel," he shot back, and took a step forward.

She back-pedalled so quickly that she almost fell over. "Do *not* kiss me right now."

He snorted, super lover-like there. "I wasn't planning to." His voice was sardonic. "Strangely enough, I like my testicles where they are and would rather not have them kicked into my throat."

They glared at each other, and she suddenly made a sound that was perilously close to both a laugh and a sob. Her hands came up to her temples. "It's only been—"

"It's been a decade."

She fought for cynicism; it made a useful safety net. "We have not been building towards this for—"

He faced her fully. "Haven't we?"

"It's too soon." Trix stared down at the mat, focusing on a small rip in the surface. She closed her eyes for a moment. "I can't."

If she could hear the stark truth in her words, then so could he.

It was very quiet. Somewhere above, there was the muffled noise of a phone ringing and a door closing. Their breathing was louder than usual in the stark echo of the gym.

When he spoke, it was abrupt and rough. "I've been offered a contract in the States."

Trix's heartbeat was a hard, sickening pulse in her stomach. "What?"

"When I met with Sylvia George, she offered me a special effects role on her latest series."

Her mind seemed to have frozen. "For how long?"

"Initial contract for twenty-four months."

"Two years." This was how *uncomplicated* their relationship was. He was leaving, and her world felt like it was caving in. "You didn't tell me."

A renewed spike of anger was working its way through the blank shock.

"No." He didn't move his eyes from hers. "I didn't." There was an uncompromising note in the bald statement. "Because you would have cut ties between us before I'd finished the sentence."

"That's—" *True. Let's face it. That's true. And you're better than this.*

Trix's lips felt dry when she pressed them together.

"I know you've been hurt," Leo said grimly, "and if I could change that, I would. I *hate* that it happened to you. And I'm sorry for any part that I've played in making you doubt yourself. But I'm not him, and you can't keep avoiding this. You have to stop shutting me out."

Okay, yes, she had been running away from this, but—seriously? Fucking seriously. He'd been making plans to leave the country. "Yeah, I'd simmer down on the accusations there, Captain America."

"I was going to tell you—"

"When? While you were waiting for your boarding call?"

The outside door swung open and Steph came in, juggling a stack of papers and a mug. Strands of blue-tipped hair were sticking out of her bun and bobbing about with her movements. "Hiya," she called cheerfully. "Natalie said you had the practice space this morning, so I'm here to put you through your paces. Just let me dump this stuff upstairs. Paperwork is doing my head in. Hi, Leo, how's it going? Harry was wondering what time you were coming in. I think he wants to discuss the lighting changes." She managed to shift the weight of the files without spilling her drink, and finally looked up. Her smile faded. "Uh… am I interrupting something?"

Trix stared down at the floor. Eventually, she heard Leo sigh.

"No," he said. "I don't think you are."

She raised her head.

Without taking his gaze from her, he said to Steph, "Is Harry in the lighting office?"

"Lighting box." Steph was darting swift peeks between them.

"All right, thanks." Leo stood completely still, except for the hand that was flexing into and out of a fist. Then he turned and strode outside, without looking back.

"Raincheck on the practice?" Steph asked at last, quietly. She put the papers down and reached out to lay a gentle hand on Trix's shoulder. Habit kicked in and her fingers moved in a slight massaging motion, with her indefatigable knack for finding the most knotted muscle straight away.

Trix blinked through the stinging at the backs of her eyes and steeled her spine. "No. I'm here. I need to train." *I need to think about nothing outside of this routine, before I lose all professionalism and cry at work.* The panic attack had been bad enough. "Let's do it."

* * *

Leo banged open the door and walked into the grey drizzle, blind to what was going on around him. He cut automatically towards the theatre, then stopped. His heart was thumping, and his stomach felt raw and acidic.

He wasn't technically on the clock until two-thirty today. Harry and the relentless minutiae of lighting changes could bloody well wait.

He turned and headed for the busy street, and he walked. In the rain. For a long time.

Turning everything over in his mind. The past. The future. Ripping into it, shredding it, and piecing it back together into the picture of what he actually, truly wanted.

He ended up at Westminster Pier, watching tourists clustered in the dismal weather to board the sightseeing boats that cruised up and down the Thames. A faint smile turned up his mouth when a young girl with pink streaks in her hair tiptoed across a narrow plank like she was walking a high-wire. Resting his back against a barricade, he pulled his phone and his card case from his pocket. Once more, his keychain came out with them, and he turned the old game console over in his hand.

Then, removing the business card he'd tucked away, he checked the number and dialled. A polite, professional voice answered.

With his thumb on the tattered old bee sticker, he said coolly, "Sylvia George, please."

Chapter Fourteen

The evenings were getting cooler as they moved towards autumn, but after the rain earlier, it was very mild tonight. Trix lay on the rooftop, flat on her back in the fake grass. Her body was lax, and even her mind was sluggish. She kept turning the same thoughts over and over, but couldn't seem to connect them into neat questions and answers. Lots of questions. *Lots* of worries. Not so many answers.

She slid one foot up, bending her knee so she could rub away a twinge in her hamstring. After a casually soul-stripping encounter with Leo, two more useful chats with Marco and five hours of training, she was shattered. The practice sessions with Steph had somewhat justified Leo's know-it-all comment that it wasn't Trix's technical ability that was holding her back, because when her brain had bigger things to worry about, her body was all "Why the fuck have you been making this so complicated?" and flowed into each transition seamlessly.

She lay there, feeling the light ruffle of the breeze across her bare legs, and her mind flirted with the memory of Leo's skin sliding across hers, his weight heavy on her in this very spot. The hard thrust of him inside her, the pads of his fingers running lightly across fine hairs, the intensity of pleasure.

More than that, the understanding in his face when she'd talked about her childhood, the laughter in his eyes when he'd coaxed her into her impromptu concert, the love when he'd told her about his grandparents.

The grimness when he'd told her about his job offer.

He was leaving.

She was going to lose him.

Trix pressed her palm over her closed eyes.

She heard the footsteps on the metal stairs inside before the door opened, and she knew it would be him. He was barefoot when he stepped out into the garden, one arm bent to cradle Reggie against his chest.

He gestured at the snuffling hedgehog. "I've brought a mediator."

She sat up. "Has he recovered from the indignity of being photographed in a tiny top hat outside the Tower?" Thanks to his feckless hedgie-minders, Reggie had been living the high life over the weekend. He didn't seem too traumatised, possibly because Scott had fed him a week's worth of his gross snacks in less than two days.

"He's fine, although I've apologised to him for leaving him alone with the incompetents." He held out his hand and she reached up to scoop Reggie into her palms, bringing him down to rest on her lap.

Leo hooked the tip of his boot into the wooden crate he'd used the night she'd sung for him and the rest of their unfortunate neighbourhood. He dragged it towards him, then sat and clasped his hands loosely between his knees, rotating one thumb around the other. She watched his fingers.

"Sorry I just walked out this morning," he said, and she shook her head.

"What else were we going to do, with Steph right there? It was probably smart, anyway. We were about ten seconds away from breaking out the boxing gloves."

"Mmm. You *are* bloody aggravating sometimes."

She side-eyed him and the corners of his eyes crinkled with a fleeting smile.

When it faded, his expression was unusually serious. "Trix."

Trix mentally braced herself and looked up. She tried not to compulsively squeeze Reggie like a stress ball. The result would be disastrous for them both.

Leo's obvious hesitancy was equally uncharacteristic. He kept turning his thumbs as he seemed to debate what to say and where to start. Finally, his gaze searching hers, he said, "Pretend I'm someone else."

Well, that was…not what she'd expected. And she hoped he didn't mean sexually, because this was really not the time, and role play was only one of her turn-ons if it involved superpowers and capes, not mentally swapping out two actual people. "Pretend you're someone else?" she repeated. "Er. Anyone in particular, or should I just pick at random?"

"I want you to talk to me," he said evenly, "and I want you to tell me the truth."

Her last attempt at keeping things light flickered and went out. "The truth?"

"The truth about how you're feeling. About us. About everything." His eyes held hers, steadily. "And I mean the actual truth, not whatever bullshit version of 'I'm fine' I assume you're spinning in your mandatory sessions with the theatre counsellor."

She flushed uncomfortably, and he reached out and closed warm fingers around her bare ankle, a brief touch before he sat back and gave her space again. Physically. Emotionally, he was knocking down every coping mechanism she'd built up.

"We were never just friends," he said softly.

"No, we weren't." They'd teetered on the verge of more, taken a drastic fall in the opposite direction, and then—

"And then we went straight from one end of the spectrum to the other," he finished for her. "Don't pass go, don't collect two hundred dollars, skip right over just-friends and land directly on—"

"Intense."

"Yes." His voice was very frank. "I made mistakes."

"We both made mistakes." The time was over for blaming one another. They'd both contributed to how things had developed.

Back then. As of late, most of the roadblocks were piled on her side of the divide.

"I know I'm not exactly an impartial sounding-board here, so…just focus on the friendship element of what we have now—and there is one." He seemed to be silently daring her to be the first to break the invisible contact. "Already a strong one." He was right. There was. Unbelievably, still, but there was. "And talk to me like you would to a good friend." His mouth turned up wryly. "Pretend I'm Lily."

She couldn't help a small smile. "Leo, I'd have to be blind drunk and squinting *very* hard, and even then, passing resemblance at best."

His flash of a grin was wider than hers. "Just temporarily overlook the fact that I'm not as pretty."

"That's a debatable point."

He lifted a brow. "Is it?"

"Oh, yeah." The short-lived amusement waned. With the hand that wasn't holding Reggie, Trix ran her fingers over her ankle where he'd stroked her skin. She swallowed. "I'm sorry."

"For what?" All traces of humour vanished in him as well. The question was wary.

"For…this." She flung her hand up in an encompassing gesture. "For all of this. For overreacting this morning. For pushing you away." The tears came suddenly. Fiercely, she pressed the side of her finger under her eyes. Leo made a sound in the back of his throat and moved as if he were going to reach for her, but she slid back a fraction and he stilled. "For being such a mess."

"You're not a mess." Despite the rigidity in every line of his muscular body, he said it almost calmly. As if it were a certainty, an incontrovertible truth. "You went through a really shitty time." He shook his head. "There are quite a few people in the world I've never met but still *really* fucking dislike, and your ex-boyfriend is polling high." He did touch her then, slipping his hand up her calf to hold her leg, secure and comforting. "You're so much stronger than that piece of shit. You're sure as hell stronger than his shadow. He had no idea who you are. And *you're* still not seeing yourself clearly right now, either. He tried to tear you down, and he failed. Look where you are and what you've managed to do since."

"And what have I done?" Trix asked with an edge of

derision. "Completely lost sight of myself, as you just helpfully pointed out. Freaked out at work because of a temporary promotion to a role I would have grabbed with both hands in the past. Worried that I won't be good enough to keep it. Hell, I'm worried what will happen if I *do* get it. I think I'm doing okay, I think I'm getting back on track, and then something sends me into a spin and my stomach drops out." She pinched the bridge of her nose. "I haven't even stood up to Marco because I've got this echo in my head of Dan saying I'm a hothead and will always shoot myself in the foot by mouthing off to the boss. It's pathetic."

"It's not pathetic. It's more manipulation on his part. The only thing you've lost is confidence. And you had a panic attack. So what?" He tightened his grip on her knee when she reacted to that, and gave her leg a little tug. "I'm not dismissing how fucking awful anxiety is. I *know* how awful it is. I was blindsided by it when my parents left, and I handled it a lot worse than you have. You should know. You bore the brunt of my reaction to it. And I'm not immune to it now, either. I don't keep those apps on my phone because I like the icons. You're not failing, Trix. You're not weak. You're just human, and, I'm sorry to disappoint you, not perfect."

Setting Reggie on the ground, she drew her knees up to her chest, dislodging Leo's grip, and wrapped her arms around herself. "Understatement of the century." She watched Reggie sniffing around the plant pots. "At the beginning of this year, Dan did something awful to Lily."

He leaned forward on his forearms again. He didn't say anything, but he was listening.

"And I was so mad that I had this surge of...what-

ever, and I went around to his flat, and I said every
pissed-off thing that I'd been thinking for months.
Vented like hell."

"Good for you."

"Except that the 'shadow' of him is still affecting
me, even now. So much for my great moment of em-
powerment."

"Yeah, well, it's not a film. Bad experiences don't
just disappear because of a grand gesture. Even a really satisfying one, and by the way, I would have paid a
year's rent to see that. I think a lot of the time you don't
ever get over stuff, exactly, you just—" He shrugged.
"You just live. You go on with what you have, and you
try to deal with all the bullshit the best you can when
you can, and you look for things that make you happy."

Something about that made her vision completely
fracture into a wet shimmer. "I saw him today."

Leo looked up sharply. "St. James?"

"Yes. Randomly ran into him outside my favourite coffee shop." She blotted her eyes with the back
of her wrist.

His face was tight. "What did he do?"

It was her turn to touch him. She reached up to rest
her fingertips on his knee. "He was just Dan. Slick,
sleek, total bastard. He didn't hurt me. He doesn't have
the power to do that directly anymore. But it just…re-
minded me. And it threw me for a loop." She pushed
back the hair that was falling across her brow. "I'm
really sorry I was such a witch to you about the thing
with Natalie's agent friend. When Dan and I were dating, he went behind my back."

"What, with your art?"

"No." She hesitated. She'd never even told Lily

about this. "I found out that he was having a PI look for information on my birth parents. Even though he knew full well that it was something I definitely didn't want. When I confronted him, he tried to lie and say he was doing it for me. Like I'd find it a really thoughtful surprise or something. It was what finally pushed me to make the break. And when Natalie said that today, right after I'd seen him, I just thought— I overreacted and I projected, and I'm sorry."

"Trix." Leo's features were still taut. "*Do* you see other similarities between the way we've always been with each other and what went down with St. James? Because, Jesus, I don't want to think it was ever as profoundly *ugly* as—"

"No." Her answer came immediately. "You're nothing like him. We're nothing like him. We might drive each other crazy, but it's always been open and very mutual warfare, not…not sly and manipulative and gross. It's not even remotely the same situation. It's not that. It's—" She stopped, swiped at another tear before it could fall, and tried again. "It's just everything. I feel like I'm a different person, and I hate it."

As usual, Leo caught the thread of her tangled thoughts. "And things changing so much between us is throwing you even more off balance."

She made a small movement with her head, a jerk of assent.

He was quiet for ages. They just sat there, close in proximity, far apart mentally, listening to the street sounds below.

At last, he said, "We all change, all the time, but fundamentally, everything you were, everything that matters, you still have that. That's still you." His brows lifted again. "Stroppy. Scrappy. Little annoying. Kind of insulting."

"You can stop any time."

His mouth quirked. "Also smart, and talented, and sexy, and everything else that makes people swipe right." Suddenly, he shifted his hip and tugged his keys out of his pocket. He held up the keychain, and she looked at it without much interest, then blinked.

"Is that—"

"The game console that you apparently saved for months to buy, and then gave away to a guy who'd been a complete arsehole to you? Yes."

It had been an impulse, after Allie had told her that Leo was in hospital and his parents were splitting. She'd known he would be unhappy, and the tiny, tattered memory of warmer feelings had steered her feet in the direction of the orthopaedic ward. He'd been sleeping, still conked out on the anaesthetic. She'd been too angry with him to stay, but she'd had the game in her pocket and he'd looked really…alone.

She reached out and touched it, turning it around to see the peeling honeybee sticker on the back. Marta. She felt the tug in her heart, residual grief and a lot of love. "Did you know it was from me?"

"Not until Lily told me before the wedding."

"Oh." She stroked the sticker one more time before she let it go. "I can't believe you kept it. Does it still work?"

"It died about a year after. But the day you left this by my bed was one of the most difficult I'd ever experienced, and that one gesture made a huge difference. I never forgot it. I'll admit that when I ran through a list of people who could have given it to me, your name didn't exactly leap to mind," he said with a faint smile. "But it doesn't surprise me at all now. Lily was right. This is you in one beautiful, impulsive act of kindness. Generous and open-hearted, and always doing the unexpected. Trix, I'm so gone over you."

She remained still, so motionless that she was surprised her heart was still beating.

"I'm not taking the job."

He said it so calmly that it almost didn't register. Then the words sank in, and her hands closed into fists. "What? No—"

"I already called Sylvia George."

Trix shook her head, vigorously. *"No,"* she said again. "You're not giving up your dream for me."

No question now as to whether her heart was still functioning. It slammed back and forth so hard that she felt sick.

He was so adamantly proud of her for not throwing away her career when Dan had dripped his poison. How could he think she would *ever* want to be responsible for him losing his?

"I'm not giving up anything." Leo was firm, his expression completely composed. Everything about him spoke of certainty and…maturity, somehow. "I'm fighting for what I want."

Every part of her was intensely focused on him, on the clash between the gentleness in his voice and the fierceness in his eyes.

"That TV contract isn't, and never has been, my dream job. It would have opened a lot of doors that have recently slammed in my face." A note of satire. "But you were right when you made that sarcastic comment the night of Paige's accident. My ambitions

do lie in film. That's where my passion is, professionally; that's always been where I'm happiest. And I'll
make it happen. Not in two years' time or at some point
in the future. Now. I'm not settling for second best. I
want the career I've been working towards since I was
eighteen. And I want you."

He grinned suddenly. "And after she got over the
shock of a 'thanks, but no thanks,' which I don't think
happens to her very often, Sylvia came through with
an alternative offer. Reckon she's still chuffed about
the exploding face incident; obviously no love lost
there. There's a fantasy film starting production in
December. In Scotland."

"Scotland."

"Only a train ride away, and only for a few months."

"Leo." Trix's throat felt thick and tight. "You can't
just— Not for me."

"Trix." His smile was a little crooked. "I'd do a
fuck of a lot for you. Just about anything bar murder
or signing another contract with Marco Ross, in fact.
But this? It's not for you. It's for me. It's right," he said
emphatically. "For me."

She took a deep breath, which caught as he continued, "I thought about this all afternoon. What to say
to you." He reached out and touched her cheek. "And
I guess, in the end, it's not that complicated after all.
You make me happy. It's as simple as that." He held her
gaze. "And I make you happy. Whether you're ready
to acknowledge that or not."

She tasted salt and realised that tears were sliding
into the corners of her mouth.

Leo made another abbreviated movement, as if he
couldn't just sit still and watch her cry. "You're it for

me, Tinker Bell. I think my heart probably went 'Yes. Her. This.' when I was sixteen years old and an immature prick, and nowhere near ready for you, and it took the rest of me over ten years to shut up and listen. But there's no ultimatum here. The stars seem to have aligned for us recently, but I don't believe fate is giving us a now-or-never moment. This is our choice, yours and mine, and there's no deadline. If you want me to wait, I'll wait." She saw his knuckles flex, and realised he wasn't nearly as confident as his words.

"I'll crash on Allie's couch tonight. Give you some space to just…be. If you can, stuck in the flat alone with the Beagle Boys." The tinge of humour dissipated. "If you decide that this is making things too hard right now, I will step back," he said quietly. "But not away. Not out. I'm not giving up on us without a hell of a fight. And don't underestimate yourself. You're the strongest person I've ever met. That's never going to change."

She gripped her knees as he scooped up Reggie with the ease of experience. His voice was rough when he said, "Final statement for the defence. Exes, anxiety, bad days at work, pain-in-the-arse sisters, awful bosses. It's all part of the package, isn't it? Life, in all its occasional shittiness. There's nothing that needs to be magically fixed before it's somehow okay for us to be together. I'm not exactly baggage-free, either. I've got jealousy issues that probably go hand-in-hand with the body image crap and no doubt tie into my deep-seated issues with my parents." The self-mockery was strong. "Every woman's dream."

When she spoke, the words emerged all croaky and

crusty. "I notice your jealousy issues have never extended to Ryan and Scott."

"No." His eyes crinkled at the corners. "Surprising, since judging by the procession of guys who trailed around after you at school, they're just your original type. Athletic and brain-cell-deprived."

Wiping at her face, she let her gaze slide pointedly down his body. "Hmm. Yeah. Good thing I've grown out of that one."

He grinned. "See, what would I do without you around to pad my ego?"

Crouching so they were at eye-level, he leaned forward and kissed her forehead. "It doesn't have to be perfect, sweetheart." His thumb caught a last tear. "I'd say we're all works-in-progress, probably until the day we die, and possibly after that. I wouldn't be surprised if we keep stumbling around the unknown, doing stupid shite and hoping for the best, ever after." She closed her eyes as he murmured against her skin, "But I still think we've got as good a chance as anyone at making it work, and better than most, because we're both stubborn as fuck. Hand's out, Trix. You just have to meet me halfway. Reach out and take it." He pressed his mouth to her ear. "Fight for me, too."

Trix stayed on the roof after the last echo of his footsteps on the metal steps faded.

Her tears dried into sticky trails down her cheeks and she sat very quietly, her mind working in busy contrast to the stillness of her body.

When she finally went downstairs, the flat was empty, resounding with his absence. She poured herself a glass of water, pressed it to her forehead and took it into her room.

She saw the paper on the bedside table right away.

No carefully impersonal note this time. She lifted the drawing and looked at it. It was a monochromatic pen sketch, stark lines of black filling in the latest episode in their story. The subject was simple and poignant. The Leo figure and Trix figure stood on either side of a divide, looking at each other unsmilingly. Sketch Leo held out his arm, reaching over the gap. Sketch Trix had balled her hands into fists and appeared to be flexing the fingers closest to him, deciding whether to move or not.

When she propped the sketch against her lamp, the back of her hand knocked her glass over and the water splashed across the paper. Black ink blossomed and trickled down the page like melting wax.

She stared at it for a long time.

Then she reached for her phone.

Chapter Fifteen

It was hard on the body, taking back control of her life.

Trix felt as if she'd spent the night on a medieval stretching rack.

A knock sounded at the door while she was getting dressed, and she opened it to find Cat on the other side.

She couldn't have felt less enthusiastic if the Grand High Witch herself was paying a breakfast call.

In fact—

No. Too easy.

It was ten to nine. Her audition for the casting board was at quarter past two, and she had something long overdue to do this morning before her final rehearsal. She wasn't sure there was time in her schedule to bury a body.

"Cat," she said warily.

"Hi." Cat tugged at her silk dress and shifted on her sky-high heels.

Trix would put the Warrior Fairy hotpants back on and perform circus tricks on Carnaby Street to possess those shoes, but they made Cat so tall that there was over a foot in height difference between them. She didn't appreciate having to cede any advantage in a confrontation with Leo's irascible sister.

"If you're looking for Leo," she said when the silence showed no sign of ending, "he's not here."

"No, I know." Cat's dark eyes turned more piercing in their scrutiny, and Trix started to feel as if she were being visually dissected. "He's sleeping on Allie's couch." The uncertainty in her initial greeting took on a more familiar sharpness. "If you guys had a fight, it's a bit extreme to kick him all the way across town, isn't it? You have separate rooms here to sulk in."

"Cat." Trix had been playing with the hem of her shirt; she let it fall. "I appreciate that you're Leo's family and he's your business, but this is private and I am *so* not discussing it with you." She could have added, "I'm surprised you even care, since you've shown absolutely no interest in his well-being ever since I've met you," but she exercised some self-restraint. There was an increasingly hopeful possibility that she would have Cat in her life for the foreseeable future.

Weep.

"Allie said you were in a really shitty relationship," Cat burst out, and Trix stiffened.

Cat modulated her tone, but her body language remained defensive. "She wasn't gossiping. Exactly. But she walked in on a phone conversation I was having at work—" she managed to make it sound as if Allie had committed an unpardonable solecism by interrupting a personal call on work premises, probably during work hours "—and she sort of…got the gist of what I was talking about, and said that you would probably understand better than anyone."

The inference of "Doubtful!" was screamingly loud, as was the headache emerging in Trix's temples.

"What exactly did Allie say?"

Insert mental reminder that Allie had a big heart to go with her huge mouth, and that murder was morally wrong, even with persistent provocation.

Cat wrinkled her nose in a way that was unexpectedly self-deprecating and almost likeable. "Not much. Just that you were a card-carrying member of the Bad Man Decisions Club."

"I was the keynote speaker last year." Trix sighed. "You'd better come in. Would you like something to drink? Tea?"

Cat looked like she was going to default to a snotty reply, but she also exercised self-restraint. "I would. Thanks. No milk, one sugar."

Trix went into the kitchen to fill the kettle. Cat walked restlessly around the room, picking things up and putting them down, without really noticing anything until she saw the sketch propped on the bookcase. It was one that Leo had done for Trix after the rooftop rendition of the *Galaxy Agent* theme. Illustrated Trix was singing as she danced through the sky, while cats and dogs joined her in warbling away to the moon, and illustrated Leo accompanied her on a guitar that was actually a giant beer bottle with strings attached.

Cat shook her head as she looked at it. "You're both dorks."

Trix poured the boiling water over the tea leaves and left them to brew. "Yes, we are." She held up the bagged bread. There was almost enough left for two slices. "Toast?"

"No. Thank you."

"There's a container on the table of some sort of pellets that I think belong to Reggie. I'm not sure if they're food or bedding, but you'd better take them home with you, because I wouldn't put it past the guys to eat them." She put the bread down and walked around the counter. "That's if you're taking Reggie back, I guess."

"I am." Cat sat gingerly on the couch. "I've actually missed the little bugger." She spoke without looking at Trix. "I know I've been a real bitch to you. And to everyone."

"Well—" Kind of hard to argue with that. On the other hand, Trix was on shaky ground when it came to making bad decisions because of bad men. "I'm assuming there was some catalyst and it's not solely a personality trait."

"I spent the last year in New York. Studying fashion design."

"Leo said."

"I met a man. A fashion exec. The top students on the course were selected to do a work placement at his label. He asked me out, and I thought it was a really good opportunity." Trix didn't miss the word choice there, but she said nothing. Cat snorted. "Serves me right, I guess, for being mercenary about it. Joke on me, I fell for him. Hard. And I thought it was mutual."

Trix nodded, sitting down on the edge of her favourite armchair.

"He led me on for months. I would have done anything for him." Cat's upper lip curled. "I *did* do a lot for him. If you catch my drift."

"Got it."

"Then when I'd given up my accommodation to move in with him, because I thought that's what we both wanted, he ditched me. With no warning. For this bouncy, perky, undersized little slapper in my History of Fashion class."

"One of those 'sweet-wee-me' girls?" Trix asked very drily, and Cat's high cheekbones reddened.

"Yeah. Well. I'm sorry about that," she bit out, and then continued in a rush of outrage, "I found out afterwards that he targets girls on the course. Pathetic, naïve girls, a category that apparently now includes me. It's so fucking humiliating. I can't believe I was so *stupid*. And I ended up with nowhere to live for the last few weeks, so I had to crash on this other guy's couch, and he let me because he had a crush on me—as if I'd ever go there—and his flat reeked and the plumbing didn't work properly and it was *awful*."

She swallowed. "But the worst part was that I'd been so wrapped up in Eric that I didn't finish my assignments and then I was too upset to do my exams. I failed the whole year. All that money, the scholarship and everything it cost Leo to get me there. I know he couldn't really afford it, and he scraped it together anyway, and it was all for nothing. It could have been the most amazing experience. It could have helped set up my career, and I blew it. For some shitbag of a guy. I don't— I don't know how to tell him."

Trix winced. Oh, God. She suddenly related strongly to one of the most insufferable people she'd ever met. How incredibly depressing. And how easy it was to see clearly when it was happening to someone else. "You weren't stupid, Cat. At least not during the part when you fell for that bastard. Apparently there's an endless store of manipulative wankers out there, and we're two of the lucky people who fell into their web."

She stood up and went to get the tea. When she

"Well. Good." Cat took a thoughtful sip of her tea. "I still don't like you."

Trix raised her own cup in a sardonic "cheers." "Not that fond of you, either."

"But I guess you'll have to accept my apology." Cat smirked into the rim of her cup. "If you're going to be my sister-in-law."

If anyone ever asked, Trix could now say with some authority that choking on hot tea and having it retract up her nasal passages was extremely painful.

Cat stayed until half past ten, probing for a few details about Dan and then proceeding to tell Trix *all* about Eric, in excruciatingly intimate detail. She was going to talk to Leo today, too, who would presumably receive the edited, PG version of the story.

Trix didn't have time to reflect on the latest weird turn in her life, since she was now running late to get to the theatre, and this appointment was going to be hard enough without showing up sweaty and frazzled.

When she got to the West End, she bought a bagel and ate it on the short, rainy walk to the Old Wellington. She was reaching for the back door when it swung open and someone came out.

"Paige." Trix took a step back, surprised. Recovering, she stepped forward to give her former castmate a gentle hug. "It's good to see you."

"And you." Paige's right arm was in a full cast, supported in a sling, and her black curls had the slightly matted look of someone who was having to wrangle conditioner with only one hand. Trix viewed her friendly expression with scepticism, but it seemed to be genuine. "I hear you're auditioning for the board this afternoon. It's nice to see you spreading your wings and getting a chance to show what you can do." She sighed, and raised her cast. "Although it would be *nicer* if it had happened under different circumstances."

"How are you doing?" Trix asked. "You've had more surgery?"

"Two scalpel-jobs down, one to go, but I've got a brief reprieve from the hospital for a few weeks, so I'll count my blessings where they come."

Trix couldn't think of a way to ask delicately. "What's the prognosis on getting back in the air?"

"Long-term, after a lot of physio and rehab, probably decent, if that's what I wanted." Paige touched the fingers that poked out of the plaster. "If you're worried they'll have to change your name on the programme again, there's no chance I'll be returning to the show." There was no censure in the words, but Trix flushed a little.

Paige smiled. "I'm not upset that you've taken over. This is *not* the way I would have chosen to do it, but it's past time that I moved on. I haven't been enjoying performing for a long time. I thought about leaving a hundred times, but it's scary to finally make that push to change, you know."

"Oh, I know," Trix said with feeling. She studied Paige with curiosity. "I had no idea you were unhappy with the show. You've always seemed like such a natural performer."

"No, *you're* a natural performer. You've always been one of the biggest crowd-pleasers in the cast, and it's not just because you have the technical skill. You're one of those people who have…*it*, the infamous X-factor. I'm good. But my heart isn't in it, not anymore. And I screwed up. Carly and I had a fight that day. A stupid, slam-the-doors, storm-out, overreaction of a fight, and I let it distract me to the point where I put in a completely sub-par performance that night, even before the disastrous finale."

Trix frowned. "Are you and Carly okay now?"

Some of the lines around Paige's mouth smoothed out. "We're getting there. As I said, I'm counting my blessings." She shook her head. "But that last night on the straps was totally unprofessional. I should have taken my cue from you."

"Me?"

"I know you had a bad relationship." Paige was so forthright that there was no room for residual awkwardness. "You were obviously going through a lot at home, but you left it in the wings every night. Even if you had a bad rehearsal, the moment you stepped out in front of the audience, your head was in the game and you delivered. Your work ethic is rock-solid and so are your stage instincts. From what I've heard, you stepped up and knocked it out of the park on your first night as Doralina. You're so ready for this. And you'd bring a hell of a lot more spark to the role than Jennifer. She's talented, but she's like me. Bit on the dull side to watch."

"You're not dull," Trix retorted, but there was warmth and humour in Paige's eyes. "What are you going to do now?"

Paige's dimples deepened. She shrugged the shoulder that wasn't incapacitated. "I have no idea. But whatever it is, I'm looking forward to it."

At the end of the alley, she turned back. "Knock 'em dead." She winked. "Break a leg, but preferably not an arm."

Trix watched her head for the bustling street and whatever future she was chasing.

Then she went inside to grab hold of her own future.

Upstairs, she went to the administration offices and came to a halt before a particular door.

Her stomach flip-flopped once, but she was sure about this. She knocked.

Karen, the company counsellor, opened the door with a smile. She had kind grey eyes and neatly bobbed grey hair, and an air of expectation. "Hello, Trix. Come in and sit down."

Trix sat down on an overstuffed armchair in the tiny office that Karen borrowed from the physiotherapists during her visits. The rain beat steadily against the window, a constant sheet of water against the glass rather than individual drips. She gripped her hands, and had to make a conscious effort to relax them. "Thanks for coming in specially. Sorry about the late-night call."

She'd expected to have to wait for one of Karen's usual appointment times. It was possibly not the *best* sign that Karen had immediately suggested they make a session for the next day.

Karen sat down opposite her and crossed one leg over the other. "I had a cancellation today, and if you're ready to talk to me finally, I'm certainly ready to listen." Her demeanour was inviting, but shrewd. "I'm guessing that things haven't really been 'fine.'"

Trix ran her hand through her wet hair. Ingrained habit was prompting her lips to form words like *no problem*, *don't need help*, and, yes, *I'm fine*. And she'd be stuck right back in the cycle of lies and denial, and not getting what she really wanted, and not enjoying what she already had.

"No," she said. "They haven't."

Chapter Sixteen

"So, that's it. I failed. The whole year. The opportunity's gone, the money's gone, it's all gone. Because I'm gullible and stupid." Cat sat on the edge of Leo's table in the makeup and props room, turning a bottle of foundation over in her hands and refusing to look at him. She set it down. "And let's face it, kind of a bitch."

Leo stood against the shelves full of masks and batons and giant playing cards and jester hats, and added another name to the short list of people who'd better hope they never ran into him in a dark alley or a conveniently deserted copse. Cat had prudently refused to add an identifiable surname to Eric the Arsehole.

She stood up, still averting her eyes. "I know I should have told you before, but—but now you know. And I'm sorry, okay? I know it cost a lot of money, and I didn't mean to waste it, and I shouldn't have been so awful, and I'm sorry."

Without a word, he opened his arms, and she glared at him ferociously before her expression crumpled and she stepped forward to hug him. With a deep sigh, he wrapped his arm around her shoulders and propped his chin on her head. "It doesn't matter about the money. Forget it."

"But—"

"It's gone, it's done, it's not important." He patted her back. "And the rest—we'll sort it. I'm sorry that happened to you, Cat, and I'd like a few minutes alone with that unconscionable fucker, but you're a survivor. You'll get through this. You know I'm here, for whatever you need, whenever you need it." Pointedly, he added, "And if you stop acting like some sort of primordial demon, you'd probably find that quite a lot of other people will happily be there for you also."

Cat pushed back from him and sniffed. "God," she said, "Trix was spot on about your reaction. That's a little annoying."

He shook his head. "You really spent over an hour with Trix? Alone. And nobody's bruised or missing any limbs?"

"She's...not the *worst* person I've ever met," Cat said grudgingly. "I still think you could do better than a woman who looks like the personification of a *My Little Pony*, but she obviously went through some serious shit, and she seems to be dealing with it."

"She's tough. She'll get there."

The cuckoo clock on the wall ticked over to two o'clock, the bedraggled yellow canary bird lurching out and shrilly tweeting twice. It was a lucky mascot for the props team, and if it wouldn't send the company into a superstitious *Macbeth*-style meltdown, he'd have yanked the damn thing off the wall weeks ago. Trix's performance for the casting board was at quarter past two on the mainstage, and he intended to be there to watch whether it was a closed house or not. Jennifer would be starting her routine any second now, and hopefully messing up just enough that she didn't hurt herself but still underlined her inferiority.

But at this exact moment, his concern was still with his sister. "And so will you."

"I apologised to Trix and Jono about the photo," Cat said with a combination of defiance and discomfort. "And I *am* sorry about that. The comments on the post got a bit out of hand."

"I'll say. That was the last thing Trix needs right now." He wasn't just writing off everything Cat had said and done recently, but he hadn't seen her in such a bad place since their parents had left. "Next time you're in trouble, you can talk to me, all right? You should have called from New York. I'd have flown over if you needed help. I'd at least have sent enough money that you wouldn't have to crash on some random's shitty couch. Jesus. I want you to be safe. And happy."

"I know." Cat blinked hard, but slipped her mask of cynicism back into place. "You always did. I guess you got Nan's genes and I got our so-called mother's."

"Nan wasn't perfect, I'm sure as hell not perfect, and neither are you, but you're not Mum and Dad," he said firmly. "You have some serious ground to make up with people around here, and you owe Jono a massive apology, but you're not going to be like them." He wasn't going to *let* her become like them. She'd taken too many steps in that direction recently. "And you can start proving it by taking Reggie back. As much as I like the little guy, he's not mine, and to be honest, I'm not sure Allie's thrilled about having him as a flatmate."

"I'll pick him up tonight," she said, eyeing him.

"But that's temporary anyway. Your living situation. You'll be moving back into the flat."

"It's temporary at Allie's," he agreed. "Where I move to depends on several factors." All of which came down to Trix.

Cat nodded at the clock. "Her audition thing is soon. You'd better get down there."

He studied her, hesitating.

"Go. Things are…okay, for now. Currently nothing more to see here. And I should get back to the wardrobe room." She crinkled her nose before she opened the door. "They're super dramatic around here if you're even five minutes late back from a break. Bloody theatre people."

He shook his head as he followed her, branching off at the green room. Several other members of the cast and crew were heading for the viewing platform to watch what was happening onstage.

He found Trix in the wings. Her freckles were all standing out and her eyes were large dark pools in the shadows. He'd expected to find her a bundle of nerves, but although she looked tense, she was surprisingly still. No bobbing, no hand-flapping, no jumping up and down onto the tips of her toes like a malfunctioning wind-up ballerina doll. She finished dusting chalk over the palms of her hands and turned to see him.

Her smile started small, at the corners of her mouth, but it grew to light up her whole face, and he was so fucking lost over her that he felt that smile in every part of him.

It took a superhuman effort not to kiss her, but he kept a distance of a few feet between them. He inclined his head towards the stage. "How did Jennifer do?"

"Really well." Trix smoothed back her ponytail, accidentally transferring streaks of chalk to her hair. "If she gets it, she'll deserve it." She lifted her chin. "But I deserve it, too."

He could feel his own smile reach his eyes. "Yes, you do."

She bit her lip. "I'm nervous."

He couldn't help touching her then, just a gentle stroke of her bare shoulder. "I know. But have fun out there anyway."

"I spoke to Karen today," Trix said suddenly. "The company therapist."

He registered that, and that little flame of optimism started to burn brighter. "And was it…helpful?"

"It was a start," Trix said. "A good start. I'm going to see her once a week for the time being."

"That's great." He wasn't entirely joking when he said, "Maybe I should see if there's coverage for crew. I could probably do with some sessions, too. And Cat definitely could."

Steph appeared from the stage and gave Trix a thumbs-up. "Batter up. They're ready for you." She lowered her voice, probably in case Jennifer was still within earshot. "And you're ready for them. It's in the bag."

"Don't forget," he murmured, when Trix briefly stiffened. "Just have fun. And if they give you any props to set the scene, steer clear of the dragon."

She made a face and followed Steph onto the stage.

Leo went to join the rest of the interested spectators on the platform. Jono turned his head, smiled, and shifted aside to make room for him. It was quiet in the stalls, just a few voices echoing in the massive, open space, the acoustics reaching up to the domed ceiling. From where he stood, Leo could just see Marco and Natalie in the front row, and about six other members of the management team clustered around.

Steph clapped Trix on the shoulder and jogged off-stage. Natalie turned and raised a hand, and the house-lights went down. The spotlights on the stage came on, throwing Trix into stark relief against the darkness beyond. Without the sets and lighting effects and the rest of the spectacle, she looked smaller than usual and somehow alone.

But when a recording of the orchestra came on through the speakers and she launched into the routine, whipping across the extended length of the huge stage in a series of handsprings, she suddenly owned that space. There was power and precision in every movement of her compact body, and she sailed through the back layouts before she caught the aerial straps midway through a front tuck.

She always seemed to be in her element when she was in the air, and he felt some of the tension leave his body when he saw the slight edge of defiance in the way she held herself in a painful-looking split. It was Trix's natural sassiness, outing itself through Doralina's fuck-you attitude rather than Pierrette's coquettishness.

She was having a blast out there.

It obviously wasn't a faultless performance; nearby, he saw Steph wince a couple of times, but overall, she looked pleased.

Trix moved from a difficult hold in which one arm was yanked behind her back like a medieval torture tactic, into the not at all offputtingly named death spin, her weight suspended from one ankle, her arms and fingers extended in graceful lines. She spun, building up momentum, until she was a blur of flashing limbs and pink hair. She came out of it with a flourish, moving smoothly to grasp just a single strap, while she reached for the other with her pointed foot.

And then she fell.

Trix knew she'd messed up the timing about half a second before she actually lost her grip on the strap, but there wasn't even time for a silent profanity before she hit the stage. Fortunately, it wasn't far to fall, and she mostly tumbled out of it, rolling to push off her hands into a messy somersault and coming down on her knees. She wasn't hurt; it was just crap timing to cock up a move that she'd never, ever had trouble with before. She'd just knocked out every advanced technique in the routine, only to be tripped up by the most simple skill. If she had time to care, there was probably some profound life metaphor in that.

Footsteps from the wings, and both Steph and Leo appeared before she could get back up. That scratching sound she heard was probably Marco drawing a neat line through her name on his clipboard.

"Any pain?" Steph asked efficiently, although more to follow protocol than out of actual concern; it clearly hadn't been a bad fall.

Trix shook her head, but her attention was on Leo, who had come to crouch by her side, his wide shoulders shielding her from the glare of the spotlight. "You can't help yourself, can you?" she asked with rueful amusement. "I'm not hurt. And since this is supposed to be a mock performance, you really shouldn't storm the stage. It adds a level of drama that the audience didn't pay for."

His small smile was half hidden by the beard. "Sorry. Instinct. You fall, my heart stops, and the rest of me moves without waiting to hear from my brain. You're okay?"

"Fine. I'm finishing," she said to Steph, who gestured to Natalie.

Leo straightened, but before he could make another move, Trix looked up at him—and then, very deliberately, she stuck out her hand.

His eyes went from her outstretched palm to her face, their dark depths flared with feeling, and his fingers closed strongly around hers, helping her to her feet with such a powerful pull that she almost bounced off his chest like a trampoline.

Their hands remained linked between their bodies for a split second, their fingers interlocking and squeezing tight.

Then he left the stage, and she took hold of the straps and swung herself back up to complete the routine. She finished as she'd begun, determined to throw her full personality into each move, and refusing to be cowed by the misstep. And when she was gliding above the stage, with the feeling that always felt like flying, she was even able to stop cursing herself and enjoy the moment without worrying about the verdict to come.

When her toes touched the stage, she caught the straps in one hand in a neat coil, and the houselights came back on.

Trix turned towards the wings and caught sight of Jono, Scott, and Ryan, who all gave her a double thumbs-up; then Natalie stood up from the front row and smiled at her. "Thanks, Trix. Nice job. And good recovery."

Marco was stony-faced when he pushed up from his seat. "There shouldn't have had to *be* a recovery," he snapped. "An eight-year-old could do that lift on the playground bars without falling." He closed his clipboard, which Trix often suspected he just carried for effect. "Pinky, you're continuing as Doralina for tomorrow night's performance. We'll let you know the permanent casting decisions shortly."

Well, that sounded…not very hopeful.

Everyone started to disperse backstage. Trix stood thinking, then turned and strode in the direction of the management offices, following Marco.

He was standing by his desk, sifting through papers. "Yes?" He didn't look up and his tone was discouraging.

A whisper of Dan in her head, murmuring things about insubordinate, rash employees who sabotaged their own career path by standing up for themselves; she could almost feel his breath in her ear.

"I've taken tumbles in training like everyone else, and it's taken me a while to find my feet in the role," she said, a little louder than she would usually speak, to drown out the last echo of that voice. "And I made a mistake out there. But apart from *once* forgetting a line in the solo, which I recovered from, I've turned in solid performances. Every night. Consistently. I turn up on time, I train hard, and I am *good* at this."

Marco lowered his papers. His expression was difficult to read but hovering in the vicinity of condescension.

"Yes, I have had some personal…problems," Trix forged on, "which I now realise have been passed along the company grapevine, but I've done my absolute best to leave them backstage the moment the curtain rises. I'm a better aerialist than Jennifer," she said bluntly, "and I will keep growing in this role. I will be *brilliant* in this role, and I deserve the chance to prove it." The newly cautious Trix would have stopped there, but the reckless Trix of old was rearing her head with a vengeance. "And every single person in this cast and crew deserves a pay rise for putting up with months of you crossing the line from effective management into verbal bullying. I don't know if you're aware, but it doesn't hurt to occasionally throw a bit of positive feedback into the constant barrage of insults. And if you ever call me 'Pinky' again, I'm filing a complaint. Somewhere."

She finally caught herself up and snapped her mouth shut. Well. If somersaulting onto her knees like a kid failing gymnastics class hadn't lost her the role, essentially calling him a dictatorial a-hole would probably do it. *Hello, understudy, it's been a while.*

Marco's eyebrow was just about arching off his forehead. "Are you finished?"

She thought about it. "Yes."

"You have the role." He flipped over one of the papers in his hand.

"What?"

"We're casting you as Doralina permanently. Or at least until you resign, are fired—which seems more likely—or injure or age yourself out of the role."

"I'm staying as Doralina." Trix's brain seemed to be limping along several yards behind this conversation.

"Not because of that utterly unprofessional little outburst," Marco said sourly, perusing his documents, "although it wouldn't hurt to bring a bit of that spirit to the role, since the meek little mouse routine is getting very tired. But you're correct in at least one of those statements: you *are* a better aerialist than Jennifer. You have better natural ability and, when you feel like displaying it, your performance has more personality. It's more exciting for the audience."

"I see." Trix wasn't sure what to do now, and Marco looked up at her.

"Was there anything else? Your objection to the term of address is noted, but you're not getting the pay rise if that was going to be your next question."

"No," she said, after a pause in which she decided not to push her luck. "There's nothing else right now."

He looked pointedly at the door, and she opened her mouth, then closed it and went out into the hallway.

As she walked back, she wasn't quite sure what had just happened.

Leo and Jono were coming out of the green room when she reached it. Jono darted a quick look between them and excused himself, patting her on the shoulder as he discreetly disappeared. "Nice one, Trix."

"Thanks," she said, but her attention didn't leave Leo.

"You didn't hit your head out there, did you?" he asked, frowning. "Because you look a bit concussed."

"I called Marco a bully, requested a mass pay rise, and he gave me the role."

"You got it?" A huge smile broke out on Leo's face, and he was really unfairly handsome. Like, save some good looks for the rest of the world. Without bothering to check if anyone was watching, he reached out and swung her into his arms, giving her a hard hug. "I knew it. So proud of you. Although next time you call someone out for being a dickhead, you could at least let me watch. It's probably really hot when I'm not on the receiving end." He tipped his head against hers. "Well. Kind of hot either way."

With her feet dangling, she wrapped her arms around his neck, tucked her nose into the hollow beneath his ear, and said, "I love you, Leo."

It had been so hard to recognise it, even more difficult to acknowledge it. And, in the end, it was so simple to say it.

She felt the ripple that went through his whole big body, freezing him in place.

Then, like a build-up of energy finding a release— or a metaphor that was slightly *less* sexual in a public space—he moved, carrying her with one arm as he strode down the hallway and around the corner, and outside into the rancid back alleyway where she'd had her panic attack.

She supposed it was oddly fitting that they do this here, in the grossly unromantic location where they'd first reached out to each other in a non-combative way.

Kicking the door shut behind them, he lowered her until her toes touched the ground first, then the rest of her feet. She was still barefoot. It had stopped raining, but the air had a damp, musty feel. And smell.

With no plan on either side, they reached for each other's right hand, clasping tightly as they had onstage, as if they were sealing a promise. Or were about to arm-wrestle.

She didn't feel like fighting with him.

She *would* feel like fighting with him at some point in the future, probably before the day was out, but right now she just wanted to…be.

Be with him. Be herself. Be happy.

The light in his eyes was dancing and a little wicked and a lot happy. "What was that, sweetheart? I might need a replay."

Her fingers tapped against his. "I must have a concussion after all, Magasiva, because I think I said I'm in love with you." She looked up at him through her lashes, the deliberately provocative glance that had irritated him immensely over the years. That fizzy feeling was back in her stomach. The good—*best*—sort of butterflies. "I might be a tiny little bit nuts about you."

They were both smiling.

"So," he said. "You and me."

"I know," Trix agreed. "My mind is just as blown."

He kissed her then, hard, and she breathed in his scent, her mind fixed firmly in the present, savouring the feel of his skin, the hardness of his body, the taste of his mouth.

Without raising his head very far, he murmured, "Love you, too."

A tiny negative part of her immediately whispered what-ifs. Everything else said, very loudly and firmly, "Yes. Him. This."

His gaze lifted from her mouth to her eyes. "How do you feel?"

Trix brought their linked hands to rest against her heart, and didn't miss the fact that his little finger crept sideways to cop a stealth feel. "Hopeful," she said at last. "I feel really…hopeful." She jerked. "And ticklish. Could you move the groping a little to the left?"

Her conscience jabbed, and she added honestly, "I am scared. I know everything's not going to magically fix itself, ever, and I know that's—" His grip remained firm, and she mimicked his raised eyebrow. "I know that's *okay*, and it's okay *not* to be okay sometimes, but I still don't want to mess this up."

"You won't," Leo said, with no hesitation. "We'll just take it one day at a time and…see what happens."

"I'm going to get anxious."

"Okay."

"I might get hurt. Or sick."

"So could I. We'll deal with it."

"Together."

"Together." He cocked his head. "I mean, let's be honest. The physical ailments are a given. You stress your body so much that you'll probably have arthritic knees by thirty-five and I'll be piggy-backing you up and down the stairs on a regular basis. And if I end up as bald as your comics suggest, you can continue to draw unflattering pictures of me with your rheumatic hands."

His lips moved to her earlobe, and Trix shivered. "'One day at a time' just took a significant leap ahead," she pointed out. "And if that's the most glowing picture you can paint of our possible future, we clearly need to do something to boost your flagging optimism."

"I like the way you think," he murmured, and kissed her again, coaxing her lips apart to slide his tongue against hers.

She let go of his fingers to seize handfuls of his T-shirt, gripping high up his ribs, pulling his body down into hers. His arms came around her to circle the base of her spine, lifting her pelvis against him.

He was hard, and her own arousal was an insistent tingling thrum, and someone was bound to come out of the door behind them at any second.

She tore her mouth from his and asked, "Did you talk to Cat?"

He set her back down and groaned. "Timing, Trix. Work on it."

Smiling, she pressed her cheek against his middle. "Sorry. But did you?"

He ran his hand over the back of her head, then tucked his arm around her. "Yeah. She told me about what's-his-face. Manipulative Douchebag 2.0. Thanks for not just kicking her straight out of the flat, by the way. You'd have been justified."

"Well. I don't think Cat and I will be going for chummy pedicures any time soon. But—I get it. And it sort of helped me as well, to talk about it with her."

"Good," he said softly, his arm tightening around her. "I know it probably horrifies you, but I have thought before that you two would probably get on, under different circumstances."

"Mmm." Trix wrinkled her nose. "That's what Cat said after the sister-in-law crack."

Leo coughed. "If that's a proposal, I have to say I wasn't really planning on ring shopping just yet."

She considered it progress that her reaction was to snort rather than hyperventilate. "Don't be ridiculous. A month ago, we were still mentally pinning each other's face to a dartboard. I think we should leave the subject of gold rings to the Hobbits."

"I've got about half an hour before the crew meeting. How do you feel about coffee shopping instead? I'll shout you an espresso."

"We could do that," she agreed. "Or we could go downstairs and have sex in my dressing room."

"I really *do* like the way you think."

When they'd locked her dressing room door—and pulled a chair in front of it for good measure, because Trix had already pushed her luck with Marco today without getting caught getting carnal on her vanity table—they discovered the difficulty of trying to keep kissing while also pulling clothes over heads and down legs.

Leo's hands were firm on her hips as he swept her down onto the hard surface. A bottle of water and a container of cleanser rolled off and hit the floor.

"Do you have—"

"Top drawer."

He yanked open the drawer and took care of the condom after eyeing the unfortunate colour—it was lime flavour, but they really didn't need to dye them to match; it wasn't an ice lolly. His lips trailed over the plane of her stomach, his teeth nipping at the crease of her inner thigh before he put his mouth on her and caused her to buck so violently that she almost did a yoga bridge on the table.

She fisted her hands against the back of his head, scrabbling for a hold in his hair. Her *"Fuck!"* was strangled. "All those years that I kind of hoped you'd lose your tongue in an unfortunate incident that would leave you unable to speak ever again," she managed to squeak out, "I take it all back. *Tragic* waste. I was short-sighted and didn't think it through."

The puff of his breath against her and the vibration when he laughed was another revelation, and she sucked in a breath. Curling her feet around his thighs, she sat up and stroked her fingertips down the sensitive length of his erection. She heard an audible click of his teeth when she cupped him, but when she edged down from the table and went to return the favour, he lifted her in a sudden rush of urgency and turned. One of his arms supported her back as he pushed her up against the wall; his other hand reached between their bodies as he eased into her, then came up to protect her head.

When he was inside her, the intensity between them took on an unexpected shade of tenderness. He rocked gently, his hips lifting hers, and she smoothed her hands over his shoulders, tracing his collarbones as she kissed him.

He rested his forehead on hers, and they looked into each other's eyes, rapid breaths touching their parted lips. "You know, when you're not annoying the hell out of me, you might be my favourite person." His voice was husky beneath the teasing.

"Yeah." Trix looped her arms about his neck to give him a little hug. "You're not completely awful, either."

Grinning, he kissed her again, his mouth caressing and tempting. He thrust, his palm tightening as he cradled her head, and she inhaled sharply at the spike of pleasure.

At some point, they lost the ability to speak, or focus on anything except the building friction and slide of their bodies, but when she was leaning bonelessly against him, her heart pounding in the aftermath of release, he spoke into her ear.

"For the record," he said, "if the subject of rings ever does come up in the future, it would be nice if your first thought isn't Mordor."

Epilogue

Three and a half years later.

"...to Hong Kong, now boarding at Gate—"

Right stopover destination, wrong airline. Trix checked her watch. Twenty minutes until their boarding call.

They were actually doing this.

She stuffed her receipt in her pocket and took the bag of overpriced snacks and drinks, smiling at the girl behind the counter. "Thanks."

"Enjoy your flight," the perky-looking redhead said brightly.

Trix adjusted the strap of her shoulder bag. It felt like it was full of bowling balls. She'd never travelled light, even when she'd only been packing for herself. And she'd never had to assemble enough stuff to leave the country for months. They'd spent about a fortnight's rent on the excess baggage allowance.

The nerves bubbled up again, but it was a smaller stirring next to the rush of excitement. She almost skipped out of the café and stood beside an empty table on her tiptoes, trying to see over the crowds of people dragging their bags through the terminal.

Leo was standing out of the stream of chaos, leaning against a pillar with one hand holding Martin, the
rest of their belongings at his feet. One of the many
benefits of his tall presence in her life: he was usually easy to find in a crowd. She navigated the pushy,
rude hazards between them, managed to avoid being
hit by swinging hand luggage as people stopped and
turned without warning, and watched the smile come
into his eyes when he saw her.

He never hid how he felt about her. He really loved
her, and he showed it all the time. It was something
she would never take for granted. It was also extremely
mutual. Cat had said sarcastically that she'd miss their
individual company while they were away, but welcome the temporary reprieve from their constant PDA.

Leo reached out to take her hand, pulling her out
of the battering zone when another flight was called
and people swarmed towards the gate.

She held up the bag. "We're fully stocked with
snacks."

"Mmm. That should last at least forty-five minutes."
He grinned when she mock-scowled. "I've flown with
you before, baby. No salt-and-vinegar crisp is safe."

"I'm a stress eater," she said with dignity, and pulled
out a bottle of water. Cracking the top, she handed
it to him. "Here. If you're going to make smart-arse
comments for the entire flight, I wouldn't want you
to dehydrate."

He took the bottle and wiggled his eyebrows at her,
and she leaned forward to kiss Martin's adorable little
head, smoothing her hand over his springy dark curls.
He was Leo's mini-me, from the velvety, almost-black
eyes to the warm brown skin and cheeky smile. And

possibly deviated septum, judging by the symphony of snoring that rattled the tiles off the roof each night.

Martin grinned gummily at her from his snug position against his dad's chest. His chubby little arms and legs bounced happily where they stuck out the sides of the carrier.

"That's it, sport," Leo said soothingly, patting his back. "Work off that ridiculous amount of energy you inherited from your firecracker of a mother. Just keep exhausting yourself real good there. And the moment we take off, you want nothing but boobs, naps, and silence."

"Is that his ideal flight or yours?" Trix said. "It's like you've cloned yourself."

His grin had a few more teeth and a lot more beard than Martin's, but otherwise—uncanny. He nudged her foot teasingly with the tip of his boot, and they gathered up their multitude of belongings. One acrobat plus one makeup artist apparently equalled one miniature human and a shit-ton of stuff.

They found seats as close to their gate as possible and settled in to wait. Trix tugged Martin's slipping sock back on and played with his fingers, smiling as he wrapped his fist around her thumb.

She loved them both so much that it physically hurt her heart.

She blew a raspberry on Martin's tiny wrinkled palm, and he shrieked with laughter and smacked Leo's shoulder.

Leo stroked the curve of Martin's ear and slipped his hand over Trix's leg to cup her knee. He rubbed her thigh. "Did you ring Lily before we left? Are they still coming out to visit while we're in Australia?"

"Mmm-hmm. For Easter. Lily said she'll forcibly kidnap Luc and drag him away from work if she has to, but he didn't sound too reluctant at dinner the other night. I doubt if he really needed to be sold on the idea of Lily and a bikini." Trix shifted restlessly on the hard seat. "I don't think this is going to feel real until we actually touch down in Melbourne."

Leo pulled out the water bottle again and unscrewed the cap. "Regrets?"

She didn't hesitate. "No." She couldn't stop smiling. "I can't wait."

"*I* can't wait to see you in the new show. Although since the Red Queen apparently looks like my girlfriend, I'm going to have to switch my allegiance away from the Obsidian Knight, and I don't know how I feel about that."

After two years of playing Doralina, a little mix-up on the subject of birth control had resulted in the gloriousness that was Martin, and Trix had left the Old Wellington. She'd been ready to start auditioning again a couple of months ago, and the stars had aligned for them again with the announcement of the *Galaxy Agent* stage spectacular. The musical had a huge aerial component, and the tour was beginning in Australia and moving to the West End after a six-month run in Melbourne. She'd auditioned for the Obsidian Knight, but been cast as the Red Queen, and she sure as hell wasn't going to be picky about it. Dream show, dream job, and they would be back in the UK in time for Leo to start work on a major film project shooting in London and Prague in autumn.

She looked at Leo, her fingers still stroking Martin's hand. It was mad, how differently things could

turn out from what you expected, and how radically
it could all change in just a few years. For all the crap
decisions and difficult days in the past, and the ones
she would have in the future, she was still having the
most amazing, perfectly imperfect life. Sitting here
about to embark on the next phase of it, she was so
profoundly blessed and grateful.

Leo's arm flexed as he raised the water bottle, and
she shook her head at the sight of the Tinker Bell tattoo
on his biceps. He'd smirked for a week after he'd had
that done in permanent ink as a really crap surprise
for her birthday. The honeybee tattoo he had over his
heart had made her cry; the smart-arse tattoo had almost relegated him to sleeping on the couch.

"By the time we get to Melbourne, we're going to
lose Saturday to the time difference," he said, taking
a swallow of water. "I'd better get the weekly proposal
in now. Marry me, sweetheart?"

"Sure," she said, leaning forward to tickle Martin's
pudgy chin. "Why not?"

Leo had just taken another mouthful of water, and
he spat it all over their son's head. Martin, with some
justification, immediately started bawling.

They probably weren't going to be the popular pas-
sengers on the flights.

"Gross." Trix pulled a tissue out of her bag and
dried off Martin's curls. "Did Daddy spit on you, bum-
blebee?"

Leo set the bottle of water down on the floor with
a thump. "Did you just say yes?"

She found Martin's pacifier and stoppered his
shrieking mouth. "Yes, I did."

There was a momentary silence from both her boys.

Martin, mouth busily sucking, looked with wide eyes from one of them to the other. He was clearly very invested in the moment.

"After a *year* of asking, you're finally saying yes?"

"Mmm-hmm."

"And you're choosing this particular time and location?"

"I am." She watched as his mouth twitched into a small smile that widened into the biggest grin.

He was laughing when he cupped the back of her head and brought her mouth to his. Between them, Martin grumbled again.

Leo kissed her, multiple times, ignoring the hundreds of people around them. "God, you're such a pisser. You're going to knock my feet out from under me for the rest of our lives, aren't you?"

"Hey, look, the vows just write themselves." Trix ran her hand over his hair. "Love you, Magasiva."

"Love you, too, Tinker Bell." He kissed her once more, and then Martin, as the voice over the loudspeaker announced their boarding call.

Trix reached for her handbag and pulled out their boarding passes. A piece of folded paper was tucked around them, and she opened it. It was the next panel in their ongoing comic strip. Illustrated Leo and Trix stood hand-in-hand, cartoon Martin between them, holding on to each of their legs. They were about to board a spaceship, heading for the unknown.

Flesh-and-blood Leo stood up and adjusted Martin's carrier, then slung the heaviest of their bags over his shoulder. "Here we go." Cocking an eyebrow, he held out his hand. "You watch my back and I'll watch yours?"

She picked up her handbag and shoulder bag, and the rest of the snacks, tucked Martin's blankie under her arm, and took Leo's hand. "Deal. But we'll be okay."

Leo pressed his lips to her cheekbone. "You think?"

She smiled. "I've got a good feeling."

* * * * *

To find out about other books by Lucy Parker, and to sign up for her newsletter to be alerted to new releases, please visit Lucy's website here or at www.lucyparkerfiction.com.

Read on for an excerpt from PRETTY FACE by Lucy Parker, now available at all participating e-retailers.

Author's Note

Trix and Leo inhabit a London that is vast, rich in culture, expensive to live in—and doesn't entirely exist on a map. The Old Wellington Theatre, Grosvenor Arena, *The Festival of Masks*, *1553*, *Galaxy Agent*, the period drama *Knightsbridge*, and Trix's favourite restaurant, Tragicomedy, are among a number of fictionalised elements in the book.

Acknowledgments

As always, many and sincere thanks to my editor, Deborah Nemeth, whose expertise and advice is absolutely invaluable, and to the entire team at Carina Press for their continued support.

Thank you so much to my family and friends, without whom I couldn't have written this book. I love you all unconditionally and endlessly.

And there are no words for how grateful I am to you, the person who's reading this book, for taking a chance on the story and letting it be part of your life for a little while. Whatever form your idea of happiness takes, I hope you always find it, recognise it, and make it.

Now available from Carina Press and Lucy Parker.

The play's the fling.

Read on for an excerpt from
PRETTY FACE.

Chapter One

It was the last straw when she seduced the vicar.

In the space of nine painful minutes, the asthmatic blonde had stolen a cheap reproduction of a Gainsborough, mistakenly spiked a martini with arsenic instead of a sedative, and accidentally ploughed a Hispano-Suiza into a Cabinet Minister. In between acts of homicidal lunacy, she fluttered improbably black eyelashes and danced an enthusiastic Charleston.

Luc wasn't surprised she was continually short of breath. He was pretty bloody speechless himself. He froze the clip on an artistic shot of a suspender belt catapulting towards a crumpled, abandoned cassock, and didn't waste words. "No fucking way."

His stage manager tore his gaze from the screen with obvious disappointment. "Not *exactly* what I was expecting," David Benton admitted. "*Knightsbridge* seems to pull a decent cast, in general. My wife's obsessed with the show. Never misses an episode." He wiggled his eyebrows. "Might do my husbandly duty and keep her company on the couch now. I've obviously been missing out." With a return to seriousness, he added, "Although, as much as I appreciate the young lady's dexterity with feathers, I really don't think…"

No. Neither did Luc. And nor would any paying punter with functional ears and a brain working somewhere above the trouser line.

It had taken two months and an extortionate increase in salary to coax Amelia Lee away from the casting department of the Majestic and onto his own staff. If Luc had realised she was in the midst of some sort of psychiatric episode, he would have added a few weeks' holiday to the incentive package.

Seeing his expression, Amelia put down her coffee mug. "I'm assuming you haven't actually watched the audition reel I forwarded. Three days ago." She looked dismissively at the large screen where he'd cut short the debauchery of the dog collar. "Obviously you can't make a judgement on the basis of that performance. The script is pants. And that character is a generic, two-dimensional male fantasy. Bat your lashes, girls, hitch up your skirts, get your tits out and the ratings up. Meryl Streep would be stuck paddling in the shallows, given that material to work with."

Luc glanced down at the headshot he held. In static black-and-white, the blonde's face was cast into clever shadows that carved out a few interesting hollows and angles, rescuing the end result from vacuous beauty. Her eyes were dark, and this time appeared to contain at least one thought. He turned it over, looking for the photographer's credit. He or she might be worth cultivating, if they could coax that from what he'd seen on the screen.

Then he tossed the image onto a growing pile of unsatisfactory faces. "I believe the whole point of—" he checked her résumé without much interest "—Lily Lamprey's inclusion as a possible was her role on *Knightsbridge*. What was your helpful contribution,

Eric?" He didn't wait for a reply from his marketing manager, who had reached out to rescue Lily from the slush pile and was staring fatuously at her photograph. "Hottest now on TV? She might attract the younger demographic?" He flicked the headshot out of Eric's hand. "I se we can add the middle-aged, overworked, and easil impressed to the list."

"Says t man who keeps clutching her photo." Amelia grinne t him. He'd known her for fifteen ve— he could t the gibe coming haf

"You migbe middle-aged and overworked, but I'd never hav alled you easily impressed. If I'd realised you were t susceptible, I'd have sent you Lily's latest magazi spread and considered the matter settled."

Nothin ke working with friends. Everyone appreciated aint that the Grim Reaper was breathing down their eck the moment they turned forty.

"Remin me again why I wanted you on board."

"My wit My charm? My compromising photos of you from T: *Importance of Being Earnest* opening night gala?"

Luc shoo his head, reluctantly and only slightly amused. A kadache was beginning to form behind his left eye, though his vision was clear so hopefully it wouldn't turn into a migraine. He'd been woken at six o'clock by a call from his contractor, cheerfully informing him that the delivery of Italian tiles for the theatre foyer was short by about three hundred, which followed the cue of everything else that had gone wrong this month.

He was more concerned about the flesh-and-blood problem than the bricks-and-mortar one. If they didn't recast this role in the next couple of days, there weren't going to be any people in the theatre to *require* a tiled foyer.

Eight tedious days of workshop auditions, sitting through scene after scene of botched Stopard and stilted Shakespeare, sifting through talet, looking for potential. He could usually tell withi five minutes if an actor was suitable for the part ty wanted, and which people had the right connecti to form a company. Chemistry wasn't rehearsed; iparked into nule, and contact or not at all. But nobc was infal-

And at this point, he might as wellve walked into Piccadilly Circus at rush hour and idomly contracted the first dozen people to cross path. He'd already lost his first choice for the role oary, thanks to Margo acting like an infatuated teener, and now his Elizabeth had fallen off a stepladdwhile painting her bedroom ceiling. She'd broken bh ankles and would be immobile for at least six wexs. He'd sent flowers from the company, calmly acced her regretful resignation, and mentally throttleder.

They were starting rehearsals in les than a fortnight. For a number of reasons, the min one being expense, changing the schedule was ot an option. His second-choice Mary was alreadyosting a fucking fortune and would happily seize ay opportunity to indulge in temperamental bullshit.Luc had no intention of giving her legitimate reasn to complain. Next week he was taking the entire cast away for a long weekend in the country. Enforced bonding and a lot of alcohol usually cut several corners in turning a roomful of individual egos into a working ensemble.

It also usually kick-started at least one co-star romance, but sex was an inevitable complication in every production. He seemed to have the unwanted knack of putting together lovesick idiots who laboured under the delusion they were the next Burton and Taylor. It almost always ended in tears, and occasionally meant recasting one of the roles before the end of the run.

In this case he hadn't even got to the start of rehearsals before he had to recast. Five business days to pick a new Elizabeth I from the reserve list. Which did not include Flapper Barbie, despite the best efforts of the board to convince him otherwise. He had no problem, *in theory*, using the celebrity pull of a screen actor, providing they were right for the part and could make the transition to the stage, but this was one of the key roles in the play. There was only so far he was willing to compromise artistic integrity for profit.

He hadn't invested this much time and money into restoring the Queen Anne only to see it founder on the rocks of an opening-night flop.

For the second time, he tossed Lily Lamprey's photograph aside. "No."

"If you'd actually looked at—" Amelia was interrupted by a quiet knock on the door.

A catering assistant came in with a trolley of sandwiches, pastries, and the makings of tea and coffee. Ibuprofen and a pint of lager would have been more welcome.

"Should I serve, sir?" the young man asked, impeccably polite. He was slightly built, freckle-faced, and Luc couldn't tell if he was actually fifteen years old or if he himself had just become so fucking old that every person under the age of twenty-five looked as if they ought to be at home playing with blocks.

"Thanks," he said, keeping his increasing irritation out of his voice. He wasn't going to vent on a kid earning minimum wage and obviously battling a severe case of nerves. "First day?"

Another quick glance. "Just temping, Mr. Savage."

When the tea things had been transferred to the conference table, David reached for an eclair and took a large bite. Wiping cream from his mouth, he said, "Where are we, then?"

"Lily Lamprey." Amelia raised a pointed eyebrow at Luc. "Yea or nay? And *nay* is an unacceptable answer until you've watched the reel, dropped the attitude, and given her proper consideration."

"*Yay* was certainly my reaction." Eric was drooling on the headshot again. For the love of God. The guy needed to get out more.

The pressure in Luc's eye socket was spreading to his temple. "On your recommendation, I sat through almost ten minutes of jazz hands and the corruption of the clergy—"

"Actually," Amelia said, "you watched ten minutes of one previous body of work, with your nose in the air and your mind on construction bills, and wrote her off after the first simpering thirty seconds."

Luc took another brief look at the headshot. Lily Lamprey was exceptionally pretty—and, from what he'd seen so far, nothing more. "She has limited stage experience. Her only major role to date is on the worst show on CTV, in a part that could be understudied by a blow-up doll, and vocally she sounds as if she should be charging by the minute. Either she runs up eight flights of stairs between takes or she's taking the piss out of a character pulled straight from C-grade film noir, in which case I privately applaud the sentiment, but it's not exactly a professional approach to—"

There was a clattering sound near the door. The catering kid ducked his head and fiddled with an empty cup. It seemed to be taking an unnecessarily long time to rearrange and remove the trolley.

Pressing his thumb and forefinger against his eyes, Luc let out a short, hard breath. "I do not need a breathy Marilyn Monroe impersonator to add a bit of sex appeal in case the critics get bored. I'm not sure where you got the impression that I'm restoring the Queen Anne as a day-care training scheme for overly ambitious teenagers, or that I would be interested in an escapee from utter shit like *Knightsbridge*, but—"

"She's twenty-six years old, Luc, and you're not a misogynistic prick. You're a businessman. From a marketing perspective, Lily Lamprey would be a cash cow. *Knightsbridge* was the second-highest rated show in the country last week—"

"Then in the interests of the viewing public, I truly hope she's the worst actor on it."

Don't miss
PRETTY FACE by Lucy Parker,
available now wherever
Carina Press ebooks are sold.

www.CarinaPress.com

About the Author

Lucy Parker lives in the gorgeous Central Otago region of New Zealand, where she feels lucky every day to look out at mountains, lakes and vineyards. She has a degree in art history, loves museums and art galleries, and doodles unrecognizable flowers when she has writer's block. When she's not writing, working or sleeping, she happily tackles the towering pile of to-be-read books that never gets any smaller. Thankfully, there's always another story waiting.

Her interest in romantic fiction began with a preteen viewing of Jane Austen's *Pride and Prejudice* (Firth-style), which prompted her to read the book as well. A family friend introduced her to Georgette Heyer, and the rest was history.

She loves to talk to other readers and writers, and you can find her on Twitter, @_LucyParker, on Facebook, www.Facebook.com/LucyParkerAuthor, or on her website, www.lucyparkerfiction.com.

Get 4 FREE REWARDS!

We'll send you 2 FREE Books plus 2 FREE Mystery Gifts.

Harlequin® Desire books feature heroes who have it all: wealth, status, incredible good looks... everything but the right woman.

FREE
Value Over
$20

Get 4 FREE REWARDS!

We'll send you 2 FREE Books plus 2 FREE Mystery Gifts.

Harlequin Presents® books feature a sensational and sophisticated world of international romance where sinfully tempting heroes ignite passion.

FREE
Value Over
$20

Get 4 FREE REWARDS!

We'll send you 2 FREE Books plus 2 FREE Mystery Gifts.

Harlequin® Romance Larger-Print books feature uplifting escapes that will warm your heart with the ultimate feel-good tales.

FREE
Value Over
$20